Daughter Of Arella

Daughter Of Arella

Karin Hunt

To order additional copies of this book, contact:
Xlibris Corporation
0-800-644-6988
www.xlibrispublishing.co.uk
Orders@Xlibrispublishing.co.uk
301064

Dedication

Dedicated to my mother who loves a good story.

Is iontach an rud Léitheoireacht a bheith i do shaol.
Oscail do mheabhair agus taitneamh a bhaint as.

Acknowledgements

Many thanks to:

Many thanks to my husband Patrick for his love and support. He has the patience of a saint and certainly knows what it is to enjoy his own company. Thank you I love you. To my brother Lee who did the most amazing art work on the cover and spent days reading to help me out. To everyone who read all the roughest drafts and always gave me feedback. Finally my thanks to Eden Marzando, Rhea Villacarlos and the rest of the team at Xlibris.

Prologue

Looking out over the horizon he smiled to himself at the chaos caused by his hand. Fires blazed high into the sky, women and children screamed and the men who were stupid enough to fight were struck down, cut to pieces and scattered to make examples of. Tonight was a good night and he was in a pleasing mood. News of the change of hands in Arella came today. Finally the day he had been waiting for. Running his fingers along the length of his face were his eye once had been, clenched his jaws until they went rigid. Stopping just above his mouth were the scar finished he dropped his hand away and walked towards the village. It was time for him to take his pick. His men would be getting anxious which meant they got argumentative and always seemed to ruin the good ones in the heat of the moment. He knew who he was looking for tonight. He had seen her the night before washing at the stream. The point we're she'd knelt merged into a part of the pool that in turn merged into an alternative route. The water seemed to run smoothly as it flowed into a deeper segment, and even smoother as it ran over her body. He had watched her for a long time hidden from her line of sight until he decided to join her. During the time he had forced himself upon her he could have sworn he had never been called such names. An uncivilized barbarian, cruel bastard, brutal and his favorite the most insensitive person she had ever met. She was untainted and wholesome he reflected licking his lips. Even though now she was what most might call ruined, but he was still the only one she'd had. This gave him a feeling of possession and ownership over her. Tonight he'd take her and following if she refused to join him he'd kill her. Stepping over the body of a young boy he paused and moved back to position himself above the supposed corpse. Tilting his head he frowned. The child was still breathing. Taking his dagger from its holder he knelt down and pulling the boys head up by his hair he drew the razor-sharp blade of ten inches in length across his throat from corner to corner. A curve that left the knife balanced from handle to tip was deadly as he pulled it away. Having cut deep enough the boy's eyes shot open and in opening his mouth blood spluttered out through wheezing breaths. Letting go of the boy's head he fell back limp and lifeless onto the earth leaving his bodies blood seeping through the cavernous hole. Rising he called to one of his men and on arriving he punched him as hard as he could screaming to make sure they are dead! The man left holding his jaw on the ground nodding as he scampered off to relay the message. Heading for where he guessed they were holding the women and young girls he walked with deliberate and calculated steps. Looking around he was thrilled to see that his men had ventured out and the hanging of the villagers was well under way people. 'Definitely less blood,' he thought. At long last he seen a gathering and as predicted there were a few already fighting over who gets who. Moving through a crowd of punches and men rolling in the dirt he spotted her. She was hiding in the corner looking petrified and he found himself feeling unruffled about taking her again, she had fought so ferociously. Having kicked, struck and nearly managing to strangle him while he was preoccupied he found himself being slightly optimistic he wouldn't have to kill her. Walking with purpose towards her he could make out the bruising on her face. 'Surely that wasn't me,' he said while hiding a snigger as he reached for her. She screamed and tried to wrestle her way free earning her a hard clout across the face. Grabbing her by the hair he jerked with brutal force drawing an agonizing gasp from her mouth making him snort out loud with glee. Pulling her back with force he turned her towards him and kissed her remorselessly and roughly, picked her up and flung her over his shoulder to the cheers of his men. He raised his hand theatrically and shouted 'take your pick, and when you're done burn it.'

Leaving his men to do as they pleased he could hear the screams of the women in the distance as he made his way back up the hillside with his prize. The smoke and the rising ash from the homes and bodies mixed and bellowed as it elevated high into the sky left a vile taste in her mouth as she contemplated what was before her.

Chapter One

Nox stood on the hill looking out over the land that separated her from what felt like the rest of the world. Why had her parents ever live in such a place? She had to admit that growing up surrounded by the boundaries of the castle wasn't too bad as her father said it was for her own safety so she by no means argued. Thinking on it now she knew that it wouldn't have accomplished anything. Her father was not the type of man that would back down on a decision at the thought of causing his only daughter and child displeasure. The man was stubborn but she loved him deeply. Ensuring that she could fight as well as any man if not superior left her to ponder weather that maybe was why she still found herself lacking a husband or children to speak of. Not that she never had men in her life, but it never seemed to venture further than a kiss and a sneaky cuddle in the sables. Smiling to herself she realized that they were more than likely terrified to approach her, which in a way she was thankful for. Her male friends all seemed to connect to her like the sister they never had, and she was more than comfortable to tolerate it considering any uninvited attention was met with a very antisocial and an unfriendly attitude from her adopted kin. Besides why would a woman settle for being dictated to by a man whom she could lay flat on his back without a second's deliberation. Her father was right to leave her to choose a husband for herself; it definitely saved him the arguments that would come with forcing her. Unfortunately she didn't really get to know her mother as she died when she was young enough not remember the important things between mother and daughter. But even so she felt she had been old enough to remember her smile and to know she would have approved with her father's decision if she had of lived. Never thinking the day would come when she would be looked upon to take her father's place, left a sickening feeling deep in the pit of her stomach had worsened over the last few days. He died to young and left a lot of things unfinished and even though he had told her it would fall to her when he died some day she never really thought the day would come. 'Not this soon damn it, it was too soon.' Thinking of it now it made her hands sweat and her heart accelerated with anticipation. Could she be the leader her father expected of her? Would his men look on her with pity and maybe even distrust that she was forced into a position she wasn't ready for? So many questions ran around her head that it was making her feel dizzy. 'Damn it, I know the land, and the people and I've fought with these men since I was a child, why would they not accept me? She was beginning to feel the pressure and she didn't like the feeling of losing control. They trusted her with their lives in battle now of all times they would have to trust her now. Clenching her jaws at the thought of any of these men thinking her inadequate made her blood boil. She could relieve them of their swords as more as fast as any other. They helped teach her to fight; they must know she's ready. Relaxing she took a deep breath closed her eyes and leaned her head back towards the suns heat. Opening her eyes she took another look out over the land that would now be hers, and she realized just what her father had seen when he looked out the day he became chief. Her heart never failed to swell with the fondness she felt when she thought of her father. More than just a father to her, he was her protector, a loyal friend and always the man she could depend on, it would be a great man indeed that would take his place in her heart. She could hear her father's voice, 'A man will not choose you but when you choose him may god be with him for he'll need to be a better man than me.' she smiled at the memory. She would have to make her way back soon but the thoughts of it didn't appeal to her; she was enjoying the peace and quiet. Already today she had to settle an argument over meat and a child's bad behavior. Being pulled in all directions was making her feel exhausted but it also made her speculate how her father did it. Surely he never let himself get caught up in such mediocre things. She was getting angry. 'A child's behavior indeed' she said as she kicked a stone as hard as she could. She agreed with Maggie about the meat, it certainly wasn't cooked through and the whole castle would be sick by morning. She decided to have a stern talk with the chef about his drinking so early in the morning while preparing food, but the man was her husband surely she can handle him, and the child in question was young Tressin her only son and definitely his father's son. The castle was buzzing with anticipation.

They would have a feast tonight to formally name her as the new leader of Arella. Never before has there been a woman to take this place until today and it made her feel a bit giddy and sick to her stomach at the same time. There would be many who would not agree with such a decision as she has many male relations but none stepped forward to voice their opinions or disapproval on the matter which gave her a bolt of satisfaction that they genuinely did believe that she had what it takes. After all she might look like her mother but she was her father's daughter.

Making her way back through the field she stopped to look at what was now her the castle from a distance. It was an intimidating building to gaze upon. Its stone walls towered on both sides breaking off into twin towers which were coupled together by the wall that branched straight across the vast wooden gates. The windows were of all different sizes and shapes, while the stained glass left shards of colour running along the walls. She loved to watch them as a child. To the east of the castle there was a huge array of colour from the shrubs that to her astonishment were still in bloom. The garden was full of Linnaea Borealis her mother's favorite.

Her father had told her how every morning when in bloom her mother would be up before the castle woke to pick and place them throughout. She looked upon them with great satisfaction.

This led onto a well kept gravel path that was bordered by a stone wall no higher than knee level.

Even though the wall was low the shrubbery that lined it always offered a chance for privacy. A place to escape, to relax and most of all to hide when she felt the need. As she grew closer she spotted the stables. 'My sanctuary' she thought affectionately with a smile. They were attractive buildings that were covered by ivy adding to the atmosphere of the whole surrounding area of the gardens and training area. Unexpectedly she heard a yell that could only mean one thing and that was young Tressin had got into the stables again. The child loved the horses but one of these days he was going to get himself killed. Picking up her pace she turned the corner and walked straight into the child who was in a great rush to get away from his father who had been called to deal with him. She tried to give him her best you're in trouble look and he took a step backwards away from her, making her feel sorry for frightening him. Nox was never one for keeping to the rules set out by her own father so she couldn't find it in her to punish him or even think of castigation for him. Instead she bent down seized him by the shoulders, drew in a deep breath and whispered to him 'never lose your sense of wonder for the world is exciting and you need to take pleasure in it all. Cause trouble for that's what you will remember,' her smile grew wide as she looked into the innocence of a child's eyes but saw the devilment which they held, yes his mother and father had their hands full. 'Go and assist your mother Tressin and tomorrow,' she paused and looked around her and then playfully rubbed the top of his head. 'Then tomorrow drive your father crazy.' At this the both of them laughed loudly they drew the attention of the passers, making her feel like she was a child herself being reprimanded for misbehavior.

Thinking she should at least look to be dealing with him she stood up pointed her finger in the direction of the castle and told him to 'Go' in her most stern voice which seemed to impress those looking. Giving Tressin a sly wink he ran off and she continued towards the stables. She was left wondering if her father would have been as lenient, but this also got her wondering if it was being a woman that she was so soft on the children around the castle. 'Surely not' she said out loud enough to cringe at her own voice. 'He's barely able to hold up a sword, but damn it he could be killed messing around in there.' She stopped walking realizing she was still talking to herself but the damn child had her questioning herself again, she'd really need to think about what to do with him. Quickening her pace and replacing her inadequate feelings she was having with determination, she had a job to do and she also had to look to be doing it to the best of her ability. Besides tomorrow when young Tressin is driving his father crazy she'll be nowhere near.

As she walked into the stables Hakan was standing looking flustered at everything that had taken place. Hakan her first in command at the wishes of the father on his death bed, and besides who was she to disagree with the wishes of a dying man and who else would she have chosen he was her cousin after all and they were very close. She trusted him with her life and that was all she needed. 'Yes I know, I'll make him a stable boy that should keep him out of trouble, and make him happy in the long run' she said before Hakan could say a word. 'Hmm, could work I suppose' he said rubbing his head still looking at the mess. 'I should have made him come with me to clean up, if I'd known how bad it was I'd have reddened his arse for him' she realized she sounded like her father and laughed making

Hakan look at her as if she were crazy, waving her hand at him she started to clean up Tressin's mess. The last time this happened she had walked into the stable to the sound of a child's laugh. There he was legs in the air at the back of the hay giggling so hard he snorted loudly and, there was Snowflake licking his face.

The horse was as bloody bad. Telling Hakan to head back to the castle to check on the plans for tomorrow's journey to the North she decided to leave a message for Tressin to clean the stables in the morning which right now left her time to settle Snowflake for the night before making her way back to the castle herself. Her nightly ritual since he arrived but at least now she slept in her own bed and not in the stall. She drove her father to drink more than he should have, which lead her to think that perhaps that's why she liked young Tressin so much. Standing with her eyes closed she took in the smells around her, the horses and the thickness of the air surrounded her and she suddenly realized that the calm that was established earlier abandoned her and with it came the wave of nausea, fear and anger which coiled in her stomach. She shut her eyes tighter against the tears streaming down her checks that she was unable to stop. Her father was dead.

She rubbed her eyes hard and then her nose with the back of her hand and walked slowly to Snowflake. He had been given to her father by Anso of Zantar after they finally signed a treaty of peace after one hundred years of war between the southern borders. Of course when she seen him she decided with determination that he was going to be hers regardless of her father's feeling in the matter. Knowing how he hated to argue with her she screamed at him, kicked him in the shin as hard as she could and disappeared for three days that when she finally came back her father was passed being angry with her; instead he was so happy for her safe return he handed the horse over as if that was what he had planned all along. She smiled as she ran her hand down behind his ears and felt his quiver of contentment und her fingers. 'My father never stood a change did he' she said into the horses ear and laughed as he shook his head in what seemed like agreement. Letting her mind wonder she returned to the day her father handed her the reins of the one year old white stallion. She remembered feeling that she should at least feel a little sorry but she didn't and she took the horse with great pleasure. Having spent two months solid being thrown with great vigor from his back and on this one particular day she had, had enough. Slumping to the ground in the stables against the stall she folded her arms, glared and pouted as she looked at the horse in question chomping happily on the grass. 'Bloody damn horse,' she said with venom as she rubbed her buttocks which she assumed by now was black and blue not to mention tender. A sudden thought came to her and up she stood with determination grabbing and apple on the way out. Coaxing the horse to her with the tasty treat she grabbed his harness as he moved close and tied him to the fence. When he was secured she sat onto the fence directly in front of him and stared him straight in the eye until water ran down her cheeks. But she'd be damned if she blinked first. 'I'll break you, you stupid beast,' she had said with so much anger towards the horse but more so towards those who said wouldn't succeed. Six months later and she was riding him with ease. After another six months she brought her father out to show him what the horse could do and what she had achieved. He trotted, lowered himself to the ground to allow her to mount him, descended on one leg in a curtsy that made her father clap and voice his elation at such a wonderful feat. Finally she brought Snowflake out into the clearing and left him to stay there which totally confused her father. Until what she was doing was obvious. She whistled the loudest whistle and in turning in the direction of the horse ran as fast as she could. She could hear her father yell for her to stop as the horse barreled towards her head down. Without stopping she jumped, grabbed the reins and swung through the air in one sweeping motion onto his firm back. When she made her way back to where her father stood he was pale and shaking and ordered her never to do that again. Of course she listened and obeyed, well until he wasn't looking at least. Another darker occasion came to her mind and her back stiffened. She had taken Snowflake half way along the foot of the Floyden Mountains. As she constantly reassured herself as long as she went no further there was no harm in it. When she had just reached her point of return she seen a single horse and rider on the hill. First she assumed he was just a hunter until it came obvious that he was more interested in hunting her. Turning she fled with the rider on her tail and making the biggest mistake of her life she turned and looked over her shoulder only to be hit full force by a low hanging branch. Falling hard and Snowflake unable to stop on time kept going. Before she knew it he was on top of her raking at her clothes, and rummaging under her skirts. She screamed, kicked, bit and struggled with great ferocity. But he was so much bigger and stronger than she was. Just as he had lowered his trousers she remembered her blade that was always attached to her thigh, she grabbed it and waited for him to come closer. When finally he lowered himself and with one hard jab she stabbed him and dragged the blade down along the left side of his face. He let out an unmerciful painful scream as blood squirted from his eye and ran through his hands and along his arms. She struggled out from underneath him and scurried to her feet calling for Snowflake. Breaking away from her memories she looked at the horse now that had saved her life on more than one occasion and she grew sad at his aged face. He was agile, had great speed and his alertness was uncanny, but she knew that eventually the time would come when she would leave him out to stud and begin with another. Running her hand down the length of his thick cresty neck and muscular physique she seen how it gave him such a formidable advantage over the other horses. She had found over the years that he had a tendency to be particularly aggressive towards other stallions, much to Hakan's annoyance of having to have another stable built to house Knor her father's deep brown stallion. 'This will be our last adventure my friend,' she said as she ran her hand down along his nose. 'It's time you retired.' She gave him a final pat on the shoulder and made her way to the castle. It was time. But first she had to find Hakan to talk about the final journey plans through the West. She would have preferred to take the east coast and into the Northern Territory over the mountains but from experience she knew it was too harsh a land and very difficult not to mention extremely dangerous. Not agreeing with the decision to form an alliance with the Mickisi in the first place didn't help when she thought about how difficult it was going to be. Nox found them brutal and ignorant to the next level and the less she had to do with them the better she felt. 'A once off offer is all they'll get' she thought to herself 'murderous bastards.'

By the time she returned to the castle Hakan and the rest of the men had already made their way to the gathering hall for the feast leaving her to get ready as fast as possible and join the celebrations. She decided on a sky blue gown, left her hair down flowing and white satin slippers. All together she was happy with her appearance and headed for the hall. When she arrived both sides were lined with men in full battle uniform which left her speechless. A fine sight to be taken in, as it happened so very rarely that on the odd occasions which it did she found herself unable to take her eyes from them. A snug fitting deep red with gold buckles lining the hip to which their armor would attach to. Taking care to look more carefully to the details of the uniforms she could just about make out the two coloured pattern of gold and black that lined the sleeves. Circular shields lay against the right leg of each man, which left them facing her directly as she walked through the gathering hall. Their sizes were the same but she knew their weights varied depending upon the warrior's preference but all was made of the same metal. Her father never thought it right to force a smaller man to use a bigger man's shield. 'It would hinder him in battle' he had said looking at her seriously. Like the archers of the Crowden the Arellian warrior's shields held their own story. Beautifully decorated and skillfully crafted, each was distinctive and unique. Like her comrades her shield had its own story but also held its own shape that differed entirely from all others. Longer in its appearance, it dipped to a point at the underside and curved to some extent into a partly circular shape at the top. This permitted her to see her opponent easily but also had the protection needed. Noticing people she hadn't seen since childhood made her feel self-conscious but with her chin held high she headed for the top table and took the seat that was once her fathers. Her skin itched at the intrusion she felt she was making by sitting in his chair but forced herself to control her inner thoughts. The feast went as planned. The food was in an unmerciful amount, the drink was plentiful and everyone in the place seemed to be aglow with excitement. Problems and upsets were forgotten for a time and people took the gift gratefully. Soon she found that she herself had relaxed to a significant amount due to a deadly concoction she had been given by Gaius. Toasts were made in her honor to the extent she was glowing with both merit and embarrassment, but sobered in a reasonable time when toasts were made to her father followed by their condolences. Glasses were lifted in his name on more than one occasion which pleased her no end. Gathering her feet under herself she moved a little unsteadily towards the window. 'Wow, what is in that drink,' she said as she hiccupped slightly and stifled a giggle. Looking out into the night her mind drifted to a day that seemed a long time ago now. Kiril son of Anso came to the castle. She had watched him closely as he walked through the grounds. His stride was extremely graceful for a man his size and she found that she wasn't the only one to notice. Many of the women followed, giggled and outright flirted to near falling at his feet, which made her want to go and beat them but stopped herself not wanting him to know it bothered her. She couldn't blame them he was like something sculpted to the highest standard. Black shoulder length hair, high sharp check bones that were covered lightly by a growing beard that made him look ravenous, full luscious lips that always seemed to result in her lick her own in wonder, and those eyes. Having often wondered what colour they were. Definitely not blue or green and too dark to be brown. It wasn't until his eyes met hers directly did she realize with the help of the sun they seemed to hold no colour. Blinking at the memory she turned her attention back to her guests. 'I wonder why Anso didn't travel this time,' she thought a little anxious at the thought he disagreed that she was the right choice.

Thinking of Anso and how she found him always to be in a great mood unlike his always frowning son. His father was never overly domineering and seemed to give him whatever he wanted. She was there the day he presented him with a sword she still thought of. It had a long edged blade with a high grip. The blade itself must have measured at least thirty inches, and designed for sufficient killing. Formed at the end of the blade was a piercingly narrow point that was an absolute thing of beauty and craftsmanship. She was so jealous of him that night. Anso had put a great deal of time and thought into his gift and the fact that he had hand crafted the sword to specially fit Kiril's hands made the jealousy go further. But did he know how to use it. she thought in awe as she recalled watching him the next morning out in the training field thinking he was alone. She had never seen someone with so much power behind him and grace in his movements. He had great training she knew. He spent at least five hours a day with his sword and the rest of his time he worked on hand on hand combat. She always wondered if she'd beat him but never got the chance. 'Always bloody frowning,' she said and yawning she turned suddenly bid a goodnight to those closest and walked with purpose from the hall, leaving many disconcerted by her departure.

~

Turning the corner to take the stairs to the highest part of the castle yelling brought her out of her thoughts and straight to her senses. The noise of breaking furniture, cursing and fists hitting faces in which it sounded like at least thirty men echoed around the hallways. Picking up her pace to a near jog she suddenly found herself bounced off the back wall as the door flew open and Toran fell upon her with such force he took the wind out of her. He was so damn big and heavy she groaned and pushed with all her might to move him, and getting a kick at him in the process.

She could feel her warm blood trickle down the back of her neck and smell the metallic scent of it. The fool had split her head. It was Hakan that she heard first and above the rest as he grabbed her by the shoulders and shook her gently. Then turning on Toran he let a roar that silenced everyone in the in close proximity to them. 'You big idiot, you've cracked her head open.' When she finally was able to focus her eyes she had Toran and his deadly bigger twin brother Gaius standing beside him looking down at her. They were ruthless and a huge commodity but in all that was good they were a definite challenge. Stillness filled the halls as the men watched and waited to see what she would do. At the very moment she was thinking the very same. Pushing herself away from the wall she looked at the blood on her fingertips and then up at Toran with those glistening green eyes of hers that said it all. He was in trouble. 'So what was it this time?' she asked incredulously in that quiet voice that put everyone on edge straight away. Why couldn't she just scream, shout and hit him back? It drove him crazy. 'Well he shouldn't have taken my drink should he' he said utterly abashed and seemed like a genuinely hurt expression flittered across his face making her wonder how drunk he really was. Quirking her eyebrow at him Nox wasn't sure if she had even heard him right. 'Let me get this straight, you demolish what seems like everything in the hall caused a near riot and left a remarkable gash in the back of my head over a fucking drink? 'Am I right? she said licking the blood from her finger prior to pointing it at him. 'For you Toran it's going to be an especially long trip, now clean up your fucking mess and get settled in for the night we're departing early. 'Yes sir' he said in a feeble voice as his brother sniggered at him and tilted the rest of the beer down his throat which amazingly he managed not to drop. Rotating she called for Hakan to tag along with her, they had issues to discuss.

Chapter Two

Kiril couldn't believe his ears. She was the leader of Arella. 'Are you positive' he asked Arnav his first in command in a rushed manner that sounded almost shocked. Making him cringed at the sound he heard coming from his mouth. 'Oh yeah' Arnav answered with a motion of his shoulders. 'Seems no more than two months past. Her father took bad in the night after an illness of some kind. He didn't have it in him to struggle against whatever it was that ailed him. Shame really a fine man from what I can recollect, and from what I hear Lady Nox isn't taking to the role as effortlessly as foreseen.' At this Kiril turned quizzically to him with a raised eyebrow.

Arnav continued 'Seems her father had very big boots to fill' he said with minor interest. Kiril shook his head in sympathetic understanding. 'Ah my father will be sad to hear the news he had grown fond of Mickel. By this stage Arnav was after growing uninterested with the current conversation and decided to see what Kiril thought of her plans to head North with a small army. He found it intriguing that Kiril was showing such bizarre and peculiar emotions as they spoke of the lovely new leader plus Arnav was curious. 'So I hear she is taken a small army of seventy men over into the Northern Territory.' 'Why?' Kiril answered in an extremely odd voice that was almost verging on desperation to Arnav's ears. Smiling to himself he continued with a similar line of conversation as if noticing nothing unusual in Kiril's taunt form. 'Well it seems her father was trying to conduct a Treaty with the Crowden Clan because let's face it they are the closest to the Mickisi and they need all the help they can get if you're following me. Anyway I'm guessing she's in the mind to thinking what better place to start. When you think about it she's in the right of it. You know with being a woman in such a position regardless of her influence and skillfulness with a blade she's still going to be tested to her limits. Our Lady Nox will need to be on top of her game so to speak.' At the frown on Kiril's face made him wonder what torment was going on with his captain and best friend's head. 'Are you well Kiril, you seem a bit . . . ' he stopped then and shrugged not knowing what else to say, but stared at him until he answered. 'Why do you think I look ill? he answered looking out the window into the distance. 'Well no you look fine' he countered resignedly. 'Then what's the problem?' Kiril spat out in a clipped tone not meant to cause offence, which he knew it didn't as Arnav just rolled his eyes and smirked while he mumbled something about not having a woman for such a long time was bad for a man's soul. As an alternative he just took one last look at his friend and went to inform the men they were to saddle up. Turning from the window he threw himself into the huge chair behind a massive oak desk which held nothing only a heavy piece of rock that he had found wandering the hills just beyond the fold. For some strange reason he was confounded to bring it back with him. He sat back and closed his eyes letting himself drift into his own thoughts bringing him to twelve years earlier when he accompanied his father to finalize the treaty between himself and Mickel Roundgate. Only ten at the time he was pissed off about being made go in the first place. Arguing profusely and constantly with his father over his gift this earned him a hard slap behind the ear and a scowling. He recalled how this cute and sweet young girl strode into the stable. Smiling at his father before turning to her own and demanded the horse. When he refused she kicked her father hard in the leg and screamed until his ears rang. 'With not even the least bit of remorse for her actions' he thought to himself. He had wanted so much to punch her as hard as he could in the face, but thinking of his arse with no skin for months stopped him. He had bit his lip and frowned at her instead, earning him a wicked and devious smirk. He smiled to himself now as he remembered the cunningness in obtaining the animal 'cheeky bitch' he thought. Suddenly without forewarning his mind went to the day he'd seen her walking along the upper wall of the castle. He couldn't take his eyes off her. Hair as black as mid-night, skin as white as porcelain with just the right amount of flushness and those eyes. He had never seen eyes like them before. A piercing green that seemed to shimmer in the sun light, and like a hawk she watched everything. She stood proud and straight backed but her femininity made his hands sweat. Petite in stature but the lines of her body showed her delicious curves making him understand why the men looked at her so fondly.

Thinking about the men who lived and shared her life made his own cheeks flush. The internal fury towards men he didn't know was immense. In all the years of visiting Arella he always felt the same towards the men in the castle. No matter how welcome they made him feel his gut twisted whenever one of them was missing from a meal or a breakfast. His mind always raced with thoughts of her being intimate with someone other than him. She strolled along talking to on-one but acknowledging everyone. He was bowled over and felt like a fool but still couldn't prevent himself staring. Looking away for a brief moment he was taken unawares to have her staring directly back at him, making his heart race and his breath catch in his throat. Beautiful was the only rational thought he had and right then he tried to remember why it was he wanted so bad to thump her. Someone shouted to him and in turning to see what the big ordeal was, he could have killed Arnav when he seen she was gone when he looked back to where she previously stood. He had kept his eyes roaming constantly looking for her for the rest of the time he was there. Never once did he catch a glimpse and to his utter annoyance he was beginning to feel totally taken back at the thought that she was being entertained by some man he didn't know, and particularly didn't like. Finally it got so unbearable he had to ask her father about her continual absence. She was rarely seen within the castle as she was in his words 'always with that bloody horse, a damn curse your father set upon me. U know Kiril I've watched my daughter turn into a strikingly attractive young woman but missed her immensely. She'd rather spend her days, evenings and nights if she could at all get away with it in the stables, and practicing with the men on the field. Wouldn't you think that a woman of twenty would be wanting to find herself a decent and well thought-of man to look after her and give me grandchildren. Don't u think that a strange thing? He had asked him in a bewildered voice. 'I wouldn't know sir for I don't know your daughter and haven't had a chance to speak with her' he said so frustrated that Mickel rubbed his fingers over his mouth to hide his smirk. 'But in all respect I don't think she is the sort to be in need of a man 'besides me' he thought before he continued. 'Surely you wouldn't force her to marry any man? he asked suddenly as his eyes widened in shock. Mickel laughed and shook his head as he took in all of Kiril's little displays of hidden affections towards his daughter. 'Not that she doesn't reap in their attentions. I've seen your men trip over their own feet to walk beside her.' He stopped once again clenching his fists, drawing Mickel's attention to what he thought he was hiding. 'But I'm sure the horse enjoys her companionship.' At that Mickel broke into a humors and contagious laugh, as he looked at him with a sly eye that understood when a man's heart was struggling. Even now made Kiril smile to himself. A booming knock came to the door drawing him out of his mind and back into reality as Arnav entered. Chewing on a big leg of chicken, while he tried to talk and gnaw at the same time he nearly choked and went into a fit of coughing. 'Men are ready and waiting whenever you are.' Kiril pressed down wearily on the table with big hands and strode over to the wall.

Taking hold of the hilt of his sword while positioning it snugly into his belt he stalked out of the room with Arnav on his heels. 'Hey do you think you'll want to punch her this time?' Arnav asked jeeringly as they walked down the crammed hallway. When Kiril just laughed Arnav slapped him on the back with his free hand and gushed with the excitement of causing a bit of trouble. 'This will be fun don't you think? turning his smirk away from his lifelong friend to wink at a buxom blonde that strode by leaving them both laughed. 'Oh yeah starting an argument with the new leader Lady Nox or the Crowden Clan is a great idea if I may so say myself.

Definite way to break the ice.' This left Kiril considering both options before speaking. Deciding on lending a hand to Lady Nox Roundgate and causing a few arguments with the Crowden's if they got out of line. 'What of the Mickisi Clan, Arnav have you heard if she intends to continue on that road? He asked with sudden weary interest. Arnav rubbed his clean shaven chin as he spoke about what might happen is she was to venture so far North. Of course her men were well capable of fighting and they're loyalty was surely as passionate if not stronger to her than once her father. But the Mickisi were a sly and war loving breed she would need to tread with extreme caution. From deep within, Kiril felt a sudden necessity to want to shield and protect her with every part of him. He'd seen her fight, the woman was well capable, a fierce creature with the courage of a lion or the stubbornness of a bear, he couldn't quiet determine which it was. He didn't realize he was day dreaming until Arnav gave him a punch to the shoulder that nearly drove him through the wall. 'What are ye thinking about now; I'm trying to tell ye about the young wench I brought to me bed last eve' he said with a turn up of his lip. 'How young' Kiril asked looking at him from the corner of his eye. 'Ah young enough but old enough to know exactly how to satisfy a man's needs, the girl had skills I'll tell ye without blushing.' Kiril just shook his head in disbelief, 'I really don't see how you've not got a hundred little bastards running around your feet.' At this Arnav just sighed and stated how crafty and inventive a woman can be in such matters which made them both erupt with laughter when they looked at each other. 'Thank to the stars,' said Arnav more seriously. 'Thank the stars is right, Kiril said, 'one of you is enough.'

Chapter Three

After three days in the saddle and Snowflake in not the most obligating of humors Nox was definitely at the end of her nerves. They would have to set up camp for a proper night's sleep and some food before the men started to kill each other. They were agitated, weary and listening to nonstop childish remarks about who was the superior fighter, who could drink more and then it happened—the colour of the bloody sky of all things. She was prepared to scream and kill them all. Seeing it she visualized herself doing it and didn't even feel repentant for the thoughts going through her head.

The scout she had sent riding up ahead to check for the best possible locations finally came hurtling back through the field before them and she prayed to the stars for something positive. Stopping to the left of her on an exhausted horse that snorted loudly and shook his head in pure annoyance and being ridden so hard. He told Nox of what he found leaving her to deliberated for some time before she finally decided to head in the direction of the Zantarian campsite and she hoped they would be hospitable enough for one night at least. As they came up over the hill she spotted one large and two smaller ones short distances apart gave a welcoming felling who's light and warmth called to her. Tents of all sizes littered the surrounding area and from the smells floating through the air they had a great hunting expedition. Fish and meat aromas filled the air and her mouth watered. At least thirty men she counted, as some stood and began to make their way towards her group, she tightened her back but to her delight she received warm smiles. Dismounting she decided first things first and that was to make plans for a place to settle the horses and set up their own camp. Not especially wanting to push her look she thought it best to get settled straight away. Much to Hakan's annoyance that she refused to eat something he backed down as quick as he opened his mouth when he received a look from those emerald eyes that said 'don't press me.' Turning sharply she called to Toran and Gaius who Kiril had noticed had been loitering near her ever since she dismounted and seemed to be shadowing her every move. After a fleeting conversation that seemed to comprise of no more than a sentence, the two men obediently stalked off through the trees with determination. 'What's she up to? he wondered as he followed her with his own eyes.

The woman hadn't even asked to converse with him. His camp and she didn't even have the decency to seek him out' Now he remembered why he had wanted to punch her 'seems some things never change.' Realizing what he was thinking he had to sniffle a laugh by rubbing his hand under his nose. The camp was in sudden uproar between the horses, the men settling in and Nox screaming out her orders, he decided he had to put a stop to the chaos and maybe offer a helping hand. Which by doing so earned him a few choice and memorable very unladylike words that he swore never to repeat. After he was stung by her tongue and had the embarrassment of his own men laugh at him and following with arrays of 'what were you thinking, trying to help a woman of all things.' 'Do you not know anything Kiril?' Arnav laughed when he picked up pace beside him. 'Obviously not' he retorted as he turned a frosty stare back over his shoulder at the little spit fire. 'You're a fool to think she can be seen taking orders from you. She's their leader. What possessed ye to tell her she was doing it all wrong?'

Arnav said with a shrug of his shoulders and a slight shake of his head. But before he could continue he was stopped when Nox called for Kiril from behind. On seeing her walk with purpose towards them he gave Kiril a pitying look and walked back towards the camp giving her a weak nod and a cheeky almost sly wink as he passed her. She found herself looking after him to the extent of stopping altogether to take him all in. Tall, lean with sandy hair that hung glistening past his shoulders. A fine specimen of a man she decided. She wondered if all the stories of him and the many women were in fact true. 'There were so many and what kind of man would allow himself to be accustomed with so many women anyway? She asked herself.

Pulling her eyes from him and back to Kiril who she found glaring at her. Making her become very uncomfortable and she had a horrible thought that maybe she had been dribbling over the man. When he raised his eyebrows at her she suddenly remembered what it was she wanted to say to him. 'I want to express gratitude for allowing us to camp with you. We will be sure to be gone by first light, save things don't flow as efficiently as I'd like. I've still to come to a decision on a small number of issues that might take some time longer than I anticipated,' she said wearily rubbing her hand along the back of her neck. 'Have you eaten' he asked hoarsely drawing her eyes back to him. When she smiled and shook her head he led her back to the camp and settled her with a plate of potatoes and a meat of some sort that she didn't even care to ask what it was, but it was the most delicious thing she had tasted in days.

When she was finished she suddenly remembered the two men she sent off to set up a watch out point, not that she didn't think Kiril was on top of things but she really didn't like being so close to Shia. Without any warning she stood and walked off without a word to anyone as she made her way towards the trees that littered the horizon. Thanking the moons light for the way she finally found Toran and Gaius and sent them back with a message that she would be here for the remainder of the night and would be down by sunrise. Much to their arguing on the matter they returned alone, only to have Hakan unleash his annoyance at their stupidity. Kiril noticed even though he wasn't pleased with the situation he didn't move to interject her decision.

~

He couldn't sleep and was really getting pissed off tossing and turning constantly, until finally made the way towards were he knew Nox would be. He wasn't sure what kind of a response he would get from her following their last encounter but he didn't really care, he needed his mind set at ease. Taking lengthy meaningful strides up the side of the hill, his calves burned with complaint as he continued until the sound of sharpening swords stopped him in his path. She had let her long black locks descend loose covering her shoulders on all sides and down her back until it was just touching the ground where she sat cross legged. He watched as she ran her fingertips along the sharpened blades with absolute care while looking upon it in the luminosity of the first shards of light. Without any forewarning she spoke faintly, catching him off guard.

'You know you shouldn't sneak up upon me Kiril, it's a good thing I recognized your heavy feet.' With that she was standing facing him. Forcing himself not to retaliate with a jibe of his own he strode towards her and began to speak of small, minor and un important things. He discovered she seemed to enjoyed speaking of when they were younger, him in particular. Soon she was rolling on her back laughing so hard she had to grip her sides as the tears ran down her face. 'Oh Kiril that is just terrible' she said still in fits of laughing. 'I can see you mean that' he replied a little gruffly. 'Did you at least get Arnav back for setting you up? She demanded giggling. With the expression that formed upon his face she knew he did and it was far from pretty. 'What did you do? Suddenly composed she sat up and moved nearer which gave him a feeling that he fought to control. 'You'll scare her off you fool' he shouted to himself as he tried not to allow her to affect him in any way, it would definitely not help at the present moment. 'I sent him to my father telling him he wanted speak with him, only when he got there my father wasn't this left Arnav by himself and with no witnesses.' By now Nox was totally engrossed in his tale and without him noticing she had edged closer making his hands sweat. 'There was myself and four others hiding within the alcoves and when he turned to leave the hall we emerged and grabbed him. It was a good thing I had help, don't let him fool you he's a strong one.' He said all convincing as her eyes widened with excitement. 'What did you do to him?

Kiril's eyes shone as he remembered and she laughed taking him by surprise. 'What? he asked shyly as she stared directly at him Face flushed from laughing she laid her hand upon his thigh 'Nothing it's just you looked so devious. I've never seen that look before' she told him tilting her head to one side as if inspecting him. Feeling self-conscious he cleared his throat. 'So we stripped him naked and took off with his clothes' he said in a rushed voice as she exploded with laughter yet again. 'Only it didn't work out how we had hoped' Kiril said as a smile spread across his face. 'Why? Nox asked while wiping wet trails of tears from her face. 'Do you always cry when you laugh? He asked her seriously. 'Only when it's really funny. Never mind that tell me why it didn't work out? She pushed. 'It seems we helped him gain his reputation for chasing the women. He was five minutes out running through the castle when he fell into someone's bed' he said shaking his head in disbelief. When he was finished his story everything seemed to turn into an uncomfortable silence. Taking a deep breath she sighed and looked at him only to find he was already looking at her. She could feel herself blush and when he seen it his heart raced in his chest. 'Do you remember the first person you ever kissed Kiril? she asked looking at him from under her eyelashes. 'Do you? he replied curious but also a bit pissed off that someone else tasted her lips. 'Of course I do, it was Gaius' she said picking a blade of grass and running it through her fingers. 'Don't look so shocked Kiril. He's a handsome man is he not? She teased.

'How should I know' replying as he contemplated what this meant. Gaius was here with her.

'Does that mean they have always been together? Damn it I knew she had a man in her life' he thought as he clenched his fists. 'I'm going to fucking kill him' he said to himself as he thought of all the times he was in Arella and Gaius was the one who told him Nox had no interest in any of the men in the castle. 'When you say first kiss? He asked indifferently. 'I was twelve and he was fourteen' she said laughing. Taking a deep breath he relaxed no end as he thought of the man sitting in the campsite arguing with his brother came to him as a young teenage man. He looked a lot different when he was younger. I think I should have waited' she said smiling as she glanced at him. 'It got a bit strange especially when he would introduce himself as my bother when I was approached by any other boys in the castle or even those that visited. Then the same person would see us together, and I would end up making up stories to calm my father's temper.'

Seeing his expression she laughed. 'It's not like he never wanted me to have a boyfriend it's just . . . well he thought I was too young to have sense' she said shrugging her shoulders. 'So what about you? Do you remember? Is there a lady in your life? 'What is wrong with you, just tell her how you feel' he said to himself just as her stomach growled loudly resulting in her blushing and saving him embarrassing himself. 'So Gaius is the man in your life I take it' trying to be calm and collective he smiled at her. 'Of course not. I don't think we have kissed since the day I turned thirteen.' She answered with a wave of her hand. 'Why? Are you jealous? She jested with him as her laughter seemed to run through his veins and the warmth that followed made him so self-conscious he rose putting a hand out to her to help her up. 'So you don't think he has feelings for you now? He asked trying his best to remain casual. She grinned and turning she faced him directly and stopped walking so he had no choice but to look at her. 'Kiril do you remember the last time you visited Arella? I do' she said before he had a chance to answer. 'I recall having a very heated discussion with Gaius about him warning you to stay away from me, am I right? Nodding he waited for her to continue. Smiling and without warning she sat down once again and stared up at him smugly. 'What did you want to say to me that night Kiril that he stopped you to extent that both of you nearly killed each other? 'Nothing' he said gruffly as stepped around her. 'We need to talk' he said as the realization that the noise coming from the camp meant the men were up and moving and it was time to get on with more pressing matters.

'Funny I thought that's what we were doing' she replied with a hint of sharpness that made him rotate back to where he left her. 'Damn it, it's as good a time as any to acknowledge the true reasons for being on the road to the Glens of Crowden.' he reasoned with himself and began to tell her before he changed his mind. He rushed through his confession as they walked hoping she wouldn't interrupt and by the time he was finished he found his hands were sweating and was left considering that maybe he didn't like her being so quiet. To his total bafflement she scrunched up her nose slightly giving him an urgent want to touch it with his finger but at the risk of maybe losing a finger he decided against it. Unable to wait any longer he pushed her for her response, and was quiet surprised when she agreed that it wouldn't be an all bad situation to arrive as a unified front to the Crowden Clan Elders. 'We'll talk more on it later, but first I need to eat,' she said and with a flash of a mischievous grin she put her hand over Arnav's shoulder, grabbed his bread and took a bite out of it leaving him open mouthed at the pure audacity to do such a thing.

By the time conversation over breakfast turned to fighting all hell broke loose. Arnav who was still clearly upset over the early morning thieving of his food grabbed his sword and demanded Nox fight him, to a chorus of cheers from her own men and a deadly look from Kiril directed Arnav's way. Not hesitating to accept his offer she started tying her hair up as tightly as humanly possible. 'Always a welcoming activity to pass the time.' she called to her men who laughed again louder. Continuing to tie her hair into a tight braid as she walked out into the field, she eyed Arnav and was pleasantly surprised that his form had changed from being angry to having the essence of pure cockiness about him. 'I'll enjoy beating you,' she thought with an inward smile. When he decided they had come far enough he stopped and faced her sword drawn. Just to make certain he was in no doubt she wasn't one for following or taking orders from any man she continued to walk until she was of the opinion her point was made. 'Was that really necessary? Arnav asked as she began untying the strings of her cloak from around her neck. The heavy black velvet fell from her with a heavy thud as it hit the grass beneath her feet.

Smirking at him as she displayed her two most deadly weapons. 'Yes it was' she said lifting her hands to take hold of the smooth handles that fit her hands perfectly, she molded her fingers into place and gave a pull that brought them from their home off her back to pointing them directly at

Arnav. 'First blood' was all he heard before she was upon him in an array of slashing, plunging and dodging. The sound of clashing swords rang out in the clearing and went on for quite a long time showing how well matched they were, until finally Arnav gave a startled yelp and jumped back. A large gash was torn across the mid-section of his shirt leaving it completely open to the elements. Stifling a giggle she held up her sword and pointed it at him daring him to attack. With that he rushed her and swiped down missing her by mere inches as she turned like lightening and drew her swords together across this throat, stopping just as a hot dibble of bright red welled up and flowed down his chest. Eyes wide with disbelief he went straight as a board, dropped his sword and let out a short but thankful sigh that she had such great control. Looking up at him she threw him a mock kiss and lowered her swords. 'Would you like to try again? She asked in a tone that he could only call sadistic if he was being totally honest with himself, and at that moment in time he didn't care about the noise coming from behind or the comments to come about being battered by a woman he simply smiled and declined. Just then she spotted Kiril making his way towards her, sword in hand and a gleam in his eye. 'Surely not' she thought to herself, taking in the big man walking with purpose. She had never realized until now how much of a domineering prowess he had radiating from him. Her emotions ran off her like water that sent a shiver down her spine. Looking the true warrior he obviously had a point to prove best let him try her inner voice said with a sigh, and by the time he had reached her Arnav was gone leaving her in the shadow of his fearless captain. 'Can I help you?' she said teasingly, craning her neck upwards to look up at him. The heat came off him in waves making her light-headed.

'First blood was it not? He returned just as teasing and before she knew it her arms were beginning to feel bruised and battered. He was powerful she thought as he rained down blow after blow to the extent that she was just ready to give in to defeat, until 'Ouch' was all she could form with her words. Her whole face throbbed and as she felt gingerly at her nose she tensed at the pain that shot all the way to the back of her head, and heaved at the taste of blood going down the back of her throat. Quietness filled the air as the men held their breath and Kiril was suddenly beside her trying desperately to look upon the damage. While he was fusing over her she seen her chance and in bending down she swiped her blade from the strapping on her thigh, grabbed a handful of his hair and pressed the cold metal under his chin. He couldn't believe it, and as he went to pull away she pulled harder on his hair forcing him to kneel lower so that her lips were brushing against his making him swallow hard. 'He has no feelings for me as I have none for him.' Moving away she rested them against his ear and with that she whispered 'I may be bleeding, but your dead' releasing his hair she walked off towards the river to a series of meaningful looks and bowed heads. She had proven herself twice over. While he stayed on bended knee with his fingertips against his mouth he was in a daze as he tried to recapture the feel of her lips so close to his.

Chapter Four

How could he have been so stupid? He cursed himself. What had possessed him to hit her?

Damn fool! Following her to the river after nearly having to fight for his own life when Hakan,

Arnav and the hovering twins advanced on him with one thing in mind. He ached all over but was glad they held back somewhat. Breaking through the bushes he spotted her knee deep in her under garments having left her deep green gown dangling over the branch of a nearby tree. Her hair now hung freed and untied again he noticed and as she started to venture deeper into the water she shivered as the coldness bit at her thighs. He watched her silently willing her to turn and look at him, but willing her not to at the same time. He couldn't bear the thought of seeing the damage caused to her by him. By his hand, no others. She had to forgive him. 'Damn it I'll make her forgive me' Finally gathering his senses he walked towards the river's perimeter.

Damn it he'd apologize, grovel or if he was completely stupid tell her it was in fact her own fault after all for letting her guard down. On hearing him approach she turned giving him the look he was dreading. Horrified shock inched into his features. She was still bleeding, and in no humor for anything he had to say. 'Come to finish the job, have you?' her tone harsh and crisp to his ears, and it stung his heart like a lightning bolt. 'How could she even think he had done this on purpose? Without realizing he had dropped his eyes from her face, and was actually staring at her breasts she thought with great displeasure. 'What the hell was wrong with this man?' Biting his bottom lip the only rational thought that came to his head was 'why would she wear such an undergarment, 'Give me strength' he whispered and looked up to find her glaring at him. 'I think you'll find that my eyes are higher than you seem to think they are' she almost hissed at him. To her utter annoyance he wasn't even the least bit repentant. Drawing in a short horrified gasp that he would blatantly gawk at her 'arrogant son-of-a-bitch' she thought and it took no more than a single final glace his way to bring him back to the reason he was there in the first place. Before he could summon the words she spun around and glided effortlessly through the water leaving him standing looking after her. 'Damn woman's going to make me follow her' he said as he placed his hands on his hips. 'If I have to get wet your really will regret it Nox' he bellowed after her. After an infuriating minute as he waited to see what she would do, he pulled his boots off followed by his shirt and stalked into the water. The water was so cold he had to stop himself from believing his testicles would never recover from the shock. When he got close enough to reach out and grab her he did, pulling her back to him with such force her face ended up totally submerged under the water forcing her to fight to the surface, spluttering and coughing until she nearly choked. Holding her firm and determined against his chest he prevented her from getting away as she killing him, leaving him struggled against her protests. 'Let me go this minute' she said under her breath as she fought to release herself. 'Stop struggling!' he shouted at her. 'For all that is good will please stop I only want to talk to you! Knowing there was no other way to get emancipated from his grasp, she stopped wiggling and looked up into his eyes, and at that very minute she didn't have a rational thought in her head. Bringing up a gentle hand with caution he wiped the blood from her upper lip. Some profound uncontrollable thing happened deep in her stomach forcing her to close her eyes as she felt his heart race against her chest. His breath was warm on her face and she did everything in her power to prevent herself from shaking. 'I'm ashamed I hit you' he said in a torn voice that made her open her eyes and stare directly at him. Dark eyes glistened with more than words meant to be spoken. 'It will never happen again' he said releasing her gently as he moved his grip to her hips keeping her held against him. Unconsciously he rubbed his erection against her thighs and became aware of how uncomfortable he was getting. His trousers were plastered tight to him and with the urge that was taking over his body at that moment in time wasn't helping matters at all. It definitely didn't help matters that he was deadly aware of her erect nipples standing taunt against his chest.

He desired her more than anything. Lifting her chin tenderly he lowered his mouth to hers and began to kiss her, molding her lips to his. She didn't fight and when he felt her tongue flick against his he lost his control, and began to ravish her with his kiss. She groaned a delicious sound and wrapped her arms tight around his neck drawing him in deeper, while wrapping her legs around his waist. He brought his hands from around her back and ran them along her thighs and around to her soft buttocks. She felt like silk in his hands, but her undergarments were driving him crazy, twisted around her in the most inconvenient places, he thought he would lose his mind if he didn't get them off her soon. Without thinking he slipped his finger into her moist entrance and all of a sudden went stiff, when her eyes flew open and she drew in a breath, her face no longer showing any expression he could figure out. She was a virgin. 'Shit!' he thought what was he doing? As gently as he could he removed his hand and broke the kiss. 'Don't stop' she said breathless. 'I . . . I can't, not like this' he said in return just as breathless. With that she pulled from his grasp and swam towards the shore leaving him standing shoulder deep in the water speechless and very confused. Why had she recoiled from him? He knew she wanted him as much as he wanted her that was evident. He watched as she left the water and walked towards her dry clothes and when she looked back at him her green eyes blazed with danger.

'Surely she's not angry with me' he said in total bewilderment as he took a second look to make sure he'd seen correct. No, there she was bustling around as fast as she could to get away.

Making his way out of the water he went to her and gently turned her around to face him only to be met with a slap that definitely would have hurt if his face wasn't already so damn cold. He stood shocked 'What the fuck was that for?' he said through clenched teeth. As tears welled up in her eyes his anger faded. 'Nox' he said in a soft voice almost a whisper as he placed his hands on her face forcing her to look at him. 'Tell me please, have I hurt you so badly that ye can't look at me?' he asked pleading. Without warning she burst into loud hard sobs. 'Why did you have to be such a gentleman?' Definitely not the answer he was expecting forcing Kiril to burst into laughter which was not the most ideal thing to do at that very moment. Slapped his hands away she looked totally humiliated, that when he went to hold her again she shuffled fast out of his reach. Wiping her hand across her face to clear her vision she braced herself, fists clenched and let him have it. 'Are my tears something that would cause you such humor' she shrieked. 'You would kiss me and touch me in such a way and then refuse me as if I'm a cheap whore that you've grown bored of? Past crying now she was furious. 'What, you don't want me anymore? Because I know you've wanted me for years. Even my father informed me of that, but no you'd always just stand staring at me like a little love sick pup, who forgot what it took to be a man and go for what he wanted. Now you could have had me and suddenly I'm to pure for you? Your pathetic' she screamed. Taking a deep breath she watched as his face changed from red to pale in seconds, and at that moment she realized she wasn't the only one that was angry.

'Bloody woman, what is wrong with you? If I was to have taken you there in the river, you'd have been nothing but a whore as you so nicely put it. Which by the way it went against every ounce of my power to leave you intact. As for my remembering what a man is about I don't think you realize how close you came to finding out, and then what would I be but nothing but a ruthless rouge in your eyes.' He was shaking now unable to stop himself from continuing.

'Besides what the hell do you think you're doing anyway teasing a man to near bursting and then leaving him staring at your back?' 'You fucking bastard' she whispered gaping at him open mouthed, she couldn't decide if he was serious and her heart was pounding so hard that she thought it might stop beating. 'It was you who pushed me away in case you've forgotten, but make no mistake it won't be ever happen again' She straightened her back, lifted her chin and pierced him with those green eyes. Turning then on trembling legs she left him looking once again at her back. He couldn't take it. 'I should have hit you harder' he screamed at her as he pulled at his hair with both fists. Suddenly she wheeled on him and all he could think was how damn beautiful she was until she struck him with what seemed to be the biggest bloody rock she could get her hands on. He cursed and shook his head. 'I hope you fucking drown' she yelled, and right there she didn't know whether to laugh or run for her life. Within two breaths she was spun around and caught once again in his vice iron grip, as he gathered her firmly and proceeded to kiss her with such force she thought her jaws would break. Forcing his tongue into her mouth, and to her annoyance her own traitorous mouth responded with such fever that she felt her knees go flimsy and fervor so uncontrollable shot down between her legs. As fast as the assault began it stopped leaving her laying languorously comfortable in his arms eyes closed and quivering like jelly. Just as she had forgotten where she was he took a deep breath, put her firm on her feet and said 'now you can go' with such male smugness, not even bothering to conceal his satisfaction, this infuriated her beyond words. But this time it was her that was left watching his back as he walked back to the water to cool down.

~

By the time Kiril returned to the campsite fully dressed, but with shaded eyes that would have impaled her if she had not been sitting already. His dark locks fell loose, but strangely he seemed to have lost his rut fullness and just looked sheepishly at her. Nox didn't think she would be able to stop herself blush with embarrassment if he had looked at her as he had before she left him at the water's edge. Heaving, and ready to take her be damned. Instead the tops of his cheeks glowed a bright pink, and she found herself gawking at him in surprise. Only noticing what she was doing when her mouth grew dry, she clamped it shut and grew self-conscious.

Had anyone noticed? She would be horrified. Just as the thought entered her head Malachi broke the silence that seems to have engulfed her as he looked directly into Kiril's face and noticed his probably broken nose. 'What happened to your nose? It's broken for sure.' At this Arnav looked up at his friend only to received a mumbled 'Were even' before he sat down by the fire. Feeling uncomfortable she rose slowly as if she had been sitting for hours and stretched herself and turned towards the lookout point. She had to stop thinking about what had happened earlier today and concentrate on what lay ahead. A treaty would have to be signed or even agreed to at the very least to ensure future peace. Damn it she needed some advice, and that of all things stuck in her gut. Spotting Gaius walking towards her from which she assumed had been taking a piss greeted him with a smile and asked him to accompany her. He gladly agreed and wrapped his arm around her shoulder giving a gentle squeeze. She was by no means put out by his casualness with her and allowed him to lead her away further up the hill. It was comforting and he was so huge to her five foot three inches, for which reason she had found herself at the receiving end of many a joke over the years but she never really minded. Gaius constantly seemed to end it all with a few choice words and a few split lips. Finally she stopped and faced him, and for the first time in a long time he could see how torn her emotions were and he didn't like it. 'I need you not to look on me as your friend, but as your chief, your leader and comrade, and tell me the truth' she said in a serious tone that he understood and just gave a slight nod for her to continue. He would oblige her with his truthful answer. 'Do you trust the Mickisi?' she said straight to the point, and as the moon shone over their heads she could see the frown grow across his brow and his lips tightened. 'No!' was all he said and that was all she needed. 'Thank you' she replied and laid a gentle hand on his arm and squeezed. 'We'll leave for the Glens of Crowden first light. We need to get things into motion and then decide what to do if anything about the Mickisi.' She felt lighter and knew she'd sleep well. As she turned to leave he took her tenderly by the hand and kissed her knuckles, 'you're doing exceptionally well Nox, stop questioning yourself. Your decision is a good one and definitely the best route in such matters as these.' He released her then and smiled at her 'but I tell you now' he stopped and looked down onto the campsite to where he assumed Kiril was still sitting by the fire, 'I promised your father I'd protect and keep you from harm's way against any enemy with my life, and that I'll do till my last breath. But, if the man lays a hand to you in that way again forgive me when I kill him.' He was intense, in addition to being very serious and she didn't know how to feel. 'You don't trust him?' she asked uneasily, hoping she was wrong. He sighed and shook his head 'Oh I trust him that's why he's still breathing,' he said with a slight smile in his voice. 'But a man in love is a dangerous thing' and at that he hooked her hand through his elbow and walked some more. Finally for the first time today she felt in control, but at the very same thing Kiril thought he was going to go on a murderous rampage. 'Where were they going?

An hour later returning to the campsite feeling truly exhausted and ready to settle in after the trek beyond the trees. She felt liberated until she felt as though someone was baring holes in her back. Spinning fast to where she felt the most tenseness, she slumped her shoulders and placed her hands on her hips as she rubbed the bridge of her nose with pinched fingers. 'Enjoy your walk did you? Kiril asked in a quiet over controlled tone as he walked towards her. Why did he think she had to answer to him. Damn him! Who does he think he is? Stupid man! So instead she said in the most ladylike voice she could muster so late at night, through him a sly smile and said 'Yes thank you for asking,' but noting the veins that bulged from his neck as she did so left her a little apprehensive and without thinking grabbed a fistful of her gown. He had stopped walking towards her now and where he stood the overhanging branches of the trees left small areas of his face and chest alight. She noticed initially the intensity of his eyes that seemed to look straight through her, the molding of his lower lip that was just that little bit thicker than the top and from what she could recollected were lethal in their taking. His shirt was opened just enough to catch a glimpse of the outline of his strong shoulders and exceptional shaping. Her hands were starting to sweat as unreserved lust seemed to be taking complete control of her whole body. 'I'm sorry I hit you with the rock' she blabbered out fast and turned before he could respond.

Following her to the fire he took the mug offered to him by Hakan and sat down.

Crossing his legs relaxing against the ground, leaned slightly so his shoulder was touching hers.

The heat coming from him was magnificent she thought as she unconsciously shifted closer to him. Hakan if he did notice any of the small subtle hints choose to ignore them and bid good night and went to retrieve his place by the tree facing east. 'Gaius thinks much of you,' he said breaking the silence that was driving him insane. 'Hmm?' she said as if she hadn't been listening when really as soon as she heard Gaius's name all she could remember was their conversation. 'He loves you, he'd told her. 'Gaius' he said again this time pointing at the huge bulge asleep snoring loudly. She smiled at the image in front of her and contentedly explained how since she was very young Toran and Gaius had been what seemed her bodyguards. This made her express her amusement considering they were only two years older, but because of their size no one opposed them even as children. They'd pretend to play the role of brothers when she received unwelcoming attention. 'He's protective' she whispered but a glint of apprehension shone in her eyes. 'He'll die for you' Kiril said more seriously now that made her turn to him with sadness that touched her soft features. 'Just as I will die for any of my brothers' she spoke in a low voice that didn't hold fear but acceptance of faith.

~

When silence fell and they slipped shyly into an uncomfortable situation she started to fidget and cursed herself for not having the ability to read minds, so instead she just came out and said what was on her mind. 'Oh, this is stupid! You listen to me, you took me by surprise, and what were you thinking anyway following me into the water, which by the way you could have drown me in the process,' stopping to catch her breath she turned her full attention on him and pointing a finger menacingly 'And by the way! She said in what seemed to not even sound like her own voice. Was cut off when his huge hand shifted behind her neck and drew her into a wonderfully, sweet and delicious kiss that she had to admit had been missing since the morning.

He kissed her with passion and such gentleness that she followed his mouth when he tried to move away, leaving him with a joyful expression that filled his face. 'You're so beautiful,' he whispered into the hours of darkness. As he laid his head against hers. 'Forgive me,' he said as he gently licked across her bottom lip before he drew it between his teeth and nibbled it. 'He's not the only man who will die for you.'

Chapter Five

After spending the night curled up with Kiril by the fire she woke feeling warm, giddy and a little bit bold if she was being honest. They had been awake for most of the night talking, cuddling and kissing until at one point she thought she might actually fall asleep with his mouth on hers. Bringing her fingers to her lips she smiled secretly and felt that familiar warm feeling she felt when she thought of him. The sun was going to be up soon and she had a horrible feeling of falling back to sleep only to wake with a hundred eyes on her, and she blushed a deep red. As if he could feel her thoughts he tightened his grip around her mid-section and drew her closer, letting out a sigh of pure contentment. She waited for him to relax enough to ease her way out of his arms, leaving her sitting staring at his form. So strikingly handsome she thought.

His face half covered by an unruly mass of soft curly waves that edged his solid jaw which stuck slightly to the soft black beard that seemed she realized to materialize over night. His long black lashes grew a lighter shade by the time they reached the ends. They lay like feathers against his cheeks. Her fingers itched to touch his lips but she knew he'd awaken and she'd get nothing done so instead she settled for the gentlest of touches to his cheek, and left as quietly as she possibly could.

By the time sunrise came horses were being tended, saddled and plans she was happy to admit were finally coming together. She found besides a few knowing nods and a comment about her sleeping arrangements the night before which she felt the necessity to point out it not being any of their damn business, the morning went without being too much of an annoyance. Finding it surprisingly reassuring to see that no-one actually seemed that surprised by the developing relations between herself and Kiril. By the time he woke and found her they seemed to be doing nothing but finding little hiding placed to enjoy a few moments in private, entwined in strange and questionable embraces when they assumed they weren't being watched. She wanted him so badly but now was definitely not the right time.

'When would be the right time' she wondered with a slight pout that she would have got away with when she was a child but now she just looked pitiful. Finding herself following his every move with her eyes, she began to notice little quirks she hadn't given herself a chance to see.

When he was clearly not interested in listening to someone he'd look out over their heads as if something in the distance was needing his attention, until they finally got bored and walked away. 'How ignorant' she thought but found it to be deeply amusing. He raked his fingers through his hair with great vigor she noticed when he was trying to figure something out in his head, and how he would bluntly laugh up in someone's face at the most inappropriate times, causing near arguments. But yet as she stood watching him go about his business she couldn't help having felt like she had won some fierce battle for his affections. He'd never tried to hide his feelings from her, well at least not after he'd kissed her for the first time in the river, if he hadn't had done that she honestly thought she would have gone mad by now. Shaking her head as she drew her eyebrows up slightly when she remembered how out right blunt and forceful he had been that day. He nearly knocked her head off, drowned her, and she actually thought she recalled him calling her a whore but damn it she couldn't not acknowledge how strong her feeling were for him. How could she deny it but to lie to herself. 'I've certainly picked a strong one, if not pig headed,' she thought with amusement, only to be snapped out of her thoughts again by what seemed like an argument in the making between Gaius and Arnav. 'Bloody men! saying it loud enough to get a few bashed if not hurt looks from those passing her. 'Oh, come on,' she said just as loudly as she looked at them. 'How did your sensitive natures ever make it past puberty?' she asked in a mocking tone that just earned her a few tongue clicks and grunts as they continued on their way.

When arriving at the point of controversy she noted that the two men were disagreeing over the best way to travel, the best paths, the food that would be needed, the camping equipment, who should take the lead. Finally she could keep quiet any longer and jumped straight in with 'You realize you two are travelling in separate ways, right?' Taking in their questioning gazes she informed them of her decision to travel along the East until they reached the foot of the Shia Mountains. It wasn't an easy path but it was at least one day faster and because of that worth the chance. Gaius was the first to object which she was expecting as soon as she mentioned the Shia, but when Arnav jumped in with his opinions which to her annoyance only consisted of 'Kiril won't agree to that.' She exploded at both men stating that Gaius should first remember that although his opinions counted and were always taken on she was chief and her decisions were final. Then turning on Arnav she spoke to him in what seemed to sound almost hiss like, and spat the words 'Kiril has no choice in the matter, he can do as he pleases, take the road he chooses, and come to it I don't remember ever asking for his permission,' at that she turned her finger at both of them 'or yours.' She was fuming and during the whole alternation she never realized she had been thumping her hands on the maps in front of her, until she noted a questionable look thrown her way by Hakan who received a glare that would have made her father proud. With that she beckoned Toran, told him the change of plans and gave orders to get the men ready to leave. Walking away from the two stunned men she made her way to retrieve Snowflake, only to her amusement Hakan was already saddled, with Snowflake chopping merrily on the fresh grass. 'Thought you were changing your mind?' he said as he caught a glimpse of her coming towards him. 'Some would hope so' she returned with a sarcastic laugh. 'Oh? A certain big man with a face like thunder maybe? He said nodding over her shoulder, making her wince even before she turned. And there he was, face like thunder indeed. Suppressing a sigh she headed back the way she came to head him off. 'Not now,' she thought pleading. Only when she actually did look up at him he gave her a brilliant smile and a slight shake of the head that only could imply one thing on his part and that was, he should have known. Feeling a gush of delight she quickened her pace and widened her smile, and before she had a chance to think of anything to say she found herself up in his arms being kissed so passionately that she forgot to breath. Grabbing his hair to force him deeper, she suppressed every instinct in her to remember where she was and that they weren't alone. He caused her to lose all her senses and she loved it. Finally realizing her he kissed her gently on what seemed to be very swollen lips. Pulling back to look at her, he ran his fingers gently along her jaw. 'Are you sure about this?' he asked her, letting a hint of his concern fill his voice that didn't go un- noticed. Taking his hand she kissed his fingers and laid his hand gently and snugly against her now flushed face, 'I've never been more sure of anything,' talking in a slight voice, leaving him wondering what question she was answering and his heart swelled. But he had make her focus.

'You know what I mean Nox, it's an unnecessary risk. There are other paths you could take.'

Leaning up onto her tiptoes she leaned close enough to just float over his lips 'I know what I am doing,' kissing him with just enough pressure to leave a tingling feeling that burned in his loins.

As if knowing his growing need she placed her hand behind his back and cheekily squeezed his buttocks while rubbing herself against his now growing erection. 'Mmm! Seems I'm leaving you at the wrong time completely' she said teasingly, while he groaned placing his forehead against hers. 'You're killing me' he replied, making her laughter fill the air. 'I hope not' she responded leaning back displaying a wide smile.

KIRIL

'Blasted woman will be the death of me,' he mumbled as he watched her leave. Her erect back showed her confidence as well as the unwavering strength she possessed. Giving him a sudden feeling of proud-ness that she was a force in her own right. 'Foot of the Shia Mountains, give me patience,' talking more loudly this time that he drew concerned looks from his men who obviously agreed with him. Arnav came up behind him and caught him unawares, 'If Anso couldn't rein her in Kiril, I hate to break it to ye but it's very unlikely you'll do it in one night,' he stated matter of fact, which to his distain secured him a meaningful scorn from his already very pissed off friend. 'I don't want to rein her in Arnav, she's not a fucking horse,' he replied heatedly and stomped off towards the remaining men that were to his total annoyance, and bewilderment were still not bloody ready. Was he going to have to crack some heads before people listened to what he asked of them. 'Hurry on!' he bellowed, 'were leaving,' and with that he was on his way to retrieve his own belongs from where he left them from the morning.

Thinking back he couldn't fathom how she had managed to untangle herself from his grasp, gather her things, and be nearly on her horse and gone by the time he realized what was going on. Refusing to think that she was trying for a quick escape and regretting her feelings for him, he shook himself and remembered how she had kissed him so hungrily. Bending down to pick up his sword from the broken off tree stump when something caught his eye. 'What the . . . ? he frowned as he plucked it from under his saddlebag. Opening it with no great finesse he nearly dropped it again when he read the words inside;

Kiril, my love

> *I feel I have left much unsaid between us, and find I am incapable of putting my emotions into words. But know this if you know nothing else*
> *You are forgiven.*

Nox

Raising her note to his lips he closed his eyes and breathed in trying to catch a small token of her scent but only the smell of the morning drew rushed from it filling his senses. Smiling like a fool and not caring he folded the note and placed it within his shirt pocket were he could feel it against his chest. Hating the fact he had to return to his father as he required to be filled in when it came to important matters such as a Treaty of the Peace. Realizing with a bitter taste in his mouth that she'd arrive in the Glens of the Crowden nearly two days and nights before him.

'Damn it,' he huffed and screamed for his men to move their arses or be left behind. Grabbing his saddlebag and flinging it with as much grace as a bear he mounted his horse, faced it in the direction of home, setting his mind on getting there, doing what needed to be done and leaving for the Crowden as soon as possible.

~

From the distance he could make out the outline of what he could only describe as mammoth trees that lined the road at the side of the cliffs, which had claimed many lives from what he could recall. Just beyond the clearing to the left of the cliffs was home. Zantar.

His home since his birth would someday be the home of his death but for now it was just home. He had rode hard for six hours straight with only one break to water the horses and to stop his men from moaning about the pain in their arses. But now with a swell of sudden pride he brought them through the gates unharmed and in surprising good spirits, which he was putting to the fact they could dismount. His father would be pleased as always to see him so deciding not to waste any time he headed straight for the stables, gladly handed over his exhausted horse, which he patted with great acknowledgement for his achievement and headed to the castle.

Taking a deep breath, he braced himself and pushed open the doors. He moved inside to a well lit room that held two giant impressive columns on either side of a huge archway that lead to private rooms. His father held gatherings in the private rooms when important visitors arrived or for special occasions. The last being when Mickel Roundgate joined them to celebrate finally putting a stop to the war that had gone on for just over a hundred years between their clans. Of course he spent all night playing with his food, ignoring any woman that showed him any interest in case Nox was looking. He smiled at the memory of when she walked into the hall in a dark red gown that emphasized her curves to an unmerciful amount. 'Mmm,' he whispered at the hidden memory he kept, until finally he arrived at his father's bedroom door. Wiping sweating hands along his legs, he knocked louder than he wanted to but before he put his hand down his father had the doors open and erupted with a joyous 'whoop,' crushing him to himself in a tight embrace. Clapping him on the back he drew him in and closed the doors behind them leaving them in quiet privacy. After what seemed like a lifetime Kiril emerged mentally exhausted from his father's gauging abilities. The man was ruthless to the extent Kiril found himself changing positions and regularly curling and uncurling his fingers until his hands began to sweat again.

Realizing his father had clearly heard something of Nox he rolled his eyes when Anso scowled at him clearly unhappy that he refused to talk about it with him. 'Do you realized your cousin has made my brother a grandfather yet again' he had said sourly, clearly jealous of the man. 'You're going to have me die an old man with no joy in my life, is that it Kiril? He said as he continued to sulk and brood. More questions came and still he refused pointedly. But when his face burned a fierce colour red his father chuckled and let him be. He dug into his pocket bringing out the note she had left him and held it in his hand just to get the feel of her. 'So this is what love does to a man, makes him a bloody fool,' he said resigned to himself but still holding the note tight he headed for his rooms to wash, change, eat and try to sleep.

When entering his room he noticed that nothing had changed. Breathing a sigh of built up tension he headed straight for the wash basin and began to strip off his dirty clothes. Washing unhurriedly and thoroughly he paid no attention to the goose bumps that had formed all over his body. As he began to wash his testicles his cock felt the pressure of pent up want and need that came when he allowed his mind to race away with thoughts of Nox. Drying quickly he headed to the table set out with a mass arrangement of foods ranging from meats hot and cold, bread, fruits and beer. Having picked for a few minutes and deciding he wasn't hungry enough to force it he walked and flung himself on the bed. Laying naked he drew the fur blanket his father had given him after a hunting trip up enough to cover high as his hips. Placing his hands at the back of his head he stared at the ceiling wondering what had ever happened to the other fur he had obtained. He had asked Anso numerous times but his father would just shrug and give him a wink. 'Such a strange man' he said out loud as he tried with all him might to relax. Before he knew it his inner mind had other ideas and memories of Nox in her wet undergarments in the river came rushing back. Her hard nipples, her tongue, how she pulled his hair in her fists, the night by the fire when she whispered how she wanted him to please her, and before he even realized he was pleasuring himself with the very images she had so nicely put inside his head.

Erupting with his climax and groaning out what sounded like a painful groan, leaving him breathing in deep breaths laying lymph and still with his eyes closed for an exceptional long time. The fact that he couldn't sleep and being constantly aroused with thoughts of her in harm's way was leading to an already wearisome and restless night. Even if he could force sleep it would be unbearable now. 'This is ridiculous,' he said in a tired voice and left his warm statuary in search of something stronger than what was now warm beer. Knowing exactly where to find it, and not bothering to put anything other than his trousers on he headed bear footed along the cold stones to the meeting hall. The fire would probably be still lighting and the change of scenery would help he thought hopefully. A voice sent a shiver down his spine when he entered the room. Not noticing Arnav and his father of all people sitting in the corner by the last flames of the fire. 'Great,' he mumbled to himself and thought of turning around as fast as he could but it was too late, making his way towards the two sets of beaming faces that seemed to know his reason for walking around half naked in the middle of the night, he braced himself when he spotted the look Arnav threw his father and sighed, rolled his eyes to the sky while he took a seat and waited for the onslaught. Arnav started in his usual subtle way of getting to the point of the matter. 'To horny to sleep?' he said with a smirk into his drink. But before he could think of something to say as he thought about what he had already done when that obstacle arouse earlier, he drew a blank but to his amusement his father seemed not a bit impressed by Arnav's line of questioning. 'You don't need to know things like that, and if ye do ye don't talk of a lady in such a way. I think that's why lad you still find yourself alone, 'he said with just enough force in his voice to try and make his point. Arnav just smiled and stated that, that was exactly how he liked it. His father regarded him closely and began contemplating what kind of woman could ever tame the man. 'Hopeless,' he said with a crooked smile. He knew his father wanted to know everything there was to know and he was sure Arnav had told him possibly everything he could. He waited until the silence got so thick in the hall that he had to speak or burst. 'She drives me crazy! She broke my nose, called me on my manhood, and who the hell tells a man he has heavy feet? I can sneak as good as any!' he was getting agitated now but couldn't stop himself. 'She calls me a bastard, wishes I'd drown and then she kisses me like both our lives depend on it.' He was stammering over his words now and tripping over his emotions when he spoke of her. Without even realizing it his father had grabbed his hand. 'Steady yourself son, I hate to be the one to tell ye but this is normal. They'll drive ye to near killing them only to rein you in and leave ye a mass of a worthless man.' Laughing then he patted his hand undoubtedly happy that Kiril finally opened up about the woman who was clearly driving him wrong. He proceeded to tell him of the time he had argued with his mother over the colour of the grass just to get her worked up so he could watch her grow angry. 'So beautiful and with a frightening temper,' he said with a rueful smile. Watching his father he wondered how he lived for so long without taking another woman. Plainly he was still very much in love with his mother but she had been dead now for fifteen years. Never having the nerve to ask him he decided since they were being honest with each other there would never be a better time. 'Father? He said looking directly at him. When Anso's eyes met his he wanted to back down immediately. How could he ask him such a thing? It was his mother after all. 'What is it son? He asked as he took a swing from his glass. 'When mother died I was very young, but why did you never take another wife as the years passed? Anso lowered his glass and to Kiril's surprise he smiled at him with bright eyes. 'Because I could never love another as I loved your mother. It would be unfair to take a wife when you still dream of you're only love.' At this Kiril nodded and drank deeply. 'You love her then? Anso asked him in a hushed voice. 'I think I love her more than my heart can stand it,' he replied torn between happiness and a feeling of pure terror. 'And she loves you in return? Laughing at how his sons face dropped at this simple question. 'Well it would seem you're in the best position to know, does it not?' his father continued looking amused.

Unfolding the letter from his hand he gave it to his father and watched as he opened and read it.

As a massive grin spread from ear to ear he said merrily 'Ah, well, that's great news,' and with that he stood up slowly, bid his son and the little rogue a good night and slipped from the hall looking like he was almost floating on air. His son was in love to a noble and wonderful woman who to his delight would watch and care for his son even if he never gives him grandchildren.

After watching his father leave he turned his attentions on Arnav who appeared to be starring into the glowing ambers of the fire. His eyes seemed in a far off place and he felt he really shouldn't interrupt whatever demons were calling to him. Arnav did this often but seldom if never spoke of the reasons behind it, which obviously meant that it was a no go area so Kiril acknowledged his right for his private thoughts. Without any inkling of a change in his humor he cast Kiril a cheeky grin that said he was going to start off were he left it before his father interrupted his questioning skills. Handing him a glass that his father had been drinking from he raised his glass in salute and toasted to the very beautiful, dangerous, short tempered and damn good fighter Lady Nox Roundgate. 'May she bring ye joy beyond measures, and many sons,' and with that he drank deep, scrunching his eyes shut at the burn that ran down his throat. Just as he was claiming back his ability to see through watery eyes, he could just make out his friends face. Worry was etched into every line on his forehead and his glass still stood full in his hand.

'Kiril, what is it man?' he asked as he lay a hand on his shoulders to try pull him out of his thoughts. 'I've only thought of the joy she has brought me in recent days, but marriage never entered my head. Don't hear me wrong, god I'd marry her tomorrow, tonight, now if she were here.' He said in hurried tone to be understood, before he took a deep breath and swallowed hard. Looking up at Arnav, his friend seen something he never thought he'd see in his eyes.

Fear. 'What if she doesn't want it all? What if, she doesn't want it to be more than what it is now? 'Stolen kisses', he said with venom as he threw his glass to the floor with a smash.

Standing and running his hands roughly through his hair which at this stage was standing out in all directions he began to pace, slow steps, head bowed. Turing suddenly to Arnav he stated that maybe he had been overly complimenting himself in the belief she would accept his offer. Had he even claimed her? She would be in the Glens of the Crowden as the new leader of Arella and at the mercy of every bastard in the place. 'And you talk of sons,' he near shouted.

Before Arnav could say anything Kiril began to rant once again. 'Did you know that Gaius, yes bloody Gaius was her first kiss? Did you know that' he repeated as he walked up and down.

'Fucking Gaius' he said in a high pitched voice as he was unable to hold back his temper any longer. Arnav had been quiet through his outburst but now made his way towards him. 'You're over analyzing everything Kiril. Do you really think that a woman such as Nox, who could have any man within this land or the next, would just settle for stolen kisses as you put it? He must have flinched for Arnav leaned forward and grabbed him by the shoulders now and became more serious than he had been all night, and spoke with earnest. 'You're a fool. Everyone who has eyes can see how the woman feels for you. As far as Gaius goes I know he only sees her as a sister. Granted that might have changed at one time but they are older now I have never seen anything to tell me that he cares for her sexually. Do you not think if that was the case he would have made his move long and ever ago. Besides Hakan , Gaius and Toran have only threatened to kill you the once, and I know they are pleased for Nox if you are what she really wants. I think they're really grown to like you.' At this Kiril looked at him shocked and reminded him that it was him who joined in the near killing of him that day, making Arnav laugh out loud. 'Ah yeah, got ye good too.' At that he dodged a punch that would have left him reeling for days. 'She loves ye, and ye know it, now stop questioning everything what ye have and enjoy it.' With that he walked back to retrieve two more drinks and toasted to Kiril and his future sons.

Chapter Six

ANSO

Walking through the fields behind the castle he smiled at the memory of the day Kiril was born.

Such a big child and his mother had fought for days to bring him into the world. Her laughter when she finally got to embrace him lit up her face as she glowed with pure love and affection for child she had waited to meet. Of course he began to cry such a earsplitting sound and he knew he was going to have his hands full with the son he could only have dreamed of. They both laughed as they looked at each other. Leaning in over him they kissed his forehead like he was the most precious thing ever to have entered their lives. As the years went by Anso had found it difficult to resist the urge to nearly kill that little miracle. He was stubborn, ill tempered and left Anso reeling on more than one occasion. He refused to acknowledge any of the girls in Zantar and as he got older and those girls turned to women he still refused. Anso couldn't understand what was wrong with his son. He was a tall handsome man who always drew the attentions of the women not to mention visiting women who were always plentiful. When he looked back on the years without his wife , he realized he had needed her help with so much. Like bedwetting, temper tantrums and the worst thing ever the mourning he faced when she died. He had never thought of re-marrying but when Kiril asked him the night before what his reasons for staying alone were he began to wonder. Not that his brother didn't try to change that whenever he had the chance. He had loathed having to visit him during the years, but Kiril had to know his uncle even if it drove to pulling his hair out. There would always be some fine bosomed woman waited to be wined, dined and anything else he had wanted. Cursing himself for doing the same to Kiril on numerous occasions he cringed remembering how he had acted . Kiril was not like him when it came to holding back his feeling on the matter leading to many woman running from the gathering hall in tears. When he finally did sleep with a woman it was after returning from one of his trips to Arella. He never understood why he had insisted on visiting when every time he returned he was in the foulest of humors and brutal on the training ground. One of these occasions he had not returned with Arnav and he was not at liberty so say where he was so Anso left well alone. 'No I could never have married another, could I Selena' he said looking toward the horizon lined by a beautiful sunset. Taking the trek to the forest he headed straight towards the gigantic oak that towered higher than any other tree.. The forest floor crunched under his feet and he had an urge to take his shoes off and walk bare footed the rest of the way. 'I used to laugh at you for doing it and now I'm considering it' shaking his head smiling he stopped and holding his head back he closed his eyes and let the air flow over this face. Totally relaxed he took deep breaths and blocked out all thoughts except for Selena. It was fruitless as his mind raced with thoughts of Kiril and his new love Lady Nox Roundgate. 'Finally' he said with a smirk and opening his eyes set them on the winding and flowing of the ground inside the fortress of trees.

'Seems all of those trips to Arella worked out for the better.' Having walked for a good hour he came to a halt and stood over a mass of stones with a heartbreaking gaze. Kneeling he placed his hand softly upon them and sighed. 'Hello my love. I have many things to tell you, but firstly it's seems our son has at last found love.' He had sat deep into the night tell her of everything that was going on in Kiril's life. 'You would approve of Lady Nox, Selena. She is a strong woman with her own mind and seems to be driving our poor Kiril insane.' laughing he drew in his breath as his eyes filled with tears of loneliness. 'You left me to soon' shedding tears he no longer felt the need to hide, and in the quietness that surrounded him he wept for the woman he had only ever loved.

~

After hours to contemplate what his son had told him of the Mackisi and the treaty with the Glens of the Crowden, he was hard pushed not to attend himself. He never trusted the Mackisi and Ulric although strict and kept their laws flawlessly there would always be something that would knock the balance of. Of course he didn't think that the chance of a treaty would be it but Nox if anything like her father, she would be likely to pursue it. He had known the girl for years and as a child she had definitely made an impression, but she had now grown into a beautiful and strong young woman who to his delight had chosen his son. By the time he had returned to the castle his mind was made up, he would be traveling with Kiril to the Glens of the Crowden.

Informing Kiril of that little matter was a different story all together. He shouted and disagreed until his face turned bright red but Anso just laughed which angered him further. 'I am the leader of Zantar Kiril in case you have forgotten yourself and have every right to be present at the sighing of any treaty within these lands.' he shouted no longer finding Kiril's unhappiness amusing. 'Arnav! What can you tell me of the Arellian's under the leadership of Lady Nox?

Arnav twitched uneasily when Kiril drew in a breath through his teeth. 'What do you want to know sir? Arnav replied sheepishly avoiding Kiril's glare in his direction. 'Everything' Anso answered as he turned his back on both men. 'From what I have seen they respect and obey her without question. She has their upmost loyalty and allegiance that I couldn't see ending anytime soon.' Not giving him a chance to continue Anso asked him to leave so he could speak to Kiril in private. Nodding he turned and left without another word. 'Father why not just ask me what you wanted to know? Kiril asked. 'The last time I looked Arnav was a captain in my army' he countered as he watched his son clench his fists. 'Besides it gives me a chance to stop your temper damaging any part of this treaty or anything else for that matter.' Not waiting for him to respond he put his hand to the door Kiril voiced his opinions loudly making Anso turn fuming.

'What? he roared. 'I said you have no place going to the Glens' Kiril responded just as hotly.

'Really? And how do you make that out? Coming back into the room he took a seat and waited patiently. 'Father please, I'm begging you to trust me.' he pleaded. Sighing Anso stood up and walked to his son and laid a warm hand upon his shoulder squeezing gently. 'Do you believe that I have no right to show myself as the man that I am? Your day will come to lead these people and with that comes with what I can offer you now' forcing him to face him. 'Son as every day passes I grow older as you grow stronger. 'Breaking from his embrace Kiril shook his head and in running his hands through his hair he laughed. 'This is about Nox' he said cynically.'I just want to spend time with her, is that so bad? Anso replied throwing his hands in the air dramatically. 'You've known her since she was a child, what would coming alone prove to you?

'That she is deserving of my only son' he yelled as he watched Kiril grow irritated. Blank faced he turned to face his father and exploded with laughter once again. 'You bloody liar, you're coming to keep an eye on me' he said with total disbelief. Grinning at his son cursed. 'This might be my only chance to have grandchildren' he reasoned in his most fretful voice.

'Unbelievable, please tell me your not serious. Your coming to badger her about grandchildren?

Kiril said amazed by his father's stupidity. 'Are you trying to scare her of? Is that it? Please help me understand what is going through your mind to think that you coming along is a good idea, if only to ruin this for me.' Kiril barked as he stormed out. 'Well that went well' Anso said as he sat back down smiling to himself.

Chapter Seven

By the time morning came the men that Anso wished to take along were saddled and ready to leave. Everyone seemed in good spirits except for Kiril who was in no form for anything least of all his father and his ideas. Usually he would flank his father's left while Arnav took his right but this morning Kiril rode behind and ignored Arnav as he beckoned him to join him. Anso turned to address his son but in seeing him glare at him with such intensity he decided against it.

Calling for them to fall out Anso lead his men out of the castle gates and towards their destination. As the hours passed Kiril had mellowed sufficiently enough to bring himself to ride alongside his father but still refused to speak with him. 'You know Kiril you get your stubbornness from your mother' Anso said bluntly clearly tiring of his sons sulking. 'Oh and what do I get from you' he replied unemotionally. 'Your good looks' Anso answered laughing.

Unable to keep a straight face Kiril smirked which was Anso's opening to make amends. 'Son I really promise you I have no intention of getting in the way or causing you any trouble were Nox is concerned' he said with all sincerity. 'Look at it this way Kiril, if your father is there she might be less likely to break your nose again' Arnav said mockingly. 'Oh shut it Arnav' Kiril replied as he re-adjusted himself in his saddle. 'Stop squabbling like two children. Your both hopeless'

Anso said as he forced his horse forward to form a gap between them all. Left riding beside each other Arnav continued to aggravate Kiril. 'So how many of the Crowden' s men do you think have been hanging out of Nox since she arrived? 'Arnav' Anso said warningly as Kiril squeezed his reins tightly imagining it as Arnav' neck.

After another two hours of Arnav pushing his buttons Kiril finally had enough and called for his father to form camp. Obligating him Anso beckoned for the men to dismount and settle in for the night. As they all went about their business the campsite took shape as fires were lit and food was cooked. Sitting alone away from the men Kiril began to contemplate what Arnav had been saying. 'Damn it, I swear I'll kill every one of them' he murmured to himself. Lying down on his back he watched the clouds through the shine of the moon and let his mind wonder. She had laughed so much during the night they had shared beside the fire, especially at the stories of when he was young and the things he did to piss off his father. Smiling he remembered how she seemed to be able to outdo him in every case. 'How did her father cope? He thought to himself as he placed his hands behind his head. The night was changing as the wind grew in force and the branches over his head creaked with the strain, but for the first time since leaving Zantar he was content. Tomorrow they would arrive in the Glens and he would see her. He was suddenly in high spirits and in closing his eyes he drifted off to what he hoped would be a restful sleep.

Unfortunately the image of her stomping of and hiding when his father began to discuss the matter of his non-existent grandchildren woke him in a sweat.

~

As they entered the Glens of the Crowden they received an escort of ten men in full uniform, bow and arrows included. It was what the Elders insisted on as they found it made people feel more welcome. Anso thought differently and frowned until they dispersed and left them to travel alone into the Crowden. Dismounting they were greeted by Ulric and his son Vidar who one day would be the Crowden's new leader. Kiril stood behind his father as he spoke with Ulric about the journey and about the reason behind their surprise visit. 'Surprise visit? Anso said taken aback. 'You knew of our arrival did you not? He continued to address the equally shocked Ulric as he insisted he knew nothing of their arrival until they came through the gates. 'Lady Nox of Arella is here is she not? Kiril said as he stepped forward. 'No she is not' Ulric replied surprised. As panic took hold of Kiril he turned looking around frantically. 'Where is she then?

Said Arnav who was clearly just as distressed as his friend. 'If she had come into the Glens on the trek you took we would have seen her. How far ahead was she? Ulric inquired. 'Four days ago' Kiril responded as he began to get flustered. 'Four days? Which way is she traveling?

Vidar asked before his father could open his mouth. 'The Floyden Mountains and into the Northern Territory' Kiril answered bitterly. 'Damn it I knew it was a bad fucking idea, bloody woman is too damn stubborn for her own good' he said turning away from the men who were now deep in conversation. 'The Mackisi have been causing out right chaos throughout that land in recent weeks. If she has traveled into their lands it will be a nightmare to get out without any harm done.' Vidar said in a loud voice that made Kiril spin around in anguish as he looked at his father. Without hesitation Anso called for his men to re-saddle and ride for the Shia Mountains.

Before the majority of the men had readied themselves Kiril was already galloping over the Glens and closer to Nox.

When reaching the base of the Shia range both the men and horses were exhausted but Anso insisted that they continued on their route. The fact that the danger of stopping so close to the Mackisi was great even with a full army behind them, but they would be slaughtered with only two hundred. Not having to explain to the men as they already seemed to know the reasons for the constant push to continue they powered on in search of the missing Arellians and their leader. Not sure if they would encounter any of the Mackisi as they travelled Arnav placed himself and twenty others as the rear of the company just in case of attack. While Kiril placed himself in front and centre forcing Anso to take up ranks in the very center of the men.

Protecting him at all costs was their main priority until they were safely out of the predicament they had found themselves in. Kiril was unable to stop himself imagining the worst as he travelled quickly through the harsh landscape, but he knew is she was at all injured everyone of them would suffer for it. 'Surely they have to be close enough to the Shia Mountains' he thought to himself as he looked around briefly. Smoke bellowed in the air far off in the distance and his heart leaped into his throat. Changing course he headed in that direction followed by two hundred of his father's best men.

Even though no smoke was visible by the time they arrived the smell of it hung so heavy in the air that some of the men covered their nose and mouth with a free hand if they had one.

The silence was deafening to the extent it seemed un-natural. Breaking the men into groups Kiril led the main army forward and into the opening, while Arnav had taken his men towards the stables or what could pass for stables. Anso was kept to the back as always when entering hospitable areas which he was not too pleased about but he stuck to the rules. Dismounting as to not make as much noise in their approach as he knew whoever was here would already know of their arrival. Growing closer to the residence he caught a glimpse of white flashing past at a great speed. Turning quickly he seen who he knew as Snowflake making his heart leap in his chest.

Taking off after the horse he left the men looking at him questionably until he returned smiling broadly. 'She's here' he said taking off towards the house at a great speed. As he was just about to jump onto the porch and barge through the door he stopped himself rethinking the situation.

'What is it? Anso said coming up close behind him. 'It could be a trap' Kiril replied moving back and beckoning for Arnav to circle the house. 'Son if the Mackisi were still here we would already know' Anso said as he stepped onto the porch and opened the door, just as Kiril made a lung for him.

Chapter Eight

The Floyden Mountain Range were a vast and harsh ground to follow on horseback so being forced to the ground on more than one occasion was taking its toll on Nox and the men who followed. As always she began to think about her decision making and her logic in leading her men in this direction. If they had walk for such long intervals at a time as they seemed to be doing they would be a full day if not more behind. 'Clever indeed,' she thought to herself and she lead Snowflake along the trek. She could just see Kiril's smug face as he pointed out how he was right. 'Damn him' she said bitterly but was unable to withhold a hidden smile at the thought of him and his graceful ferocity. They had found an ideal location to camp the previous night not that it wasn't cold, uncomfortable and outright hard to gain any sleep at all but at least they had rested. Having had a full look out over the valley below the ridge of the mountain she noticed in the distance a homestead stood by itself in among a range of trees and makeshift sheds. 'Interesting,' she thought making the decision at first light they would venture in that direction, she noted that her mental image of the area meant that the horses could be watered and if they were lucky enough to buy, bribe or even charm some food from the inhabitants all the better. Only last night under the glow of the full moon she had never anticipated the fact that they would be left having to trek down the blasted thing. Making their way over fallen rocks and small streams that seemed to branch out into smaller rivers that ran through as far as she could see, she was drawn out of her concentrating with a high pitched frightened scream. Jumping at the sound she halted and went quiet. It was difficult to pinpoint where to sound had come from as it seemed to almost echo through the valley. From all the angles she looked was covered with some sort of dead foliage that had wrapped around each other forming what seemed a visual impairment to anyone not on a height. The men had stopped right behind and were listening intently for any sound that they could distinguish as odd. Surely they all weren't going mad she found herself asking as silence fell once again. Then it came. A fear, ear piercing scream, that sent a shiver down her spine and just then she remembered where they were. No longer in the Floyden Mountains they had emerged from the gap and were now facing the breathtaking view of the Shia Mountains in all its glory. It was she decided both a beautiful and devastating formation. Cringing as she thought of the Mickisi Clan. Dangerous, out of control, war loving men who have no care for laws or any order of living. They killed, raped, pillaged and did whatever the hell they liked she thought as a feeling of pure disgust traveled up her throat and made her gage. 'Fucking animals,' she said a little anxious despite herself. Turning her attentions to Hakan who had pulled up alongside her, 'what the hell was that? She asked in a whisper. 'I don't know but I think we're going to find out. Did ye not say there was a homestead not far? He asked calmly but kept his eyes peeled in the direction the scream had come from. 'Shit, your right' she replied in utter horror. Then realization hit home and the colour drained from her face. 'The Mickisi,' she whispered in a venomous hiss. With that she took tight hold of her feeling and started pointedly in the direction of the chaos. Laying out orders to the men to break into the two groups and work their way around the homestead as carefully and quietly as humanely possible. She was both furious and terrified but she'd be damned if she would leave anyone at the mercy of those bastards. Advancing as close as possible without being seen, she noticed with pleasure that all angles were being watched.

Without any warning the most disgusting, revolting smell filled her senses and she gasped as did the men standing with her. She looked at Hakan who had his eyes fixed firm on the mound of flames just on the outskirts of the homestead. Frowning against the sun to have a better look it hit her like a jolt to her mid-section. 'No! she whispered in utter horror. 'Hakan! she said pleading. But he just stared stony faced and clenched his jaws so tight they looked ready to snap from the force. 'Give the order

Nox before I break ranks,' he stated, his back straight as an arrow and sword clenched tight in his fist. Taking a deep breath she screamed for the attack and ran barreling through the trees, towards a very shocked group of Mickisi men. She ventured of to the right when she heard a woman's cry for help. Running as fast as her legs could carry her she turned the corner of the house only to find herself smack bang in the middle of a gang of men holding the young woman captive against a tree. Her clothes she noticed had been torn off; blood ran from her lips, while the dirt and blood covered her legs from being dragged. She was frantically trying to escape her captures but to no avail. 'How could she, Nox thought with sympathy, as she took in her surroundings. Stopping just short of the gang of men she had a sudden realization that she was by herself. 'Fucking idiot, Nox you fucking idiot,' she fumed at herself for not thinking. Counting ten men she took a step backwards against her own will only to be stopped abruptly by what seemed a block wall. She froze, and sweat began to run down the inside of the bodice. Feeling the blood drain from her face, she had a horrible feeling that she was going to faint and all she could think was Kiril is not going to be happy. Damn it she wished he was here. She braced herself and turned with terrifying awareness' of her size towards this huge shadow that was cast over her. When she looked up into the eyes of her opponent she actually swayed slightly. Toran. He stood like the great warrior he was. An impressive sight to be taken in. Larger than life, dirt and blood soaked through his shirt and she had to stop herself from hugging him tight. That wouldn't do at all she thought, with a shaky inward giggle.

Walking out in front her towards the men, 'I would suggest that ye let the lady go,' he snapped in a cold voice clearly not impressed by what he was witnessing. When the men did nothing to co-operate he took a deep breath, rolled his shoulders and advanced on them. He was fast, with powerful and lethal strikes. Within three heartbeats three had fallen and at this she at last came to her own senses. Setting into a run she went to the aid of the young woman who now was being dragged into the house, by a hefty, dark-haired bearded man who had an unmerciful grip of her hair and as she kicked and screamed, he clearly had a single thing on his mind. 'Not today,' Nox exclaimed as she rushed him from the back. With an unceremonious heave he threw the woman viciously against the wall knocking her unconscious and leaving her with an additional ailment to recover from.

'You'll pay for your interfering bitch. You want to take her place, so be it,' he spat. He definitely wasn't joking she concluded as he circled around her. Fighting stubbornly against what seemed his ending conclusion she lifted her swords took a firm stance and invited him into her space. She was going to enjoy gutting him like the pig he was. Lunging at her she jumped away just as his hands grabbed for her hair and with a clean swipe of her left hand caught him across the back of his legs and he groaned with pain as the blood ran down his calve. He turned blazing eyes on her while looking frantically for a weapon. 'Stupid man! She thought with smugness. She had her bearings and as if by her own mentality she began to see things very clearly. The sweat running down his dirty face, his heart beat throbbing hard in his neck, the yellow stains on his teeth as he flashed her a nasty grin. 'If that's all you have girly I suggest you just lie on your back now,' he said in a deep breath. At this she exploded into laughter totally catching him off guard to the extent he straightened and looked quiet uneasy. Holding up her swords again she welcomed him to try yet again. This time when he advanced she turned like lightning and in raising both of her deadly arsenals she slashed them down hard along his back and reeled in the sound that came from his mouth. He fell heavy to the ground groaning face down. At that she drew back she kicked with all her might into his ribs. He turned over onto his back and looked directly up into her eyes, which must have been dancing with at the sight of him lying helpless and deadly wounded. 'I think you'll find I don't lie down,' she said as she drove her sword home. Settled into his chest she gave a final twist and let go leaving it standing prone from his body. 'Bastard!' she sighed and withdrew her weapon. Stepping back she took a deep breath and looked around at the damage. To her disgust the fire was still burning high and the smoke that formed still floated in the air. The smell of burning, seared flesh came with the wind that blew the smoke cloud in all directions. There was no escape. Without any sign her stomach twisted and she doubled over and vomited what seemed to be everything she had eaten in days. Giving one last gag she stood and wiped her mouth. Taking a look around her breath caught when she seen Toran kneeling on one knee his sword holding his weight. No longer thinking about the woman that lay by the house door she grabbed up her skirts and ran as fast as her legs would allow. When she reached Toran she fell to her knees in front of him, and began roughly taking and reviewing the damage she couldn't see. 'Toran, are you hurt? When he didn't answer she got angry and irritated and yelled at him. 'Toran, damn it were are you hurt?

Removing his hand he displayed a deep gash along his side, which blood oozed out of when he let his hand fall away. 'Oh,' she said weakly.

Forcing his hand back against the wound she stood and frantically searched the surrounding area for Gaius. 'Gaius' she screamed in a broken voice that held fear for her injured friend. Seeing him walk towards the house were the woman sat she called waving wildly to get his attention, until finally Hakan spotted her and turned the big man in her direction. 'What the fuck are you waving at? she yelled at him as she moved herself away from in front of Toran who was now lying on the ground sweating and groaning in a most alarming fashion. Gaius's hand dropped to his side and as his eyes grew wide he let out a yell of disbelief that his brother would have fallen. He came barreling towards Nox so fast she had to leap away to evade being smashed in to. 'Toran' he shouted as he knelt by his motionless body.

'How bad are you hurt man tell me? He said with such emotion Toran gave him a feeble grin.

The shaking was so uncontrollable now he couldn't lye still even with Gaius holding in down.

'I've had worse. I'm alright just a bit dizzy,' he groaned as he closed his eyes. As if unsaid words passed between the brothers Gaius rose and along with the help of Hakan got Toran to his feet and headed back towards the dwelling. Turning his attention Nox she was unsure what to do when she seen the pain behind his eyes. Staring at each other for a split second before walking away she called for the residence to be searched for a suitable space for Toran's recovery. 'I promise you he will be in good health by the time we leave here' she said passing Gaius who asked about the woman. 'Now that she was awake surely she could help in his mending. He helped save her life, now she can help save his,' he said as he struggled with the dead weight of Toran's full sixteen stone.

Standing before a room full of men and one woman who she didn't know Tianna braced herself for the unknown. She had seen man injuries before by the sword but she had never tried to mend a man of this weight or the magnitude of his injuries. Terrified she turned to the one who looked the mirror image of the man before her. Steadying her hands she placed them on her hips and drew her chin high. 'He's lost quiet a lot of blood but I don't know by looking at him how much of it is his own. We need to take off his shirt and have a better inspection of the damage. You can try and get him upstairs, but I think the living space would be a better choice.

By the looks of him he weights quiet a lot, and I don't think it would be an easy task.' She said trying to keep her voice as steady as possible but having so many men glower over her was daunting. After having the day she had anything else was going to push her over the edge. It was possibly the worst day of her life so far. 'Will you just tell us where to put him' Hakan said testily as he fumbled to retain his strength under Toran's slumped form. Pointing to the table in the room she told them she needed fresh water, cloths and whatever alcohol they could get their hands on. Leaving Toran on the table Gaius rushed off through the door in search of her demands. Nox realized that the men seemed in ferociously great spirits after the recent fight and went about the business of clearing as much of the damage as they could. Some had squelched the flames that had been burning and with great haste to prevent the ill-fated woman the chance to see what was left behind. Burying the bodies further up the hill away from the view of the house was a clear attempt to save her feelings. As Nox felt herself grow soft hearted for the men who showed they too knew of heartache, she also knew the time would come that the woman in front of her would have to deal with it sooner or later but right now they needed her to concentrate on the task at hand. Covering her resentment at being dragged into something that couldn't have been more ill-timed and outright disastrous for Toran and his life wasn't helping her mood. Nox tried to remember she couldn't blame the woman for the actions of the men that came here today to raid, molest and strike out at those who were obviously no match for their wickedness. Gaius returned with arm loads of what seemed like supplies and dumped them onto the ground at her feet, and looked at her expectantly. 'You idiot,' she said in a rebuking voice that got her a small amount of raised eyebrows including a smirk from Toran. 'What? Gaius shouted at her. 'It's what you wanted is it not? continuing to yell he squared his shoulders towering over the woman who at that very moment had been pushed to her breaking point. 'And if I wanted them soiled and filthy, I would have taken the shirt of your fucking back,' she returned shortly. Taking a step towards her Gaius suddenly stopped noticing the strength and anger that was there not seconds passed had disappeared and was replaced by fear. Her face had grown anxious and he realized she was close to tears. 'I'm sorry,' he said hands held upwards in a retreating manner. 'Please, I didn't mean to shout.' He said glimpsing at his brother who was still losing so much blood. She looked at him and gave a slight nod of appreciation at his apology. Walking towards Toran she began to cut his shirt off. 'I need the water boiled, and a fire set. He'll catch a chill. Considering the extent of the injuries he already has pneumonia is not going to help' she said in a croaked voice, which was obviously torn to shreds from her desperate cries for help earlier. Gaius obligated without question.

Later in the night Nox spotted the woman emerging from the house, looking exhausted and drawn. Standing on the porch outside the entrance she had left slightly ajar, she tilted back her head to the stars and breathed deeply. 'I'll have to speak with her' she said to Hakan in a somewhat saddened voice. Hakan nodded his agreement, but his eyes showed his concern for the woman who had yet to ask of her family. Instead Tianna had set herself to the task of helping in the mending of Toran. Over which Gaius received more than one scream to 'get out,' and 'I told you to leave that alone.' While she got 'there's no need to shout' and 'I'm only trying to help.'

'Head in and check to make sure he hasn't killed Gaius and keep your eyes to Toran, I'll be back shortly,' with that she walked slowly towards the woman whose name she didn't even know.

Focusing her gaze on Nox Tianna descended from the porch and walked with purpose in her direction. Without a word spoken between them they turned and walked towards the hill were her family had been taken and laid to rest. They emerged at last in a sheltered spot, shadowed by a huge oak tree who's branches hung like a silent guard over the freshly dug earth. Nox made a mental note to thank the men for picking such a suitable location. 'Your man is mending well, his fever has broken but he sleeps heavy,' she whispered as she forced herself to look at the site that now held everything in her life. Nox noted the strain to keep her voice from shaking until kneeling down next to the mound she crumpled into an ear piercing scream that turned into an uncontrollable sobs that hurt Nox's throat to even hear. At the best of times she would have had just the thing to say but not today. Right now what was there to say? So she said nothing. Instead she fell to her knees beside the woman and folding her into her arms she held on tightly rocking slightly and mumbling soothing sounds as if to a child. While she smoothed her hair gently from her face he nodded for the two men who had been standing just beyond the burial site to leave.

Lowering their heads in pity they winced slightly at the sound coming from the traumatized woman who lay in her arms. Moving quietly away they left her to grieve in privacy. 'You're safe now,' Nox uttered hoarsely trying with all her might not to weep for her loss and heart ache.

Pulling back the woman whispered 'Tianna,' Tianna is my name,' and with that she buried her head deeper into Nox's chest and wept with earnest, until she could feel her exhaust herself to mere whimpering. Nox had to ask. 'Tianna, why did those men attack your home? asking as carefully as she possibly could. 'I don't know, she sobbed, 'my father yelled for my mother and me to get into the house and before we got to close the door they were upon us. We ran upstairs as they approached like lurking rats,' she spat. 'My father didn't stand a chance, and they pulled my mother from the house,' she cried shutting her eyes as a painful memory of what haunted her etched into her mind. 'I couldn't help them', she sobbed. 'Tianna? Nox drew her attention back to her and looked deep into her bloodshot, reddened eyes and asked the question she dreaded the answer to. 'How badly hurt are you? she asked taking in the woman's response. Her eyes went wide with horror and she shook her head with vigor. 'No! I swear they didn't, I'll prove it, here look,' she said as she began to lift her new shirts to show Nox she had not been attacked by the animals. Her legs had been torn and battered when she seen her earlier but from what she could see of them now it stopped just short of her thighs. 'Stop! Nox said in shock that she would have driven the woman to defend her modesty to the extent of raising her skirts. 'Please,' Nox pleaded with her as she held her hands still. 'Forgive me, I just needed to know. I want you to be able to heal without hiding injuries from me.' Putting her hands to her face Tianna erupted once again in an unmerciful sob and begged Nox forgive her being so hysterical in her actions. 'You saved my life,' she whispered and hugged Nox tightly. Holding her tight to herself Nox gathered her to her feet and closely clutching her hard to her shoulder headed back towards the homestead.

~

Making their way into the home to an array of polite nods and murmured condolences in the direction of the heart stricken woman, Nox led her to the living area and a seat by the fire.

Handing her a drink and a slight squeeze of the shoulder she turned and looked upon Toran who to her surprise had his full attention on Tianna. His colour was high and she hoped it wasn't another fever setting in. Just as she was going to set about querying his well being the men from the lookout burst through the door breathing heavily and trying with all their might to speak in clear sentences. Hakan grabbed one and forced him to first breath and then focus on what ailed him. 'We . . . have . . . company!' he finally spoke in broken words. 'The Mickisi?' Nox asked anxiously as she looked around the room for her swords, and in doing so spotted Tianna without hesitation move to Toran's side and grab his hand tight. Looking at the joined hands and Toran looking up into the young woman's face she wondered what had passed between the two during the evening when no-one was around. She thought of jesting him but this was clearly not the time and moving quickly she pushed her way past the men still blocking the door, with Hakan and Gaius on her heels. An ear piercing whistle made Hakan cringe and curse her for being so damn close. Nox took off running in the direction of the barn that held the horses only to be met by a galloping Snowflake, head down and running with purpose in her direction. Neither of them slowing they moved in perfect unison with each other and in one smooth motion she took hold of his reins as he passed and glided through the air landing on his powerful back. She took off without hesitation galloping towards the highest point of the hillside. They rose like undulant mounds all around and she struggled in the dark to see even with the good view. 'Damn it, 'she hissed and just before she moved the sound of hooves came in a rush that nearly knocked her off Snowflake. Turning she screamed for every man to get into the house, no-one was to be seen outside. On hearing this Hakan and Gaius moved with speed shouting orders and hording the men into every space available inside the homestead. Dismounting Snowflake she slapped him hard and sent him off in the opposite direction. He'd know to come back when she called but for now he needed to be hidden. Entering the house she took one last look outside and closed the door with a slam. Shouting orders to dense the fire, close every window, and bolt every door.

Toran was standing now she realized with great difficulty. 'I'm sorry, if I hadn't been so careless we wouldn't be here,' he said in a broken voice. 'You have nothing to be sorry for,' she shouted at him clearly annoyed that he would take the blame on his shoulders. 'You risked your life against ten to save Tianna's life and virtue that does not warrant apology for being injured in the process,' she said a little softer, when she seen he had his sword at the ready. 'Warrior till the end,' she said drawing the attention to his sword in his hand showing his readiness to defend again. Walking towards him she took the sword from him and looking up into his eyes she said softly 'you won't be needing that go and rest.' And with that she turned leaving him in Tianna's arms as she led him back to the table. 'How many? Hakan said in a low voice. 'From what I could hear but not see, I'm maybe thinking two hundred strong.' At that Hakan pulled back to look at her and smiled unexpectedly. 'Like that is it? She smiled suddenly, an engaging grin that said it all 'let them come.'

Quietness fell as the sound of the army grew closer until it stopped outside and made her heart flutter with what might have been excitement or pure terror. Footsteps echoed on the porch and she crouched behind the door sword at the ready, hands sweating, bodice stuck tight to her torso and her hair she now realized was half out of its braid and falling wildly across her face and chest. As the door opened with a loud creak as a man who she noticed from behind held a powerful and domineering presence about him walked in with caution. Wide shouldered, graying hair and an almost arrogant tilt to his head as he glimpsed around. She held her breath He was just beyond the threshold 'a few more steps' she thought to herself as she listened intently for noises coming from outside. Stepping out from behind the door she ran her sword up along his back leaving it nestled at the base of his neck. 'You take a great risk entering this house old man,' she stated teeth clenched. 'And you take a great risk leaving your back open to attack,' came a voice from behind which made her turn and stare with wide emerald eyes.

Kiril.

Chapter Nine

Without a seconds hesitation she lowered her sword and walked to Kiril not taking her eyes from his. When she reached him he made no attempt to enfold her in his arms or reach out to her but she couldn't not be close, she couldn't not touch him, feel him, smell him, so she leaned forward leaning her head against his broad chest and took a deep breath that filled her senses. Raising her head after what seemed to long without any type of response from him; she placed her hands against his chest and looked up into his eyes. The first thing she realized was that he hadn't slept. His eyes were puffed and red and his disheveled hair seemed to be sticking up no end. He just stood staring into her eyes as emotions filled his features. He took her by both arms then, and held her close. 'What were you thinking? 'I'm sorry, but we couldn't just leave,' she said with a little snap in her voice. 'You scared me Nox! 'You'd have done the same.' She said a bit softer when she noticed his face held nothing but concern for her wellbeing. Mindful of all the eyes watching she pulled back slightly, but her stomach gave a sudden lurch when he took hold of her hand and led her from the house towards his horse. Lifting her gently into the saddle he nestled comfortably in behind her and with his free hand took a tight hold around her mid-section, turned the horse in the direction from which they came and rode off with her in tow.

With an embarrassed look on behalf of his son Anso turned to Hakan and scratched his head and gave a weak laugh. 'So I'm guessing we are staying the night then? Hakan who was still looking out in astonishment that Nox would just leave shrugged his shoulders and nodded in agreement. 'It's about bloody time. If I had to listen to you for one more night tossing and turning and snapping over the least little thing I think I might have killed you,' Arnav called after his friend as he descended over the hill. Anso laughed and followed Hakan into the house.

Closing her eyes she laid her head back against Kiril's chest. She had missed him, more than she thought she would. This had left her wondering a many night why he had such an effect on her, and just then the thought of him not being there with her at that very moment her eyes welled up and left her thinking that she might actually cry. He felt her tense and tightened his grip as he leaned down and kissed her on the head softly. 'How did you know where we where? she asked. 'Well it would seem that when we got The Glens of Crowden no-one even knew of your arrival. Of course when they heard of your travel plan everyone got exceedingly worried as it would happen the Mickisi have been wondering a bit these days.' He leaned forward to look at her 'as you've seemed to have found out,' he said sounding a little testy.

Instead of getting into the whole ordeal now she placed her hand over his and squeezed. This seemed to do the job she realized when he began to kiss her neck and her nipples tightened with the sensation that followed. When she squealed and shook herself he stopped and laughed an exhilarating sound that made her turn and stare blankly at him. 'It tickled,' she said as she leaned forwards and began to kiss the base of his throat. She felt him swallow hard, and she gave an inward smirk as she flicked her tongue out and licked the lob of his ear making him shiver. 'Ha! She bellowed with excitement at her skills. 'You have an advantage; I have to concentrate on both of us staying on the bloody horse,' he answered in a level voice that she had to give him credit for in his current state. She could feel his excitement since she was put on the horse between his muscular thighs. Turning again she eyed him with intensity that made him look slightly uncomfortable. Running her fingers up along his shirt she began to undo his buttons one by one until the upper part of his torso was fully visible. 'Do you remember that night by the fire? She asked in a seductive voice that grabbed his attention away from what her fingers were doing to his nipple. When she had his full unwavering attention she smiled and with great detail recalled to him what she had said. Leaving him struggling with great difficulty to hold the horse still when he dropped the reins. When she seen her chance she jumped from the horse leaving him looking after her as she walked towards a mass of trees. With a nervous laugh he dismounted and followed her. His heart was beating frantically the woman was driving him insane. Coming to a clearing he spotted her pressed against a tree trunk that seemed solidly reassuring. The ground was over grown with heather that felt soft beneath his feet as he made his way towards her, never taking his eyes from hers, he noticed how she played with the strings of her bodice still looking at him from under her eyes with a slight quirk of one eyebrow. Just as he made it to her she pulled with one hard yank and her bodice fell loosely to her hips leaving her breasts out and ready for the taking. Cupping them gently in each hand he took her nipple in his mouth and sucked hungrily making her moan loudly and arch her back to bring him closer. She wanted him so badly. He pressed firmly against her and she knew how he was at his own extremity of physical pain. Reaching for him she worked her fingers on the rest of his buttoned shirt and with both hands slipped it down over his shoulders, letting it drop to the ground at her feet. He moved up to her neck were he ravished her with his mouth as his hands fumbled within the folds of her gown. Cursing through kisses he pulled back and knelt to the ground in front of her and tugged what remained of her gown down over her hips displaying her entire beauty. He began kissing her with slow and meaningful kisses along her upper thighs until he worked his way between her legs. She gasped as he took her in his mouth, licking, sucking and nibbling gently on the nub of her affections. She felt devilish as she took hold of fist full's of his hair, but she didn't care as she prayed and beseeched everything known to man for taking such ecstasy in his mouth. When he felt her tense he stopped 'Not yet, he said to himself as he rose to face her once again. As he stood she reached for his belt and trousers which to her annoyance seemed to cause a problem, it was taking too damn long. She cursed, he moved back and to her amusement basically ribbed the trousers from himself, causing her to laugh out loud and him blush slightly. Pulling her to him he lowered her to the ground and began to kiss her gently. She widened her legs for him and as he lay upon her she was suddenly very nervous.

'This is it,' she thought anxiously. 'What if I'm not what he expects? What if he doesn't like it?

What if he's disappointed? She must have looked terrified for he began to smooth the hair away from her face. She began to feel very self-conscious but had to speak before he thought the worst. 'You'll tell me if I'm doing it wrong! She muttered beneath her breath. He kissed her so gently she felt herself wondering if she imagined it. 'Oh, my love, if it feels wrong it's because I'm not doing it right by you,' he answered in a soft voice that melted her heart. 'Such the gentleman,' she whispered while she ran her finger along his lower lip pulling him down to her.

He knew he had to be gentle with her; he couldn't hurt her more than necessary. She was moist and willing and he entered her as slowly and gently as he possibly could for such a big man. At the point that he stretched and ripped her he bit his lip so hard he tasted blood. She cried out a painful whimper and he felt her bite down on his shoulder. He moved slowly in fear of hurting her further but when she began to move with him his slow strokes turned into meaningful measured trusts that made her moan louder and rake his back and buttocks as she held on tighter. Raising her hips to draw him in deeper made him near lose his mind but he obliged as his deeply charged energy vented with his demand and pure lust went through her.

The pain had passed well beyond the boundaries of pleasure and with every powerful trust, kiss, nibble she undertook at his mercy she fought for more. Until at last he felt her legs tighten around his hips and her breath caught as she lost the last piece of abandonment and she screamed out his name. Her entire body convulsed in a continual shudder. As if her climax pulled with force he gave one last muscular trust driving upward as far as she could take him and exploded his steaming seed deep into her, accompanied by a groan of pure satisfaction that accompanied an unwarranted climax. Both were breathing deeply and they were left trembling and damp with sweat but he had to ask. 'Did I hurt you badly my love? He was leaning with his forehead against hers, his hair fallen around them like a veil, leaving nothing but his eyes to look into.

She smiled and without warning ran her fingers gently across his eyes forcing him to close them.

'There hazel,' she whispered as if to herself. Leaning up she kissed him tenderly. 'You're forgiven.' With that he opened his eyes and smiled that knee shaking smile upon her. 'I have something I need to ask you,' 'Oh' she asked a little weary. He sighed, she laughed. 'I'm sorry, ask me anything,' she said amused. Will u do me the honor of being my wife? It almost seemed surreal when he heard the words coming from his mouth and it didn't help when her face went completely blank and he could almost hear her swallow, as her eyes bore into his. He could feel the panic rise in him and he flushed hotly. 'Idiot' he thought to himself as he rose up off her warm, soft body. He began to fumble in the dark for his clothes 'fuck' he yelled into the forest, 'fuck, fuck,' and without even hearing her rise she came behind him, closed her arms around him, and laid her head against his back. 'Are you going to let me answer or are you just going to leave me here,' she asked with a smile in her voice. Turning he looked at her. She could see his internal struggle and longed to end it. Hair flowing loose, eyes wide with a hidden emotion that he wasn't sure scared or excited him, flushed and looking more beautiful than he had ever imagined she could look. Silence fell between them then and he fought to control himself. 'I can't do without you,' he said in a half muffled voice. Taking him by the hand she led him back to where they had just made love and pulled him down onto the ground with her.

Straddling him, she kissed him long and soundly making him forget momentarily what had just happened, but when she stopped it all rushed back. Nox cuddled up to him sending the warmth that radiated from her through his thighs and he could feel his erection begin.'Try stopping me,' she said with a wide smile that sent his heart a flutter and his loins burning. Kissing her deeply while he slid his hands to her hips gripping hard, he sheathed himself deep inside her with one hard trust, and she responded tenfold.

~

Excitement was pulsing through every part of her body. Without warning thoughts of things leading up to this moment ran through her mind she had killed, been attacked, scared for her life and the lives of her men, made love to Kiril and agreed to marry him. Kiril's fingers traced up along the outside of her thigh as she sat nestled in between his legs once again, making her smile a silent smile to herself. Pulling her hair back she clipped it at the nape of her neck to let some air run over her skin, as a large warm hand rested on her shoulder and eased her neck over to the side, as he made his way down along the back of her ear kissing gently and worrying her ear lobe with his teeth, whispering how much he loved her. As they came over the hill towards the homestead she noticed how things had changed since she left earlier in the night. Campsites were set up in various places, with tents or just men lying out under the stars, drinking, talking and enjoying the break from the saddle she presumed. The smell of food was overwhelming and her mouth began to water at the thought of having something substantial in her stomach. As they drew closer she was happy to see that Toran was out sitting with Gaius and the man who looked like the man she threatened who she now recognized as Anso. 'Great,' she mumbled almost to herself. 'I forgot about having to apologize to your father.' Kiril buried his face into her hair and what sounded very like a snigger came from behind, and just before she could formulate a reply to shut him up they were spotted by Anso, who with the delight of seeing them return waved with great excitement, and bellowed for them to come rest with at the fire. 'I hope you're ready for this Nox, it's going to be a long night,' he said holding a suppressed sigh of resignation. But then cursed when he seen Arnav smiling up at him. Unable to help herself she threw him a cheesy grin, dismounted from the horse before Kiril had even stopped, and walked with purpose straight for Arnav who seemed to think she was intending to sit beside him so moved slightly to give her space, he was in total shock when she swiped quick as lightning and grabbed his food in passing, giggling as he jumped up after her. 'No! he growled. 'Have you not learned your lesson yet Nox? he shouted. She turned around and stood facing him and took a bite of something she thought might have been chicken and smiled wickedly at him, 'I think I remember it was you who learned a lesson when our swords last met. But if you want to try again we can after I eat.' She said and sat beside Hakan and Anso who was truly enjoying the display, but more so that Nox sat beside him so freely and comfortably. 'Where is Tianna? She asked worriedly as she hadn't seen her since she arrived back and remembering how upset she was before Kiril arrived she was beginning to feel bad for leaving her by herself. As if by radar Toran stopped his conversation and turned to her. 'She's sleeping, I convinced her I was fine and told her to get some rest. It's going to be long journey back to Arella she'll need it.' Nox tried to stop her lips from quivering before she responded. 'Oh! So she's coming with us then?

It was nice to be informed that Arella was going to have another resident.' she retorted a little snappy which she noticed made Anso sit up a little straighter and Toran's face turn a little pale.

She could sense Kiril staring at her and was finding it hard to keep straight faced in the circumstances. She was going to insist on Tianna traveling with them as she would never consider leaving her anywhere near this place and definitely not anywhere near the Mickisi.

They would be back looking for the men who never returned. 'We'll be leaving in the morning, she said changing the subject and getting up from the fire she walked towards the house, leaving Kiril looking after her along with the rest of the men. 'Seems you did a great job at quenching her temper' Toran spat as he looked at Kiril who just looked back at him not caring either way, leaving Toran digging his knuckles into his temples. Nox would talk to Toran in private. 'What makes you think I want to,' he returned in what could have been an opening for the conversation to continue but instead Toran got up and stalked towards the house in search of Nox. His father looked worried. 'Will she be able to handle the big man? he asked looking around at Kiril, Arnav and Hakan who seemed quiet amused by the entertainment. The three men just looked at each other and laughed a full hearted laugh making his father frown at his son who seemed not to worried for the woman he nearly killed himself to get to. 'So then are you to marry? Hakan spluttered out as he drank a good mouth full of beer. This got his father's attention and Arnav seemed to have stopped giving out about his food being robbed again. Poking the fire with a long stick Kiril smiled and told them that she had agreed to marry him but they had not talked of when or where, but it would be after they get back from the Glens of Crowden. He reminded them that it was not as easy as they seemed to think it would be, remembering that Nox had just been named new leader of Arella, she had her place, her lands to run and her own people to care for. Looking at his father he reminded him with no offence to be taken that he would not live forever and his place was in Zantar. Quietness filled the air as the men took in what he was telling them. 'Shit! What a load of fucking crap! Arnav exploded. 'There has to be a way around it! He said facing Anso. 'Surely you knew he'd marry some day? 'Oh don't you worry,'

Anso said with a stern voice, 'they'll marry.' And with that he laid his hand on his sons shoulder and smiled 'you couldn't have picked a better woman.'

~

A loud commotion sounded from the house that made Kiril and Gaius stand with weariness. The window facing the front of the house suddenly exploded sending glass shards everywhere and following it came Toran. He fell with a loud thump and moaned as he rolled onto his bad side and held it tightly against himself. Gaius shook his head and sat back down mumbling under his breath about keeping his mouth shut. 'Bloody fool! Hakan said joining in with Gaius who just took another look over his shoulder at his brother. 'That'll hurt tomorrow,' he said with a smirk and looked up at Anso who was in shock and obviously not following what had just happened.

'It would seem Toran pissed off Nox.' He said as if that explained everything. Anso's mouth opened but nothing came out until Kiril sat back down beside him and gave him a smile that held a twinkle in his eye. 'That was Nox? he asked in shock, only to have his son laugh and nod.

Right there Anso understood. This is what Kiril has wanted; this is who he can't be without, this small but fierce force of nature that can put any man on his back and his son loves her for it.

Without noticing her decent from the window Anso was surprised to see Nox standing over Toran hands on her hips and lips pouted. 'Remember who you speak to! she shrieked at him. 'I was never going to leave her here u bloody fool, what do you take me for? You don't think I can see what this place is doing too her. I was the one holding her when she cried for her family; I was the one mending her wounds that she received from those animals. Wounds she tried to hide for shames sake.' Putting her hand to her forehead she rubbed hard with the palm of her hand as if it would take away the thoughts she had building up. She was angry, tired and expected more especially from Toran. 'Damn him! How could he think me so cruel? What did you think she just turned up to help mend you before she had been taking care of first. I'm not blind man; I can see how it is between you both. I have fucking eyes! Now get a grip before I do something I regret.' Taking a deep breath she through her head up to the sky and cursed, turning she walked away leaving him as he tried to stand and hoped that Tianna would be out to help the poor fool.

Chapter Ten

Three days later the silence in the house woke her and she bolted up to find Kiril already gone from her bed. She trotted across the cold wooden floor on her tiptoes towards the window, and there down in the front of the house stood Kiril, Anso and Hakan deep in conversation. 'What is that all about? She was curious but not annoyed at being left out Hakan was her first in command after all he should be involved in any big decisions. Going to gather her gown to get dressed she saw something lying on the table by Kiril's sword. Going over she picked it up and recognized it straight away. Her letter. He kept it. Battered and well read she determined and felt a flutter in her stomach. She never even expected that he would have found it let alone still have it. Putting it back she headed for the dresser and using the very cold water that had been there from the night before washed herself quickly to avoid feeling the cold all the way to her bones. 'Damn, I should have just heated it,' she said as she got dressed teeth chattering. On leaving the sanctuary of the room she walked into Tianna who looked as if she had been awake for hours. 'Nox, may I speak with you? She asked in a quiet tone almost weary and Nox kicked herself for being the reason behind it. 'Of course, walk with me.' She replied in what she hoped was cheerful voice and when they arrived at the bottom of the stairs Tianna turned to her and spoke with more confidence. 'I want to apologize to you for assuming that I could just come to your home before asking your thoughts on the matter. I never meant any disrespect. You've been so good to me when you didn't have to, and showed great concern for my wellbeing and feelings.' Nox tried to interrupt her but Tianna raised her hand to stop her and continued. 'I've never felt this way for anyone before,' she said with a smile that lit up her face. 'He's a good man, and I feel he really cares for me. But I never wanted the both of you to come to blows over me in any way and I feel responsible for the atmosphere that is between you.' Now Nox jumped in when she had felt Tianna was finished. 'Firstly it is me who should apologize to you. I had no intention of ever leaving you here by yourself to live in this place where memories would be so bad it would ruin you, secondly, I should have known not to jest with Toran of his feeling for you when clearly I can see how he feels, and never witnessing him in such a situation where his heart is out in the open for all to see I should have been more sensitive, and lastly you are and always will be welcomed in Arella. It is your home now.' Seeing the relief on her face Nox moved in and hugged her tightly. 'He is a good man, and you need not worry there is no atmosphere between us,' This was received with a bright smile. When they were finished Nox headed outside in search for Kiril only to find the three men were still deep in conversation but stopped abruptly when she walked over into their circle. She gave Kiril a small smile and ran her fingers lightly over his. 'So are you going to tell me what's going on? The three men just looked at each other and said it was nothing of importance, just discussing the best way to address the Crowden Clan once they arrive. It could take two days but at least they would be ready for their questions. She frowned at Hakan but decided to talk to him in private whenever a chance arose. When she announced that she wanted to leave within the hour things were set in motion when Anso called for some of his men to start the packing and to ready the camp to depart. The fact they didn't want to be there when the Mickisi sent more looking for their men, meant things were moving at a good pace to her delight. Not that they wouldn't be able to fight against them but like Anso pointed out 'To have no association with what went on here would be better for all. The girl is going home with young Toran so she'll be safe; and being here for the last five days means we need to move so when the treaty is signed with the elders we can all head to the south. So the sooner we are out of here the better.' Agreeing with everything Anso said she snapped into full concentration when he mentioned travelling to the south. 'Why the south? Well I know why I'm heading south but why you and your army? She said facing Anso who turned abruptly towards Kiril and Hakan for support. 'Ok, enough! Speak! she said facing Anso not allowing the others advise him on his answer she stood in front of him and glared.

Seeing him look over her head she took a menacing step closer making in focus on her again. He placed his hands on her shoulders gently and smiled down at her like a father would smile at a daughter and she had a sudden want for her own father at that very moment. 'For the wedding of course,' he said with delight. Turning in a swirl of skirts she set her sights on Kiril only to find him frowning pinching the bridge of his nose between his thumb and forefinger shaking he head. He knew she was looking at him but refused to look at her afraid of what he'd see in her eyes. When she got no response and Hakan seemed to be looking behind his shoulder as if nothing just happened she took a deep breath and turned back to Anso who was staring at his son. Nox forced a smile and took hold of his hand. 'We'll talk more on it but some other time, we have a lot to organize and we should really take our time in discussing something so important.' This seemed to please him no end for he gave her an ear splitting grin and squeezed her hand gently. Turning she sidestepped past Kiril who was now looking sheepishly at her but she was in no mood to take any pity on him. She was angry and he was going to know all about it.

The bushes crackled behind her and even without looking she knew it was Kiril. She swiveled on him instantaneously. 'I thought it was understood that I would not be forced into a time, date or place,' she said with a snap. 'What so you no longer want to marry me is that it? he said heatedly. 'What the hell do you want? I said I'd marry you did I not? And now you're going to push and push is that it? she shouted. 'I thought what I wanted was obvious. I want you! Nothing else, just you,' he bellowed as he turned from her rubbing the back of his neck. 'I told you last night-'she started before he cut her off. 'Yeah you told me, but you never asked me,' he said red faced from trying to keep his anger under control. 'But I –'she said moving towards him. 'But you what Nox? he shouted still not backing down. Instead of being intimidated of this big man that stood in front her straining to keep his temper in check she grew angrier and exploded. 'I will not be forced into a marriage do you hear me you fucking arsehole.

Who do you think you are standing there throwing out orders and demands? What you think, because you've fucked me you own me now is that it? She stopped herself and inhaled deeply fists clenched. He had gone completely taunt she realized and was glaring at her jaws clenched.

'If that is how you feel leave,' and with that he stepped out of her way to allow her to pass. She stared at him wondering if he was bluffing but when he didn't move or say anything she walked past him legs threatening to give way under her, but she pushed forward and ran. Bursting through the bushes she headed straight for the horses. She needed space, needed to feel the wind in her hair, feel free, cry, and scream, anything as long as it was away from the campsite. On entering the stable she noticed from the corner of her eye that Hakan was packing supplies to the ten horses chosen to carry the heavy loads. On hearing her enter he turned and smiled at her until he realized she was in tears and dropping the bundle of bread he ran to her. 'Nox, what is it? he asked pleading for her to speak. 'I'm such a fool Hakan,' she said sobbing into her hands.

He pulled her hands free of her face and held it between his making her look up at him. 'You are no fool, do you hear.' He said in a stern voice. 'So whatever it is it can be fixed.' She shook her head angrily and moved to Snowflake. Saddling and mounting him she erupted from the stables in a full gallop. Makin her way through the campsite nearly colliding with at least six men in the process. Hakan ran after her for a few steps and shouted for her to come back but she kept going and within a minute she was out of sight. He scanned the campsite for the reason behind the problem that seemed to be unfixable and found it in the form of Kiril walking towards him. 'Ah great, he muttered. 'Are you going to go after her? he asked the big man questionably. 'NO! was all he got in return.

~

After spending a good hour racing through the valley, pacing up and down shouting out insults at the absent Kiril, crying at her stupidity and cursing the fact that all she wanted to do was run straight into his arms and say she was sorry. But be damned if she would. Knowing that her absence would have been noticed by now and they would be waiting on her return to leave she mounted Snowflake again and headed with hast back to the campsite. Sure enough everything seemed ready and waiting. Moving to the front of the line between Hakan and Gaius who both gave her a nod and a supportive wink she gave the order to move out not even turning once to see where Kiril was. After what seemed like hours in the saddle Anso rode up beside her and said about taking a break for the horses, which she agreed to after complaining about wasting day light. 'We'll have time, he said with a smile, but the look in his eyes said it all.

As the men watered the horses she stood away by herself with Snowflake rubbing the back of his ears and whispered soothing sounds to him. 'Nox.' Arnav said in a quiet voice. She turned to face him only to see that he was handing her a piece of fruit cake. She laughed and through him a sly look. 'Since when do you hand over food willingly, and what do you want in return? He looked totally abashed at the comment and frowned looking hurt or at least trying his best to look like he was hurting which made her laugh even harder. 'Thank you,' she said and took a bite out of the cake. 'Forgive him, he's a fool. But a fool that loves you beyond sense.' He said as he moved up to pat the horse that held her full attention. Suddenly without any warning she lurched over and vomited violently, leaving Arnav shouting for help.

Toran arrived with Tianna and fussed over her. Holding back her hair, asking questions about what she had eaten, how many times had she been sick and were very upset to learn she had been ill since the night before. 'I'm fine,' she insisted and walked towards Hakan who was holing out a flask of what she hoped was something very strong. 'You're sick.' He stated in a stern voice that made her smile up at him. 'I was sick,' she pointed out cheekily and handed him back the flask and walked back to Snowflake. Mounting him she called ignoring Anso who was begging her to rest for the men to keep moving. As she turned her stomach lurched again and she cringed at the burn in the back of her throat. She was angry. Kiril didn't even come to see if she was okay. Her anger turned to pain and she thought she could feel her heart break.

By night fall she was exhausted and had to dismount a number of times to vomit much to her annoyance. She hadn't seen Kiril since the morning but learned from his over concerning father that he had taken to the back of the line to give her space and when he arrived at camp he would inform him of her being so ill. She insisted on him not to relay his message but she knew his father wouldn't listen. 'He's ruthless' she said to herself. Still not feeling her best she refused the food offered and took to her make shift bed under a horse chestnut tree well at least that what she thought it might be. Lying on her back she looked up at the stars and forced back the tears that threatened to spill out of her eyes. A commotion to her right made her come out of herself pity and looked up to see what was going on. Kiril was storming through the camp looking around wildly shouting her name. Her heart felt like it might explode when she seen the worry his face held for her. How could she think he didn't care? 'I'm a fool, she hissed at herself. She rose with difficulty but with the sudden motion she moaned and fell to her knees and unable to stop what was coming she gave in and allowed her stomach to lurch and force nothing out of her completely empty stomach. Big warm hands fell to her waist as she gripped her stomach with both hands. 'Nox! My love! What is it? said Kiril with such emotion in his voice she thought she might cry again. But before she could answer her body had other ideas and she could do nothing but allow the process to continue. Totally exhausted she lay down on the ground, her bodice was stuck to her from sweating; her hair was stuck to her forehead and her insides felt like shit. Sitting down at her head Kiril lifted it carefully and placed it across his knees and gently stroked her face and hair. 'I didn't know you were ill, I would have been here sooner, I swear to you.' he said in a torn voice. She laid her hand over his and he leaned down and kissed her fingers gently one by one. 'Forgive me.' he said pleading. She gave a weak laugh 'you're already forgiven.' And with that she fell into deep sleep.

~

Kiril came up and knelt down beside her, his bag hand on her back rubbing gently as a trickle of sweat ran down her neck. She wiped her mouth and stood up leaning against the jagged bits of bark that hung from the tree. 'Do you think you'll be sick again? He asked in a worried voice.

Handing her his flask she took a long swallow from it and shook her head before she handed it back. Glancing up the path that lead to the stream where they gathered the water she asked him if he would accompany her there so she could freshen up before they were due to leave and continue for the Glens of Crowden. Placing the flask on the ground her took her by the hand and led her away from the campsite. The air she noticed was crisp and colder out in the open and she inhaled deeper taking in all the fragrances around her. A small qualm made her pause as a sudden thought came to her like a lightning bolt. Kiril stopped and turned to her question ally.

'Don't be ridiculous Nox! she screamed at herself and gave Kiril a small smile and a wave of her hand for him to continue. Calculating in the head she went back and remembered what had happened over the last week. Until finally coming to that night in the clearing and she had to stop herself from letting her imagination wander it was clearly not the time. She groaned and put her fingers against her eyelids and pressed hard. She had no idea how to confront this obstacle.

'Give me a sword and let me do what I please with it, but this—.' She thought making a small sound in the back of her throat, apprehension or maybe acknowledgement of what she knew or at least what she thought she knew at this very moment. She hadn't clue what to do. 'I couldn't be, damn it.' Belatedly it registered that she was speaking out loud when she heard her own unmistakable voice echo through the silence. Whatever information had been passed in their exchanged look it evidently told him she was hiding something. 'Nox? he said making his way towards her. Taking in a deep breath of the cold air she dug in her feet and walked ahead with meaningfully strides. Stopping only when his big hands wrapped around her waist and his fingers inter-wound across her stomach. This gave her a strange feeling as she looked at his hands possessively protecting what he didn't know. A moment's hesitation was all it took when his hand found hers and he placed it between both his. Neither of them spoke for a time and he could tell from her posture she had something to declare, but in learning from previous experience what happens when he pushes he waited patiently until finally she spoke.

'Kiril,' she murmured

'Hmm.' he replied quietly.

'Do you think –'she stopped feeling her throat drying.

'What is it?' he said trying to keep his voice as normal as possible.

'Well do you think you will want children some day? She asked in a small voice that made him tighten his grip around her waist.

'Of course I do' he shouted in his mind but declined to say it out loud.

'Well I seem to be finding it hard enough right now to make you agree to a wedding. So I think I'll bide my time before I begin to press you for my sons.' He said jokingly.

She had the most apprehensive feeling and when she didn't respond at all he loosened his grasp and turned her to look at him. The worry on her face domineered over her soft features, making a knot form in his chest. Unconsciously he placed his hand gently along her cheek and rubbed with his thumb along her jaw. She was so pale and a bubble of fear grew in his stomach. 'Nox! tell me,' he said giving her a fleeting look with soft hazel eyes that glistened in the light of the moon.

Feeling her insides melt she knew he could handle it. 'How much do you want a son? she blurted out, no longer able to keep it to herself. 'He'd just have to deal with it, she thought as she waited for his response to her statement. Silence filled the air once again and she found that a scurrying noise of what could have been anything from a mouse to a rabbit made a great welcoming commotion. Risking a look at him she realized he was in the midst of a subsequent inward struggle with his own feeling and emotions. She etched closer and in taking his hand placed it gently against her stomach and looked up into his eyes only to see wet tracks along his cheeks. 'Please tell me you're not crying,' she snapped. Here I am a nervous bloody wreck who in case you didn't notice at this moment is in need of you, my supposed big strong man to make it all better and here you are bloody crying.' He didn't answer her and before she could say anything else he pulled her to him. Kissing her thoroughly leaving them both gasping for air but wanting more. 'Your pleased? She managed before he pulled her to him yet again in an embrace that needed no explanation and would have led to further matters had he not broke away to look down at her. He noticed she was smiling for the first in days and he laughed out loud making her just look at him in wonder. 'That was fast.' he said with all the male ego and smugness he could muster. 'Who are you telling,' she replied wide eyed. 'As much as it's going to be the hardest thing I ever do not to scream it from the highest point on that god forsaken mountain, I think we should not inform my father just yet.' Smiling up at him she agreed and with that he led her further into the forest and to the stream.

Chapter Eleven

As the army moved at a good pace Nox was beginning to see the differences between the Northern Territory and the South as this time of year. It was dry, warm, sometimes windy and it never seemed to rain. Unlike the South where you were guaranteed rain for the winter months.

Her stomach twisted and she drew in a deep breath to sustain the feeling building up inside. She began to wonder about the greeting they would receive when they entered the Glens. Not being leader of Arella for long now there seemed a great many things her father never told or prepared her for. Thinking now that maybe these things were things he could never get her ready for, things that only could be dealt with in a time and place. The tough decisions, the responsibilities, facing death and being the giver of it, forming lasting relations with distant clan and the most difficult love. Coming to a halt just they were forced to dismount and the lesson of how to scale boulders with a horse was about to begin. It held all of her attention, and the image of falling and breaking her neck went through her head. But looking behind her she realized with a smile that wouldn't happen due to the fact that she had Kiril who she noted had become as bad as Gaius and Toran for hovering, even though Toran had his sights set firm on Tianna he still had a job to do and by god he was doing it. Finally they reached what seemed like the end of a trek only to be hit with the mouth dropping view of the most beautiful waterfall she had ever seen.

Its water channeled and cascaded down the steepest slope before crashing into a rocky riverbed which formed a massive mist cloud producing a rainbow that barely rose six feet out of the water. The sound of the water was so overbearingly loud, but she was full of inquisitiveness and dropping the reins she began to climb out over the smooth rocks that lined the water's edge until she couldn't go any further. Bending down she watched as the tiny fish struggled against the deadly current that was being formed by the sheer volume of the clearest water that enabled her to see everything even the sand at the very bottom. She found herself begin to relax and lowered her shoulders and closed her eyes and just listened to the sounds around her. When she finally looked back she found Kiril grinning at her, and she was overwhelmed at his restraint to follow her out and drag her back from the water's edge. Instead he just stood there enjoining the view of her child like excitement over the natural scenery. She drew in a deep breath and with one last look at the beauty that surrounded and captured her mind she walked carefully back to solid ground. Only to receive a kiss on the forehead and whispered promise of privacy. This sent a tingle at the prospect of having Kiril all to herself and out of prying eyes, all the way between her legs. She gave him a flirtatious smile and a flutter of her eye lashes that made him laugh. As she made her way past him she reached across and gently squeezed those firm well shaped buttocks of his which earned her a snigger from behind and a slight slap on the arse for her troubles. Not being sick now for two days had certainly raised her spirits and meant she wasn't being hounded by Anso, Hakan, Gaius and Toran not to mention Tianna who was extremely suspicious but didn't voice her opinions on the matter. As they continued along the stony trek all she could see were imposing sights of a dry and dirty landscape patched here and there with both tall and thin tree that in areas wove together forming strange shapes that set the imagination to wonder.

Enormous roots had broken out of the ground and had begun to grow and wrap around the neighboring trees and whatever boulders lay in close proximity. 'How does anything grow here? she thought to herself with a slight frown that etched across her brow. Everything was drowned out and shadowed by the Shia Mountains that stood so high not even the clouds were capable of covering their peaks. Mist formed along the middle levels and moved down along the sides giving it an eerie presence that chilled her bones. Thinking back to the waterfall and all its hidden beauty she couldn't believe the contrast in this land. All she could think about were the Mickisi. She found it extremely difficult to accept that they had no inclination of their presence.

Taking in the landscape in front of them she wondered from which direction they would come.

Spotting two most likely possibilities she concentrated on them as they continued carefully pressing forward. Facing them was one of her possibilities for an attack if it was going to happen. It was a huge gap in the rock formation that could easily fit twenty side by side through at the same time, and the second was to the right of them as they traveled along. This would lead them right down off the mountain and directly on top of them. Taking a closer look at this trek she noted how the ground here was now turned more to dusk from continual use, and this made her more determined that this was one of their exit points off the slopes. She was unable to take her eyes of the trek and an uneasy feeling took over her. She had a mental picture of hundreds of Mickisi descending from the heights and them having nowhere to go but down. She shook herself and turned to Kiril who was looking at her with a slight quirk to his lips. 'What? She said with a smile in her voice. 'Just thinking how stunning you are.' He said with a wink. 'Hmm! remember that when I get fat!' she said with a pout that made him laugh. Just as he was going to lean in and give her a kiss there was a loud discussion going on up front this grabbed both their attention. They pushed through with the horses and when they came up beside Arnav he turned and explained what was going on. It was clear they had a big problem that had to be dealt with.

Looking out over the slope in that they obviously had to descend was daunting but the only alternative was to stay where they were and that wasn't an option. Taking in all the angles Hakan and Gaius looked at each other and shrugged. 'I guess straight down.' they said not even slightly bothered about any of it. 'What say you Nox? Gaius asked with what she thought was a challenge. Giving him a sly look and taking one last look out over the ledge she grabbed Snowflakes reins 'Yep! Straight down it is.' Gaius laughed with delight and took the first step off the slope leaving Hakan following on his heels. Just as she was about to leave the ledge Kiril stepped in front of her. 'Are you crazy? What if you fall? We can find another way down! He said sternly as he placed his arm around her waist to steady her this really didn't do anything for her sense of power. Anso looked at his son question ally but with the look he received in return he turned with his horse and headed of the slope followed by Arnav. 'Going soft are you Nox? he said jeeringly as he walked past. On hearing this she looked up at Kiril pleading with him not to force her to back down now but he had no more interested in arguing with her on the matter or with Arnav about watching his mouth. Realizing that they weren't the only ones still holding back when she saw Toran holding tight to Tianna's hand as he tried to decide if there was an easier point to descend from that wouldn't be putting the life of the woman he loved in danger.

'It's a bit late for that' thinking to herself returning her attentions to Kiril who was she thought starting to reconsider the possibility of making it down the slope in one piece. Finally deciding with reproach that it was the only way he leaned in and kissed her gently telling her to go safely and to stick close to him. Catching a hold of Snowflakes reins that little bit tighter she moved carefully and steadily off the slope onto the main trek. Walking and watching each step she was taking was tedious and tiresome. The ground under her feet was unstable and extremely rocky. A dust cloud formed and bellowed into the air by the time all of the men had ventured out and were making their way to the bottom. Again she found herself thinking about the Mickisi.

How can they be unaware of the presence of an army two hundred and seventy strong with cavalry and supplies? 'What are they up to? She thought uneasily as she continued. As if they had heard her thoughts an unmerciful yell came from over her head sending a chill down her spine. She froze for a split second before she looked up only to be met with an image of at least three hundred Mackisi lining the slope, the mountain side and coming down the trek in force.

'Son of a bitch, the bastards waited until we would be trapped' she shouted back at Kiril. The long haired, bearded, dirty clothed army of the Mackisi came with swords of all sizes and their screams were ear piercing, but not as daunting as their presence. With sudden shock she realized the ground seemed to be moving under her feet. Stone and dust erupted like a blanket from above and around them and she was losing her footing fast. 'Their causing the rocks to fall' she called to Kiril who had the look of pure fear cross his face as he watched her let go of the reins and lost control her feet falling hard leaving him screaming after her, but unable to reach her he leapt forward and let the rock slide take him with it. When she finally stopped falling she hit the ground so hard the thought that she was going to black out from the force she hit her head, and the shooting pain that flowed down her back reminded her that her swords were still intact. Black dots formed in her vision and she could see nothing but a hazy picture before her. Her father's voice boomed in her ears, 'Get up! She opened her eyes and as she was beginning to stand she was grabbed roughly 'Get up! the voice shouted again only this time it propelled her with force through the Glen. She let the presence take her, and was running so fast her legs ached and right then her stomach began to lurch forcing her to pull with all her might against the unknown faceless grip. She stopped just enough for her stomach to empty its contents before she was dragged again. Taking a quick glance behind her she could still make out the blanket of dust drifting over the slope and out over the boarders into the Glens of the Crowden. She tugged against the vice iron grip that had her by the wrist and turning she screamed into the commotion for Kiril. Panic took her, causing her lashing out wildly to get free. She managed to break the hold on her and went running with every bit of energy she had left towards the oncoming rush of men and horses. All of a sudden she was jerked high of the ground feet flying high in the air until her legs were left dangling. Kicking and screaming until eventually she got a hold of one of who's ever arm it was and bit down as hard as she could until she tasted blood, which ended in her being dropped hard to the ground. Turning with a murderous defiant stare that spread across her face, she was just about ready to kill when she stopped herself and jumped with a yelp of surprise and elation into Kiril's arms. 'Where were you going? he screamed at her. 'I was looking for you, you-'she couldn't find any words to say, she was just so elated to see that he was safe. 'Come on,' he said to her taking her by the hand and leading her towards where the men had begun to gather. 'Kiril, I'm sorry, she got away from me,' Arnav said apologetically as he made his way towards them. She withdrew her hand from Kiril's and walked to Arnav, hugging him tightly she whispered 'thank you, you saved more than just me.' And with that she kissed him on the cheek leaving him looking at his friend in shock. There was utter chaos and in the mist a horn blew loud from the mountain side. Coming around Kiril she looked up and could see that the Mickisi were still advancing on them. Sudden awareness of her duties kicked in and in a loud scream she called for hr men to form ranks as she took off running. 'Nox! Kiril yelled as she went out of sight. A high pitched whistle came and Hakan winced. 'I wish she wouldn't do that' he scowled as he went to grab his horse. Kiril grabbed him hard making him turn to face him 'where the fuck is she gone? He said through clenched teeth. Hakan looked at him as if he should already know and shrugged 'to get Snowflake of course.' And with that he mounted his own horse and shouted to form the lines. Within minutes she was back accompanied by a once white Snowflake now covered in dirty and muck from head to hoof. He had an urge to go and grab her off the damn horse and throttle her for being so reckless but looking at her, back straight, chin up and with that air of dominance she held without even trying he could just stare at her like a fool. 'Blasted woman will be the death of me' he grumbled as he went to retrieve his horse. As the dust settled they could make out the Mackisi as they came across the Glen. They were a sight to be witnessed, and placing herself in front of her men Snowflake trotted like the proud stallion he was, as if knowing this would be his final fight on any battle field he was ready and rearing to go. She ran a hand gently down along his neck and whispered for him to be easy.

Gaius came up beside her to the right Toran to her left and Hakan moved up just close enough but far enough to acknowledge his leader belonged in front so the enemy knew who it was they were dealing with. She didn't need to be shielded as a fragile member of her army. Kiril watched as the big men of her clan protected her, how they formed into the ranks assigned of them and felt a rush of appreciation for their loyalty. He knew this was definitely not his place to interfere. She was their leader and as such this was her duty, but it didn't stop the lump that had formed in his throat and the thoughts that ran through his head. 'Damn it she might be their leader but she's to be my wife and carries my child' With all his might he fought against every twitching muscle, every finger that tensed on this reins, every ounce of will power he possessed not to grab her and run for the hills to keep her safe. Just as he considered what she would do if he did indeed do it she let a yell for attack and she was gone with seventy of her best men.

'Fuck! he hissed and took off after them, followed closely by Arnav and Anso who shouted for his men to attack on sight. The clash of swords that echoed around the Glens and the blood already seeping through the lush green grasses told her this was going to be a battle remembered.

Snowflake battered his way through leaving her to swipe and kick as required. She could barely move in a circle, men were up against her and it was becoming very difficult to fight and protect herself. She could already feel the effects of what she thought were two gashes made in her right leg just above her knee. It burned like something horrible and the swell of blood ran down her calve and onto her foot. Seeing a break in the expanse mass of men she faced Snowflake in the direction and when the chance arose she jumped from his back and landed sending a shot of pain up her leg, making her wince slightly. 'I think you may be lost little girl' came a menacing voice from behind her. There stood a huge man with long dirty brown hair, that had two plaits she noticed on both sides on his head, heavily bearded and with nearly all his front teeth missing.

She wondered if they fell out or they were knocked out but either way she thought he was one ugly man. 'Maybe you'd like to just give up now' he said raising his sword giving her an evil toothless smirk. Drawing both swords now she threw him a smirk in return followed by a mocking wink and welcomed him to attack. He lunged at her swiping madly and grunting in effort. She was so much more graceful than the big oaf allowing her to side step every swing, and laugh when he near tripped over his own feet. 'It seems you remind me of someone I met some days ago' she shouted at him, 'he was very clumsy too' and with that she turned fast and drew her sword along his throat nipping it just enough to cause him alarm. Hot and flustered now he was to mad to concentrate on what he was doing and the more he swung wildly the more injuries he sustained, until he finally fell onto his knees, breathing heavily. Looking up at her under dark eyebrows he gritted his teeth and rose again but leaned on his sword for support.

'This someone you met? He asked breathlessly. She threw him a look that made his face pale when she answered. 'Just someone who squealed like a pig when I gutted him, maybe you knew him, missing a few men are you? And there it was who he reminded her of. The same eyes, the grin, the smugness. His jaws clenched tight together and she waited for him to attack. In a flurry of hard blows he had found his strength once again and by god she could feel every single one of them that rained down on her in pure hatred. She fell to the ground and digging in her heels she scurried back out of his range as he hit the ground where she lay. Scrambling in her skirts until she found her blade always attached to her thigh she drew it out and just as he was about to strike sword above his head she threw it with all her might, and watched as it hit home straight between his eyes. She watched as the life left his eyes and he fell with a heavy thump onto his back.

Walking over she leaned down and pulled the blade free and wiped it in his shirt. She placed a hand over her still flat stomach and felt a sudden feeling of anger towards herself. 'Stupid selfish fool' she shouted, as she picked up her swords. But as she looked around she knew she would have to fight to make it out of here but after today things would have to change. She took a deep breath and ran head long into the mass of fighting bodies. Her arms ached, leg bled, she thought she definitely had a split lip and her nose was bleeding again. Suddenly there was that loud horn sounding off in the distance and there seemed to be a deflation in the mass of bodies trying to kill her. She sighed with relief. Out of nowhere horses and men rode past at such speed she wasn't sure if she was seeing correctly. But sure enough there they were. The Crowden Clan had come. The sound of arrows whistled through the air over their heads, and she watched as they hit home in the Mackisi. She had caught a glimpse of Kiril during the battle but looked frantically around now. She could feel her heart clench in her chest when she couldn't see him and tears became to form on her lashes as fear gripped her. 'Where are you? She screamed in her head. Suddenly she seen him caught between three fighting hard. Gripping both swords hard enough to turn her knuckles white she ran with one purpose in mind and that way to save her man. She entered the confrontation with a scream filled with hatred. And with all her might in her already trembling arms she attacked with force. Catching one straight through the chest she turned and with one clean swipe took his head. As she watched it roll she looked out from under her hair that had now come completely loose and was blowing across her face, and glared at one of the others who stood breathing heavily but still ready for battle. She let him come. Just as she was about to make the killing blow a mighty sword she knew so well came barreling through the air and with force of contact lifted him clean of his feet. She turned to see Kiril standing behind her with relief spread across his face. He all but ran to her and caught her up in a bone crushing embrace that she submitted to instantly. Letting her go he placed her down on her feet and looked into her eyes and she knew what question was on his lips. 'Were fine' she said with meaning and placed a hand on his cheek when he breathed out a sigh and smiled. Looking around she could see the battle had began to phase out due to a sudden retreat by the Mickisi who were not expecting extra reinforcements to aid them. 'They'll attack again' Kiril said in a quiet voice while he looked at the men scurrying up the side of the slope. 'Only next time we'll be ready' came a familiar voice from behind. On turning she was met with the image of a golden armored covered Vidar son of Ulric of the Crowden who gave her a face splitting grin that held a twinkle in his eye. 'Seems as always you bring trouble with you' he said in a jeering manner that Kiril seemed not to care for and tightened his grip around her waist making his claim known.

Seeing this Vidar looked at his arm, looked at him and raised an eyebrow in challenge. 'Make your way to the castle, they know of your arrival and you will be taken care of' Vidar said looking only at Nox. She nodded once and in catching Hakan's eye relayed the message and left it to him to gather the men.

~

She had been given a room facing out over the Glens giving her a clear view of the mountains in the distance. Kiril was quiet but snapping at everything anyone said this made her laugh inwardly at his jealousy over Vidar. She had left him with Arnav who was trying his best to speak with him only to receive a frown and a grunt in reply. Not intended on spending any time walking around the castle or its grounds but found herself being ambushed on the way to her room by Vidar who seemed in a great rush to accompany her to the training ground to show of his new mere that was in the process of being broken in. Smiling she accepted his invitation and descended the stairs she had just walked up with great difficulty. Her leg ached something terrible and she was famished. When they had reached the corridor leading out to the training grounds she pashed Kiril and Arnav and was surprised to see they hadn't moved a muscle since leaving them. Arnav she seen had managed to cool Kiril's temper but she shuddered to think what seeing her with Vidar would do to him. Trying to move faster in order to get out without been seen didn't go as she planned when Ulric shouted her name drawing unwanted attention that she could have done without. 'Shit! she said to herself as Kiril's eyes met hers and then went to Vidar. She smiled and waved at him only to receive a look of hurt and betrayal from darkening eyes that made her heart rise into her mouth. 'Nox, I'm so happy you are safe and well' Ulric said in loud voice, making her think he was over compensating for something unknown to her. She just smiled but grew anxious and found herself just wanting to get away.

'Vidar was just taking me to show off his new mere' she said in what hoped was a light tone.

'Ah well don't let me interrupt then, I'm sure we will have loads to speak of later in the evening,' and with that he turned and left. Suddenly she found herself been forced slightly towards the door by an over eager Vidar who to her annoyance insisted on placing his hand on the lower part of her back just above her buttocks. 'Kiril is not going to be happy' she said to herself and cringed at what he might be thinking at this moment.

After what seemed a lifetime of listening to the man gloat and spoon over his mere she eventually broke away and rushed to her room were a hot bath of water had been left for her.

Smiling she undressed with every intention of taking her time washing and enjoying the heat caress and spread through her giving her a feeling that her insides were melting. Closing her eyes and taking in the quiet surroundings she began to think again about the child growing inside her. She had taken many chances, many dangerous chances over the last couple of days that could have ended her life or her child's. Again she cursed herself. A slight knock came to her door dragging her back to reality. 'Who is it?' she called quiet annoyed at the disturbance. 'It's me.' Kiril's voice came through the thick wooden door sounding muffled. She smiled to herself and called for him to come it. When he entered she noticed he swayed slightly as he stood over her. 'You're drunk already' she said in amazement. 'We've only been here a few hours.' He walked, well more like stumbled she noticed over to the bed and placed himself awkwardly on the edge. She waited for him to fall but he managed to stay there and with that he began to talk to her in slurred speech. She bit her lip and tried with all her might not to laugh. 'I don't like him,' he said gruffly. 'Ah,' she thought to herself, now it makes sense. 'Who? She asked in a sweet voice as she ran the water through her fingers not looking at him. He stood suddenly and grabbed the bed post to stop from falling. 'You know damn well who, your Vidar' he hissed as he walked menacingly towards her bath. She sighed and rolled her eyes and looked up at him 'firstly he's not my Vidar, secondly before you say a word no! I have never had any relations with the man, although he has asked on numerous occasions for an audience which he never received due to Toran and Gaius, which was his jibe of bringing trouble with me and thirdly you're a bad drunk, now hand me the towel since you've ruined by bath I might as well get out.'

Reaching over he grabbed the towel from the stand trying to look as sheepish as he possibly could muster in his state. They hadn't had a chance for more than a kiss in passing for days now and he was feeling the absence. He stood staring at her naked and dripping with water that ran down between her breast, down along her stomach and through her legs. He hadn't seen her naked now in what felt way to long and he took in ever last inch of her before him. Leaning over he placed the towel back onto the stand and kicked of his boots. When he started to lower his trousers she gave him a seductive one sided smile not taking her eyes from his. As he pulled his shirt over his head slowly she enjoyed what she seen. Every ripple of muscle was perfectly formed from his waist upwards, and she sucked in her bottom lips. Throwing his shirt aside he walked and stepped into the bath tub. The heat that came from her skin made him feel like the blood was running from his head all the way to between his legs. He had to touch her. Kneeling in front of her he grasped her hips and held her firm. Be brought his cheek to her stomach and laid it there for an instant before he began kissing her gently from hip to hip. A warm feeling rushed through her and with tenderness she placed her hands on his head and ran her fingers through his hair, smiling down at him. Spotting her wounded leg he frowned up at her, but when she shrugged it off he began to kiss her thigh around the wounded area. Lowering herself down along his length until she knelt facing him. She had forgotten the pain in her right thigh until the heat of the water stung, but she didn't care this time. Placing her hands against his chest and slowly began to move her fingers teasingly over his nipples and well shaped abdomen. Bringing his big warm hand to her breasts he cupped them a little too hard and she drew in a hiss through her teeth. He looked shocked but apologized and began kneading them tantalizingly softer until her nipples rose and became taunt. He lowered his mouth to hers and as she kissed him back he drew her closer until her breasts were pressed firm against his chest. He groaned as his erection grew firmer and slid over her lower stomach. He kept forgetting how petite she was and also had to remind himself to go gently. Sitting back into the water he brought her with him until she was lying between his legs. Rising herself up using both sides of the bath tub she slid herself down over his throbbing erection. He leaned his head back and held his breath as he entered her.

While she put her head against his shoulder and moaned out loud. The feeling on entering her alone was always a thrill but with the heat and the water that accompanied his entry was unbearable. Grasping her by the buttocks he aided in her efforts as he slid in and out slowly enough that he thought he might actually burst from the wanting. She placed her hands behind his head and grabbed the frame. With one push backward she had lowered herself so that every inch of him was inside her, leaving him groaning her name. She didn't move and he could feel himself throbbing inside her, and began to hope for the love all that was good he could hold out.

'Not yet, please, not yet,' he pleaded with himself over and over. Rising off him she knelt between his powerful thighs and told him to raise himself out of the water. He did as she asked after a quick look only to be met with those smoldering emerald eyes. And when she lowered her head and took him in her mouth, he cursed out loud making her giggle which made him laugh shakily as his eyes rolled in his head. She licked, sucked until he no longer could take it and he lowered himself back down into the water feeling extremely sensitive. He needed to stop before he lost his control. Turning her around to face her back to him, he nestled her in between his knees and with big hands massaged lavender scented soap through her hair, making her give a slight moan of contentment. When he was finished he moved his lathered up hands around to her breasts and down along her hips until his hands were back in the water where he let his fingers glide up and down the inside of her thighs. She moaned again and arched her back until she was against his chest. When she felt his erection press against her she let one of her hands slip behind her back and grabbed him by his testicles. With a sudden movement that caused water to spill everywhere he was up and out of the bath tub with her in his arms before she knew what was going on? Placing her on the bed he entered her slowly at first but when she refused to go along with slow and gentle he entered her fast and hard. 'Umm! she moaned as he raised her from underneath and redoubled his efforts, to posses her, to make his claim on her known, to show his true passion for her. She moved her hips to take him further with each powerful trust which drove him crazy. Kissing her hard and eagerly he bit down on her top lip as she dug her nails deep into his back. He could feel her tense under him as her climax took hold in long powerful spasms. He couldn't hold back any longer and joining her as she called his name breathlessly he shouted hers, as his arms shook, and thighs trembled. Sweat beaded from his forehead and dripped onto her breasts. She placed both hands on his face and drew in a deep breath and kissed him tenderly. 'I love you' she whispered as she pulled him into another kiss.

Chapter Twelve

'You know we're going to have to talk about it.'

'Mmm! I know. 'It's going to cause problems; I've only been leader for a few months.'

'There is a way around everything.'

'Which is?

'Hakan!

At this she looked deep into his eyes and blinked in surprise.

'You're serious! she said a little hurt that he would have thought so much about someone taking her place. Seeing her face change he reached for her and held her close. 'You're having our child Nox, we are going to be married' he said softly as he kissed her forehead. She pushed away and glared. 'You think I don't know this already, and for the record I was going to marry you regardless even before a child entered into this fucking mess' she snapped as a frown deepened across her brow. 'We have to meet the elders' she said as she walked away towards the gathering hall. 'Why did he have to mention that, as if I haven't thought of it already.

Bloody man! she with a loud oath under her breath. She knew he heard her but he didn't push the subject, instead just follow close behind her, mumbling something along the lines of not meaning anything by it. When he got no response he pulled a face and knitted his eyebrows together as he bit on his tongue to keep it quiet. Walking through the double doors that led to the hall he grabbed her hand and kissed her knuckles without stopping or slowing down, drawing a few surprised stares from those they passed. She wasn't sure if it was just because of whom she was or he was or who they were together and what it meant. She didn't stop to ask but pushed on until they came to the corridor that led to the gathering hall. It was long and narrow with huge pieces of art work that hung from ceiling to floor. An urge to stop and admire the detail hidden within them but stopped herself and kept her mind on what lay ahead. Kiril held tight to her hand refusing to let it go. People were going to know they were set to be married by the time the day was out so why hide the fact. With confidence they entered the meeting hall to find the elders were seated around a huge rectangle table in the middle of the room. She couldn't help but notice the circular window that spanned all the way across the back wall. She had never seen anything like it before. The colours inter-wound each other and with the light of the moon shinning through, it gave the room an eerie but beautiful and peaceful feel.

'I wonder how long that's going to last,' she thought to herself. Kiril must have noticed the raised eyebrows when they entered hands clasped tight together for she felt him tense and squeeze her hand just that little bit tighter leaving her with numb fingers. 'What the –' Vidar said loud enough for everyone to hear as he looked at Kiril's fingers wrapped around hers. Kiril threw him a look of pure hate and dislike making him sit deeper into the chair. Taking a breath she looked around the room giving small nods of acknowledgment to all that were in attendance and walked with purpose to take her place among them. Anso threw her his usual smile; Arnav gave a cheeky wink, and Gaius and Toran made a face that made her smirk in their direction while Hakan who to her surprise looked worried. Sitting beside him she leaned in 'what is it? she whispered. 'The scouts have brought back news of the Mickisi forming ranks.' He told her in a hushed voice. She gasped and stared at him eyes wide. 'How many? She said as she tried to look like she was listening to what was being discussed. 'Three thousand strong' he said behind his hand. 'Three!' she bellowed before she could stop herself. 'Well that decides it then we need the elders to sign the treaty tonight. They might have come to our aid but if we have brought a war reigning down on Arella we will need them' she stated as a true leader. Hakan nodded his head in agreement. On hearing her name she looked up to find Ulric addressing her with a friendly smile.

'I said I hear you are to wed' he said in a warm tone but his face showed something else as he arched his eyebrows waiting for her reply that had her gritting her teeth in anticipation of what he might say. 'Of course we are pleased for you' he continued. 'And here it is, as if it has anything to do with you,' she thought to herself as she held her patience in check. 'But as you know with you having being named leader of Arella as your father's only living child' he stopped and looked at Anso, 'and as I am aware Kiril is you're only living heir. 'Careful little man,' Kiril hissed just loud enough for Anso to hear who placed his hand on his sons arm. 'It is a very tricky situation as neither of you would be able to step down from these positions as you know, that is unless there is someone in the bloodline to step into your place as leader.' She blushed slightly but burned as Kiril brushed his knee against her leg. Raising her chin she smiled back at Ulric and told him that she was indeed to wed and very much looking forward to the day.

This earned her a squeeze of her thigh and a wondering hand that made her squirm in her seat trying to get away. Continuing on that line of conversation she reassured Ulric and everyone else in the hall that they have discussed in great details the matter of their marriage and what it would mean to both of them and their people. 'I seem to have missed the day that happened,' Kiril said to himself as he looked at the woman he loved and moved his fingers lightly between her legs and caressed her gently making her drew in a sharp breath when he entered her, causing Arnav to look at her questionably only to turn away when he looked at Kiril smirking.

'Unbelievable' he thought to himself grinning. With great difficulty she continued to point out that their lands bordered each other, this could be only a good thing in the years to come as the peace treaties through the lands seemed so far to be benefiting every clan and village involved.

'This brings me gentlemen to the real reason behind our visit here. As you are aware my father had begun in the efforts of joining Arella to the Glens of the Crowden, feeling that as the closest to the Shia Mountains and the Mackisi a treaty could be the difference between fighting this enemy alone or fighting with comrades. As you seen from earlier today it can be achieved.'

This rewarded her with another plunge deep into her from under the table from the man in question. She could feel the heat burning and tried her best to fight against it. 'What is he playing at? she thought to herself as she tried to focus on what was going on. 'Then you are also aware Lady Nox that the Mackisi have near on three thousand men maybe even more. What you seen today was merely three hundred and as I recall you had difficulty in fending off,' Ulric blurted out. 'And you will be aware Ulric that three thousand are not a match for the armies of Arella and Zantar, as for being unable to fight off the advances of the Mackisi earlier today, we were at a disadvantage of being attacked when at our weakest but you can rest assured it will not happen again,' she said with force in her voice that could have been focused on what he had just said or the fact the she could feel her climax growing. Noticing the tightening of his lips that forced his temples to throb she continued unconcerned but snuck a glance in both directions along the table of the others present as she waited for a snide comment but none came. Drawing a breath she pressed on with her argument. 'Now just imagine what force we would be if the army of The Crowden joined these treaties.' When she finished silence filled the hall, and she thanked all that was good at that very moment as the haze came over her eyes and she gripped his hand tight to keep him there, while he leaned in and whispered how wet she felt. But for those looking he seemed to just in deep conversation with her about something important, except for Arnav who sniggered beside her. When her body relaxed he released her, leaving her having to draw in a deep breath as she watched the elders whisper and argue amongst themselves. Ulric stood and addressed the halls occupants stating that they would have further talks on the matter and would have their final decision in the morning. She nodded her acknowledgement and rose to leave only to be stopped by Ulric who once again had something to say. 'I find you deeply enduring Nox, and I wish you to know that the people of Arella have a very strong leader who I feel would be able to protect and guild them true even the darkest of times.' She smiled at him but she had, had enough of his speeches for one day. 'And may the day come when your only son and heir marries and continues on your line, as I have every intention of carrying on mine.'

At this he locked gazes with her and for a moment he thought he might explode with anger at such a bold statement. Until he tore his gaze away leaving her with a thrill of gratification that rippled through her. On hearing a snigger that was hidden behind a hand she turned to see Gaius struggle to control his face as it reddened with the pressure of holding in his joy at her quickness as much as her words that seemed to affect Ulric no end. 'That should shut him up,' she thought as she turned and winked at Anso. Your father would be proud.' he said to her as she passed.

~

'Why that ignorant little man,' she yelled as she smashed the glass against the door as Gaius entered her room. 'Whoa! You could have hit me! He said as he looked wide eyed at her and then at the glass shards that littered the ground before them. She just huffed and turned back to Kiril who was looking at her amused. 'Who the fuck does he think he is telling me my place in Arella. As if I didn't already bloody know.' She was fuming, hands waving in the air theatrically as she ranted. 'How can you just sit there? She shouted at Anso and Kiril who were sitting at the table sharing food that had been left out for her, which she just turned her nose up at when she walked in. They sat and just watched her storming round the room, until Kiril decided it was time he intervened. He rose and walked to her and enclosed her in his arms. 'I think maybe you should try and calm down my love. It can't be good for our son,' he whispered in her ear. He could feel the tension in her shoulders relax as she took a deep breath and laid her head against his chest. 'I can just sit there because I will not be seen to be undermining your place by stepping forward and voicing my own opinions. As you clearly managed it quite nicely yourself.' He said brushing his lips across her forehead. 'Besides if I don't stay calm I'm likely to go and find the bastard and kill him for insulting my father and upsetting you.' He threw her a boyish grin when she looked up and quirked and eyebrow at him. For the first time since entering the room Anso spoke with a mouth full of meat. 'I thought the little shit was going to choke,' he said with a wicked laugh. 'That would have been a pity,' she retorted sarcastically and as her gaze lightened on him she leaned her head back to allow Kiril to kiss her. Promising to calm herself Kiril took her by the hand and led her to one of the chairs. Placing her neatly on his knee he pushed food in front of her and told her to eat. She made a face as she poked the food with an uninterested finger. Kiril cleared his throat and squeezed her waist to get her attention. He looked from her to the food and back again making her sigh and stuff a piece of bread into her mouth, and as she chewed her stomach twisted in complaint. 'Oh great not again,' she said to herself as she cringed and put a hand to her mid-section as she stiffened her spine.

She looked around the room for something she could use if the occasion arose. Spotting the water basin she decided it would do when a knock came to the door. Anso went to open the door leaving them a moment's privacy. 'You're sick again,' he stated more than questioned as he looked pityingly upon her paling face. She nodded and pushed the food away as he hugged her against him. Stretching his arm behind her he began to rub the middle of her shoulders with his thumb moving to the nape of her neck sending a chill that tickled along her spine. The corners of his mouth twitched as she edged closer and dug her head into the hollow between his shoulder and neck and breathed in deeply. Hearing Hakan and Arnav entering she straightened and turned to greet them. Only to be told how horrid she looked and maybe she should try eating something, which only earned them a frown from her and a shake of the head from Kiril. 'What do you want? she snapped making Hakan raise both hands in surrender, while Arnav laughed and winked at her as he passed. Spotting the food he grabbed a hand full and went and sat with Gaius on the bed. 'What have you learned,' Kiril asked the men who had obviously been up to something. 'Well besides that idiot Vidar crying over the fact that your getting married to the lovely Nox here, didn't hear much,' Arnav said with a roll of his eyes, as Kiril clenched his jaws tight. 'Stop trying to cause trouble,' Hakan said as he threw Arnav a mischievous look over his shoulder. 'As I remember it, he said he could still make Nox here change her mind, and come to her senses.' At this Kiril moved Nox off his knee gently then smacked his hand hard on the table and as he stood up flung the chair across the room and watched as it broke in pieces. 'I'm going kill that son-of-a-bitch,' he screamed as he stormed towards the door to a chorus of calm downs and he's not worth it. But it was the sound of Nox vomiting in the corner that caught his attention and silenced the men who were all standing and looking in shock at her kneeling with her head in the water basin. Kiril ran to her and began to murmur soft reassuring things as he stroked her back. Finally exhausted and sweating she rose from the floor and opened the window to allow the cool crisp air rush over her face. Breathing in the late night air she let herself think over everything that had happened during the meeting today and realized with a shock that she hadn't asked Hakan about what else he had found. 'So' she said as she looked back at Hakan. When he looked confused she sighed and continued. 'The Mickisi of course.'

She answered a little testy but on hearing her voice she apologized and went and sat between the two men on her bed. Hakan sat back on the chair, looked her square in the eye and folded his arms across his chest. 'We are concerned Nox. So I think before we get into that you should be telling us what's going on. You've been sick since leaving Tia's homestead.' Before she could even think of an answer Arnav answered for her. 'You Arellian's aren't that smart are you? he said smirking at Hakan. 'Arnav! Kiril warned. 'I knew it! Gaius roared with delight as he jumped up and down on the bed slapping his knee hard with his hand and grinning like he had just won something important. Anso stood up and walked to his son and embraced him tightly 'You could have at least married her first,' he said smiling through tears that had formed on his eye lashes. Turing to Nox them he kissed her cheek and drew her to him with great care as if she might break. Releasing her he laughed out loud as he wiped his face 'you've made me a happy man son' he said with sincerity 'finally a grandfather.' After one last look at them both he moved back to the table and sat down and making a slight motion of his head as he was thinking 'well now, what were we discussing? Oh yes Hakan you have news.' But Hakan was just staring at Nox which made her feel very uncomfortable and she could feel her agitation growing again. At last he stood followed by Gaius and walked to her, they knelt before her, took her hands in theirs, bowed their heads, and recited an Arellian passage said to every expectant mother for luck.

> *May the moon and stars shine upon you at night,*
> *And may the sun shine its warmth upon you,*
> *Bring forth winds that carry good news,*
> *That your sons and daughters are plentiful.*

When they were finished each rose and kissed her gently on the forehead. Then turned and took Kiril's hand, shaking it hard and gave him a congratulant pat on the shoulder. Moving back to his seat Hakan began to relay what they had learned. The Mickisi had begun to form ranks but wasn't sure what the reasons behind it were. But assuming that it had everything to do with what had happened earlier today, his guess was that they know about the treaty and were trying to put a halt if not slow it down. Nox frowned and spent some time taking in the information leaving the men to discuss it among themselves. 'I'm finding it odd that this wasn't addressed with more interest today. I'd be thinking it of great importance to know what these bastards are planning and where they are planning to travel.' With a look in Hakan's direction 'I'm assuming you can handle this! she asked rubbing a hand across her face. Without a word he nodded his approval and gathered his things without hesitation and headed for the door calling for Gaius to accompany him. Gaius jumped from the bed with a whoop of excitement. 'Finally something to do.' Rushing after them Nox called for them to take Toran along. And with that they disappeared out of view.

Chapter Thirteen

THE SHIA MOUNTAINS

The men walked shoulder to shoulder thirty strong that spread the width of the mountain trek and as far as the eye could see. They had definitely come together in force. From what they could make out each man carried at least one sword. While others carried axes and large blocks of what looked like small tree trunks that had been carved into something sinister. Marching along with purpose they formed a rhythm that echoed through the mountains like thunder. Hakan was surprised that they had been able to find such a surprisingly flat surface to form camp, in comparison to the wide spance of land that surrounded them that rose and fell like waves in the ocean, it was near perfect. They had fought their way through over grown thorn bushes and clumps of trees that had grown into one another as they moved further into the thick of the mountains for over an hour before coming on a small group of Mackisi who seemed in great spirits but in a terrible hurry to get to their destination. They followed as close but as quietly as possible until at last they were led directly to their main campsite. They were unable to recognise any part of the landscape from where they had emerged, unless they wanted to count the slope that near killed them this morning, but it would do no good considering they left it behind some time ago. Lying flat allowing their bodies to sink into the stony surface beneath them, they listened and waited for an opportunity that might arise to gather some information to bring back to Nox, and give them the upper hand in dealing with whatever may come. Noticing a tent that had been erected some distance from the camp at the base of a colossal sized bolder which shadowed out the moonlight on one side, but still enough light got through to allow them to keep a close eye on the comings and goings of men they didn't recognise to their utter annoyance.

Just as they were about to edge closer towards a group of Mackisi who had branched off and where talking in muttered tones a shout came from the front of the gathered army. They jumped to attentions and all but ran back to get into line. There stood a single man that demanded ultimate attention be it through fear or loyalty but received it none the less. They could hear him but were unable to see him clearly without having to rise slightly from the ground which wasn't the best idea considering they were smack bang in the middle of three thousand Mackisi.

Moving slightly to their left they were able to make out the outline of the man, and hoping that he would sometime move more into the moonlit mountain face they waited, listened and observed.

As he raised both his arms silence fell over the mountain. Looking out over the gathered army before him he called for them to be patient. Their time was coming. 'We've been quite too long,' he roared. 'They think of us as dogs, as nothing, they believe themselves better. They come from the South and the West and enter our lands, and we are expected not to retaliate? I say we show them what happens when you cage a beast that is meant to roam free. We will no longer bide the shadows of the Shia.' The men who had once been silent screamed their agreement. Waving swords, axes and anything else that came to hand in the air in a menacing fashion as they grew excited from his words. 'If what they've been doing is quiet, I hate to think what they have in mind,' Gaius whispered not taking his eyes from who he now knew as the infamous leader of the Mackisi. An hour passed as they lay in hiding. Shouting, cheering and on numerous occasions fighting broke out amongst the men before them as they seemed to grow unstable. To their astonishment the leader of this brutish army stood and met their internal arguing with laughter and encouragement clearly finding it easier not to waste any effort in calling a halt to the madness. This led to newfound confidence in those involved. As they watched the chaos unwind they grew disgusted when they were forced to witness the winners' prize in the shape of a young girl no older than thirteen being dragged kicking and screaming from somewhere out of view, and left to the whims of a man who by now was crazed by the taste of killing, and who had no intentions of showing any concern for the young girl before him. Her screams were deafening and could be heard over the chaos. 'Fucking animal,' Gaius hissed as he began to rise to attack only to be pulled and held tight by Hakan and Toran. 'We can't! Toran near shouted a whisper into his brother's ear. He looked at both men with rage in his eyes but he knew they were right. What would it achieve? As he relaxed they released their strong grips on him and turned to face were the young girl fought against her captor. Lowering their heads unable to watch, as they found to have the ability to hear was bad enough for the men of Arella.

After what seemed a lifetime it all went quiet and they watched as the bastard walked away happy with his conquest leaving the girl now lying bleeding, beaten beyond recognition and whimpering small traumatized sobs that ripped at their hearts. Another yell came from the leader which drew their attention back to him. When they looked up they got what they were waiting for. At first glimpse he looked to have some facial markings, as Hakan pointed out in more of a question than a statement. As he moved more into their line of sight they could see it for what it was. The whole right side of his face was so badly mutilated his eye had been completely removed. 'That's pretty,' Gaius said as he frowned and made a face of total disgust at the image in front of them. 'I think it's time we leave,' Hakan said in a hushed tone, looked in the direction of the young girl who was curled up tightly against herself. 'She's coming with us.' As they waited for the first opportunity to slip from their hiding place to retrieve her. Both men noticed the eagerness in Gaius, but also noticed the growing anger the longer they had to wait. Finally the group of men moved off towards the campsite leaving the young girl sprawled out on the ground.

Moving on elbows and knees Hakan moved at a fast pace staying as low and quiet as possible. She was breathing deep shallow breaths when he reached her this alarmed him leaving him to think that she had more than just the injuries that could be seen. But then reminded himself of the brutal and savage beating she had received before the rape she then had to endure. He had to take a deep breath to control his anger and with a quick glance he placed his hand gently over her mouth to quench any verbal complaint or argument at being pulled into the pushes where two huge men lay in waiting. He tried to whisper reassuring things into her ear but she was so terrified that by the time he managed to put his other hand behind her back to help draw her closer to him to ensure he caused no more injury as he brought her with him she began to kick and fight against him with such great ferocity he felt a deep feeling of proud-ness for the strength she displayed. When he finally reached Toran and Gaius they took her between them and huddled her through the bushes and with great care placed her between them. Gaius took over mouth covering duties, as Toran put his finger to his mouth in a shushing motion. Her eyes widened and tears ran down her cheeks and over Gaius's hand. Leaving him with a sudden urge to gather the poor child to him and comfort her like a father would. But right now he knew she thought the worst and he refrained from touching her more than necessary. Hakan crawled back through the bushes and without stopping continued until he was ahead of them and moving fast in the opposite direction of the campsite. It was time to leave

Chapter Fourteen

Kiril lay with his head perched on Nox's shoulder as they sat beside each other on the four poster bed. Running his hand over her stomach he kissed her neck gently and asked her how she was feeling. Knowing what he meant she moved her head back to look at him only to find him grinning back at her. 'You know you'll get bored of me,' she said giggling as he grazed his teeth across her jaw. 'Never! he replied with a playful snarl as he bit her neck resulting in a high pitched squeal come from her as she tried to break free only to find herself sprawled beneath him as he continued his attack making her laugh so hard her sides began to hurt. A loud knock came to the door making Kiril growl his contempt at the interruption 'Go away! he shouted sharply but whoever it was just knocked harder until he finally rose with a curse to answer it. He had just turned the round glass handle and cracked the door open an inch when Tianna burst through out of breath and flushed with excitement. She looked around past Kiril until she spotted Nox who by now was standing at the base of the bed. Tianna broke into a wide smile. 'He's here! I found him in the courtyard, but we must go quickly.' Nox straightened abruptly but her manner was one of total control and composed. Kiril frowned and looked from one to the other. 'Who's here? He asked Tianna, but Nox answered for her 'Elder Dreakwood, now get dressed into something clean,' she said looked at him, 'well cleaner at least.' And with that she turned and started to let her hair down while Tianna attacked it with a comb she had found on the bedside cabinet. 'Wait! What are you talking about? Kiril asked in total confusion. But when Nox turned on him in what seemed like total bewilderment that he would stand there asking questions instead of just doing what she asked, he wished he'd just kept his mouth shut. There she was hands on her hips, head tilted to one side and glowering at him. 'Kiril, my love,' she said as she made her way towards speaking in what she hoped was a warm voice. But he knew better as her face showed a different story. Placing her hands against his chest she looked up at him and gave him a slight smile 'please get dressed, before Elder Dreakwood thinks Tianna here was merely playing games with him.' Not giving him any change to ask any more questions or argue she turned back to Tianna who by this stage so excited she was already on her way out the door and gone. Kiril walked to his dry shirt and trousers and began to dress but clearly not doing it fast enough for Nox, she near ran at him and roughly grabbed the back of his shirt and stuffed it into the back of his trousers. Swiping her hands across his shoulders and down along his back she murmured to herself as she spun him around without any notice nearly making him trip over his own feet and leaving him having to grab the bedpost to straighten himself. 'Nox! What is wrong with you? Must you be so damned rough? he asked only to be ignored as she squinted up at him and his appearance. Her nose scrunched up as she clearly thought he was an unruly mess, but he'd have to do. Laughing at her and placed his forefinger on the top of her nose making her snap out of her thoughts. Her face relaxed into a breathtaking smile. He reached for her only to have his hand grabbed tightly and pulled from the room in hot pursuit of Tianna who seemed all to have disappeared from sight. They made their way through a series of corridors and small gathering alcoves that made his mind wander with images of Nox laid against one of the walls with her skirts up around her waist and at his mercy. Without a second thought he grabbed her tightly and pulled her back into the one they had just passed and pushing her against the wall he began kissing her thoroughly even through her complaining of having to be somewhere. Which to his relief ended when she put her two arms around his neck and pulled him closer. He began to rummage under her skirts until he felt her smooth skin under his hands. Lifting her with great ease resulting in her wrapping her legs around his waist. In the excitement he had forgotten to open his trousers and was having great difficulty in getting them down enough, damn it he had no choice but to lower her to the ground. As soon as he did and the kiss was broken she pushed her skirts back down and slapped him on the arm hard. 'We don't have time,' she said in a hushed voice. 'Believe me it won't take long,' he said as he reached for her again. She laughed and kissed him briefly as she pushed her way out of the alcove leaving him with his trousers down around his ankles and a painful erection. When he didn't follow she ran back in and promised they would definitely claim one on the way back. She kissed him again only this time lingered that little bit longer leaving him fighting for self control. 'You know your torturing me,' he said with a sigh. Flashing a grin at him she let her hand slip down the inside of his trousers and grabbed him gently by his throbbing erection forcing him to draw a quick breath in.

'It won't take long, I promise,' she said as she flicked her tongue and licked his bottom lip. 'It better not! he answered as he allowed her to drag him out of the alcove. He could have stopped her sometime ago but he was beginning to grow curious and was enjoying the fact she seemed genuinely excited about it so he continued to allow her to continue on her path. Finally they came to an archway that led from the castle into a wooded area where he spotted Tianna with Arnav and his father. Now he stopped her. 'Ok! Enough! What's going on? She looked around for support and just as she was about to answer a man stepped out from behind a wall covered with ivy and bright red flowers. He had long white hair, clean shaven and bright blue eyes that held a sparkle. She pulled her hand free and went to the man greeting him warmly resulting in him embracing her as he looked down on her fondly before turning his attentions to Kiril who was staring with a frown at the man who had his woman in his arms. 'We should begin,' Elder Dreakwood said with a smile as he walked through the gap in the wall, followed by Arnav, Anso and Tianna, which left Nox to explain to Kiril as he refused to move one more step. 'You want to marry me do you not? she asked in a hurt tone. 'Of course I do you know that, but I don't understand what that has to do with anything-.' Realisation came over his face. 'Now! he said in shock. 'But how? Stepping closer she looked at him nervously 'Elder Dreakwood has the right to marry any couple who enter into it of their own free will. So since he was here I thought I'd ask and if he agreed to marry us . . . well,' she stopped talking and shrugged her shoulders. 'When I said about getting married at your return to Arella you all but torn me to shreds. Why the rush now? She smiled up at him and took his hand. 'I want to give our child your name even before he enters this world. Is that such a bad thing? And I really don't want to be looked on as a whore for getting with child before taking a husband, and I know people will be surprised when they learn of our marriage but I couldn't stand it to think that my people would think bad of me,' she said in a soft voice no longer looking at him. A smile spread across his face. 'Are you sure you want to do it like this? he asked her as he placed his fingers under her chin and made her look up at him. He was surprised to see her eyes glistening 'you've changed your mind? she said and walked away from him in shock that she could have been so wrong. Walking after her he placed himself in front to stop her going any further and gathered her to him in a loving embrace. 'All I've ever wanted is you,' he said as he bent his head to hers and kissed her with a passion that left her aching for more and breathless. 'You will never be deemed a whore or anything other than the lady you are, and if anyone says otherwise I'll kill them myself. Taking him by the hand she led him through the gap and to where she would finally be his wife.

Standing before Elder Ransan Dreakwood Nox had a unexpected feeling of triumph. She had proven she would not be dictated to and when she felt right to marry she would of her own accord. Placing two rings on the ground between them Ransan smiled and began. 'Kiril, you stand before this woman wishing to live your life as her friend, lover and protector. Walk the circle and shelter her with your protection.' Circling Nox, Kiril never took his eyes from her wanting to reveal how he felt at that very moment. When he had concluded he stopped opposite her once again. Turning now to Nox, Ransan called for her to follow in Kiril's footsteps declaring her desire to become his friend, lover and protector. Facing each other Ransan bowed and picked up the rings at their feet, handing them over to the young couple before him.

'I will form a circle adjoining both of you at this moment. As I do so place the rings upon each other's fingers.' As he walked around them he declared them eternally joined to one another.

Coming to a halt behind them he positioned his hands on their shoulders 'there shall be no falseness, untrustworthiness and betrayal between you both. You are each others, so may you support and show dedication to one another.' Breaking away he came to face them both and smiled warmly at them both. Kiril you can now kiss your wife. Not waiting to be told twice he picked her up in a swish of skirts and kissed her thoroughly to the claps as well as cheers from his father, Arnav and Tianna.

~

He could feel his muscles clench under the strain of pushing himself to the limit the night before. A lingering smile formed across his lips and a feeling of being pleasantly exhausted.

But it didn't stop thoughts of the woman naked in his bed. Taking her three times in the night one being in an alcove that he had made a mental note to return to, only to be the one with his back against the wall and a very feisty and lively Nox taking control of the situation. Leaving them both speechless and breathless. He felt he could still feel the softness of her skin and the scent of her hair lingered in his senses. She was finally his and his alone. Clenching his fists at the sudden thought of another touching her as he had done not two hours passed. He took a deep breath and relaxed his hands down by his sides. No she was his, he need not worry. He smiled again as he could see her in his mind's eye laid out before him, hair messed and fallen around her shoulders, her laughter that sent burning all the way to his balls and left him with a need that made him want to run back to the castle and to his bed. Hearing his name he snapped out of his thoughts feeling annoyed at the interruption, but made the decision to return to his bed and his new wife as soon as possible. The ache in his loins was starting to be painful. He spotted Arnav coming up along the trek and turned his smile on him until he spoke. 'You're up early; did she tire of you already then? I would have thought we would have had to drag you kicking and screaming from her bed,' Arnav said smirking in the way that said he knew what was coming and he checked the distance between himself and Kiril as he turned his frown on him. 'Oh shush up you fool, as far as she kicking me out goes you'd be wrong,' Kiril said and turned to leave it at that but Arnav continued to badger him on the subject. 'Oh so it's like that is it. Ah sure I knew you had it in you. She needed a little rest did she, to recover like? With that Kiril spun around and with the glare that came his way Arnav decided it better not to say any more or he'd end up flat on his back with a tired and very angry Zantarian warrior standing over him. 'I got word that Hakan wished to speak with me.' Kiril said looking at the castle. 'That's why I'm here. I went to retrieve your father and noticed you out here so seemed the best solution and maybe we could get all this over with and get out of here.' Arnav replied a little nervously as he looked around the glen as if waiting on an unwanted guest. Trusting himself not to smile or laugh out loud at his friend he just simply asked what he'd been up to. Not bothering to continue after receiving a 'you don't want to know' look he turned and headed towards the castle to find Hakan.

~

Arriving outside Hakan's room that he had been assigned, they could hear muffled voices from within and what seemed like a young woman crying. Looking at each other in confusion Arnav knocked and walked in. Sure enough there she was sitting in the middle of the bed, badly bruised and crying to near a sobbing that was stopping her from being able to talk in consistent sentences. Gaius was trying his very best to try and console the poor child but to no avail.

Tianna suddenly burst through the door and scowled all the men who were lurking around the bed. 'What do you think you're doing? she yelled. 'No wonder the child is terrified and you all standing there gawking at her like fools. Move yourselves this instant,' she said in a stern voice with demanded authority. 'Surely you can discuss things someplace else, and allow her to rest and me to tend her wounds.' Without another word she turned and ignoring the men sat on the bed and stroked away the tears gently from the girls face. As Kiril was about to leave she called him back. 'Nox was called to the gathering hall by the elders.' Kiril frowned 'When? 'Oh not twenty minutes past, she asked me to relay the message so you'd be aware of her whereabouts.'

Nodding his gratitude he left the room and the girl in Tianna's good hands. 'What was that about? Hakan asked when he drew close enough to talk without shouting. 'Seems the elders called for Nox, she's at the gathering hall.' Hakan scowled 'Why? If it was about the treaty we would have all been called as witnesses. 'I don't know and I don't like it but I'm going to find out.' And with that the six men walked with even paces through the corridors ignoring every passerby. They could hear Nox before seeing her and Kiril gave a small laugh and shook his head. 'I'm betting they wished they hadn't bothered now.' At this the others nodded in agreement and continued through the doors to find Nox in a heated conversation with Ulric.

'There has to be a logical explanation,' she repeated in amazement. 'I think that would depend on your definition of logical. Unsettling would be a better word would it not? She didn't raise her voice but her face flushed and her lips tightened forcing her to hold her tongue, while the whole time never taking her eyes from Ulric. A bitter laugh sounded to her left and when she glanced in the direction she was faced with Vidar staring straight at her. Turning her body to face him head on, she placed her hands on the table in front of her, leaned forward and glared at him out through her hair that was hanging loose around her face. 'Have you something you wish to say? As I don't remember referring to you.' she said with spite filling her voice. Not seeming fazed but her abruptness he threw her a sly smile that made her gut twist. 'I just find it . . . interesting,' he said as he rubbed his fingertips along the table. At this she stood up straight as shock ran through her. 'He can't be serious,' she thought to herself as she looked down at him. 'That you would send your men into the Shia Mountains without first discussing it with your host. Did it not occur to you that if things went any other way we would now be overrun with the Mickisi this very second,' he said as he raised himself from his seat descending on her his voice barely under a shout. At this she noticed a movement in the corner of her eye only to see Kiril making his way towards Vidar and felt a rush of panic. Looking at him with pleading eyes 'please don't interfere,' she thought as he slowed down and stopped just behind his seat.

Turning her gaze back on Vidar her shock faded and it was replaced by anger. She clenched her fists and braced herself as she shouted back at him with such emotion he looked to his father for help, only to receive none, he was on his own. 'And has it occurred to you, you bloody fool that what you speak of is already on your door step. Or does it make you happier to turn a blind eye? Because while you're sleeping at night them bastards are forming an army big enough to wipe out your lovely castle from over you heads. Not to mention raiding and burning down villages and homesteads along with those who live in them, raping and kidnapping the young girls and women that they wish to use as animals when they are not near beating them to death for sport.' Shrieking and not caring she was fuming. 'And don't show yourselves naïve enough to think it rumor. We have seen it with our own eyes.' She couldn't stop. Having seen the young girl. She had seen the damage done and heard of the horrific scene that took place. Damn them they're going to learn of it. Without taking a breath she turned her attention to Ulric 'we are leaving immediately. I have come to you, put my life and the lives of my men and husband at risk in order to bring you an opportunity of friendship and security from Arella. But I have found that what I have witnessed during our travels have opened my eyes wide enough to know when I am fighting a losing battle. I find it exceedingly strange that you do not seem at all threatened by this growing enemy and why you do not send your riders out in defense of those who cannot defend themselves and their own. Your ignorance on the matter adds insult to injury, as you seem to remain oblivious to the chaos. They are entering your lands are they not? she said with a snipe at Vidar who seemed to be growing angrier by the second. 'You fucking bitch,' he snapped. 'How dare you enter these halls throwing out accusations and what exactly are you suggesting? 'With a roar Kiril lunged at him hitting him so hard the sound of knuckles meeting flesh echoed around the hall. When he fell Kiril stood over him like a domineering presence lifting him with great ease smacked him hard against the wall leaving his feet almost dangling.

'If you so much as look at my wife again let alone speak to her in such a way, I will kill you. Do you understand? he hissed. As he moved away a small entourage had made their way towards him only to stop when they were approached by two more angry Zantarians, and three very red faced Arellians swords at the ready. Stepping away from the table Nox faced Ulric 'I will not stand before you again within your great halls and offer the same. But I fear the next time we meet it will be you standing before me in mine.' With one last glance around the hall she turned on her heel and walked with every bit of dignity she could gather from within.

When she got outside the doors of the gathering hall she took a deep breath and turned to the men who stood behind her all still very angry and a bit confused. Looking at Kiril she gave him a look of what were you thinking. 'What? he said innocently as he shrugged his shoulders making Arnav snigger and the twins laugh out right. 'Uh-huh' was all she said in return and headed towards Hakan's room to retrieve Tianna and the young girl who she hadn't a clue what to do with.

Chapter Fifteen

Deciding the best thing to do was ride with Kiril and allow the girl who they now knew as Nasha to ride alone on Snowflake as she was still very anxious and afraid of just about everything and trusted no one, they set out to leave The Glens of the Crowden. She noticed how uncomfortable Nasha was in the saddle and felt tears sting her eyes. 'She'll never recover' she whispered to Kiril who seemed to notice where Nox's attention had been drawn to. Not answering he pulled her closer and kissed the top of her head. Making the decision to travel down to the West and then to make her way to Arella had caused some unforeseen arguments that had been squashed by Anso before they could begin. She had a lot of things to organize that wouldn't be able to wait, and she knew she wasn't the only one who knew it even though he refused to agree with her. Beyond a small open space not even big enough to claim the name clearing they could just peer over the hill that allowed them to see the rolling mass of fields and trees before them. It was beautiful even at this time of year. She observed with great interest the assortment of plants and flowers that had managed to survive tha harsher weather. A wave of emotion came over her as she thought of the men who had died during this journey this was supposed to be peaceful and straight forward. She had been lucky to have only lost three unlike Anso's twenty one. She grew angry at herself for feeling blessed 'only three indeed, three fathers, three sons, three brothers. Three was three to many to be replaced by those who loved them' she argued with herself. She had never had to return to Arella without all that rode away with her. How could she look upon the faces as they noticed theirs weren't coming home.

'Damn it' she shouted drawing looks from Kiril and Hakan.

'Are you okay' Hakan asked in a worried tone.

'No I'm bloody not! she snapped as she rubbed her hand hard across her face.

'Are you feeling unwell, are you going to be sick again? Kiril asked looking in over her shoulder.

'No! I'm not feeling bloody unwell, if I was you'd know about it' she shouted back at him.

Clearly not in the form to be shouted at for no apparent reason he stopped the horse grabbed hold of her shoulder and turned her just enough to face him.

'Do you want to walk? he asked as his eyes bore into hers.

Sputtering a sarcastic laugh she threw her leg over the saddle and jumped to the ground, hunched her shoulders and set out on foot.

'I hope you enjoy celibacy' she shouted back at Kiril leaving him and Hakan looking at each other in disbelief.

'Blasted woman! he mumbled as he dismounted from the horse and went after her.

'Nox! he called as he grew closer. She shoved her head in the air ignoring him and walked faster.

Nox! he shouted as he grabbed her firmly by the arm only to have her snatch it back and glare at him.

'What? she snapped not taking her eyes from his.

'You know what; walk, if that's what you want to do bloody go right ahead' he said in a defeated tone and turned from her and stalked back to retrieve his horse.

Telling herself she did the right thing by dismounting from the horse instead of throwing him off, her feet and legs were telling her another story and she was even more testy than before.

It definitely didn't help that Kiril rode right past her and offered his horse to her, only to have him storm off when she told him quite nicely were to put his horse. The day hadn't cleared and she felt the first drops of rain fall near an hour past but to her relief they had ceased. She knew Anso was right about forming a camp and shelter before the evening drew closer and damn it she was still hungry. It wouldn't be much fun not being able to find any dry wood to set a fire and keep it going throughout the night, and maybe cook some food when the rain did eventually come. Besides being outnumbered by a good two hundred plus men wasn't exactly going to go in her favor so she agreed. 'Your feet have to be hurting' Anso spoke to her as merely stating the obvious, clearly not meaning offence. 'Ah . . . no, not really' she lied. He stopped suddenly and dismounted from his horse which caught her unawares and left her looking at him with a slight smile that had formed on her lips. 'Thought you might want the company, he said as he smiled back at her. They walked in silence for some time until finally she broke it and spoke to him in a soft voice.

'How do you do it?

'Do what? he asked not looking at her.

'Return home after losing men? I witnessed my father do it for years but . . . '

'It's never easy, but that's what war is. You'll have to get used to it I'm afraid.' 'Mmm! Maybe your right' she said looking out into the distance. 'But I will tell you this, it is something that never gets any easier. You're a leader now and unfortunately the burden of such things will always be upon your shoulders until you replace it with something positive' he said with a faint heart stricken smile. 'Thank you Anso, for everything. I owe you an apology' she said without breaking her gaze. 'When you arrived with Kiril' he raised his hand to stop her. 'You need not apologize for defending yourself and your men Nox. I found it deeply reassuring that the woman my son loves and wanted so badly to marry would put herself before an unknown enemy with great courage' he said with a smile. 'Even if my son insists that it was pure stubbornness' he said laughing at the face she made.

By the time another hour passed both her and Anso gave in and called for the camp to be established. A shooting pain shot up from her feet all the way to the tops of the legs and she winched bending to fill up the water jug. Just as she was about to turn she heard crunching leaves behind her and she braced herself for Kiril but on turning she found Tianna standing in front of her with her hands on her hips. 'And what do you think you are doing? Sounding displeased at having to ask her in the first place. 'You should not be lifting such heavy things' she said as she reached to take the jug only to be shooed away by Nox who clearly didn't see the need. 'It's no wonder Toran is behaving himself' Nox said with a look at Tianna who just smiled to herself. 'I haven't seen or heard him and Gaius fight in weeks' Nox said laughing.

The spark of humor that had been missing since the morning had returned and she began to feel more at ease. Finding herself being fed by every man that passed her as she walked amused her, but she had a feeling it had something to do with Kiril and his persisting on her eating.

Regardless she accepted everything with a bashful glance, and found she was more than happy to take what rations they were willing to part with. Even now the smell that came wafting in the wind made her stomach growl and her mouth water.

It had started raining by the time they made it to the camp and she found Kiril had settled down beside the fire talking with Arnav while Gaius listen contently to their conversation. She had a sudden urge to go over and slap him but decided against it because deep down she didn't know why she wanted to slap him in the first place. Instead went with the water, handed it to Malachi who was standing opposite Kiril at the fire. Without looking at him she turned and went to find Nasha. She had noticed her breasts had begun to ache terribly and the feeling of constantly wanting to cry every time she took a glimpse of Kiril made her lips quiver leaving her having to fight back her tears. Wiping rain from her eyes she squinted into the darkness. There she was sitting with a steaming cup of what could have been anything. It seems the girl had inherited more father figures than she could handle. On seeing Nox making her way towards her she gave her a sheepish look that held what she thought was fear but more so worry. Sitting down beside her taking care not to over crowd her with her closeness she spoke to her in gentle tones and was surprised that she seemed quite comfortable in speaking with her. 'How are you feeling Nasha? she asked carefully. Noticing how she looked out into the distance she wondered what horrible memories haunted her. But then Nox wondered if she had even wanted to come to with them to Arella or even Zantar. 'I should have asked! The Crowden was her home. 'I should have asked before assuming you would be happy to travel with us' Nox said in a low tone. At this Nasha's head shot back to look at Nox, her eyes grew wide 'No, I wanted more than anything to come with you. Everyone has been so good to me. I don't know what would have happened to me if your men hadn't saved me. I will never forget what they did for me. If you had of left me there . . . ' stopping she began to cry uncontrollably making Nox curse herself for upsetting the girl. She gathered her to herself and a sudden memory of the night she had consoled Tianna rushed back into her mind. Remembering the heart ache and the anger she felt towards those who wronged her was nothing like what she felt now. 'Damn it she's just a child! Angry tears ran down her face as she listened to the weeping girl in her arms and she thought of the child growing inside of her and a chill settled in her stomach. What would she do if this was her daughter, her child? Risking a look in Kiril's direction she felt elated when as always his eyes met hers. Giving him a warm smile she mouthed an I'm sorry in his direction, and giggled quietly as his threw her a mock kiss and a wink. Pulling back away from the tear stained face of a young girl who was brutally pushed into womanhood she wiped her face gently with a fold of her skirt and held it between both hands whispering 'you are a beautiful young woman and you will always be safe when you are with us.' At this Nasha looked away from her and Nox knew she had something to say.

'He spoke of you.' Nasha said looking down at the ground at her feet.

'Who did? Nox replied in an even tone.

'The leader of the Mackisi' she said now looking at her.

'Oh . . . And what had he got to say? Nox answered but noticed her breathing accelerated slightly.

'You're the one who marked him' Nasha replied staring straight at her.

As panic rose in her she ran towards the fire screaming for Hakan which made Kiril, Arnav and Gaius jump up looking around frantically moving with hast towards her. Hakan! she screamed yet again as she turned in circle scanning the campsite only to find that wherever he was, he wasn't anywhere near. Remembering that Gaius had accompanied him on when he went up onto the Shia Mountains she grabbed him with force shouting for him to tell her what he seen.

'Tell me! Who did you see? she shouted making him trip over his words. 'Eh . . . well . . . we seen the army . . . ' he stopped as she shook her head frantically 'No! the leader Gaius, I need you to describe him,' she was hysterical by this time drawing the attention of Anso and Toran. 'Gaius! she screamed up at him. 'Okay . . . okay . . . 'he said holding her shoulders trying to calm her down.

By now Kiril was standing behind her with his hands on her hips as he murmured softly to her only she wasn't having any of it. She wanted answers and wanted them now. 'Tell me.

Describe him!' she said still too upset to let go of his arms. 'He was an ugly brute, a nasty scare down one side of his face that looked to have claimed his eye –'stopping him before he could go on 'Gaius which side of his face? she said with wide eyes that were filled of something he had never seen before. 'The left side' he said with certainty. Letting go of Gaius she stumbled backwards only to be caught by Kiril before she fell over tree roots. She was in a daze as Kiril's hands touched her tenderly as he tried to calm her down 'it can't be' she repeated over and over.

She gnawed on her bottom lip as the sweat ran down along her sides making her bodice stick tight to her. Losing touch with everything around her as her throat grew tight and the world seemed to spin. Everything went black.

Chapter Sixteen

LEL – THE SHIA MOUNTAINS

He sat watching her as she lay upon the blankets on the ground. Her bruised face had healed well leaving only a dirty yellow swelling around her right eye while her lips no longer split and bled when he forced her mouth. She had also he realized stopped trying to bite his cock off whenever she had the chance him which pleased him no end. He smiled to himself at the strength she still showed and he found that he was growing quite fond of her. He had noticed a subtle change in her demeanor when he had taken her the night before. She didn't seem as angry or fearful of him as she had done since taking her by the stream and he was a hundred percent sure that she had climaxed in the midst of their love making. 'Love making' he said to himself sarcastically. It had given him a sense of power. He had broken her. Of course he knew it wouldn't stop her from trying to injure him if other occasions arose, and secretly he hoped she wouldn't. He enjoyed fighting with her, he enjoyed how she bit and slapped him when he drew to close. But then to break her down and force her body to respond to his was a great victory every time. A gust of cool air rushed into the tent through the open flap accompanied by Kovit his first in command. 'They've left the

Crowden' he near shouted with excitement only to have Lel look from him to the woman who was beginning to stir with in the blankets. 'Kovit, if you wake that woman and I have to listen to her' he turned his full attention to his captain 'I won't be held responsible for what I do' he said as he made his way towards the table that took up most of the tent. Kovit apologized and laid the maps out in front of them both. 'When did they leave?

Lel asked not taking his eyes from the maps as he took in the lands before him. 'Just before noon, they headed West' he stated as he ran his finger down along the Western root. 'Hmm!

Well I didn't think they would come back along this way especially without their full armies behind them' he said as he scratched his head in thinking. 'Lel, you should know Lady Nox has wed' Kovit said looking directly into the face of his leader who seemed to be frowning deeply at the news. 'Who? He asked without breaking eye contact with a tone that held bitterness. 'Kiril, son of Anso Zanni of Zantar.' Walking away from the table leaving Kovit looking after him in shock that this news would cause him such unrest he paced up and down mumbling things not loud enough for Kovit to hear. 'What would you have us do? his captain said in an all business like tone that drew Lel's attention back to the situation at hand. Walking back over and looking again over the maps he sighed tiredly and told him they would not attack them now, they would wait. This didn't go down very well with his captain who was in the mind that the best time to attack was now when they were weak and at their worst. Only to be met with a very angry Lel who rushed Kovit and grabbed him tightly against him. 'I will not take my victory over Arella by bringing three thousand down on two hundred. We will wait' he said in a hiss.

Kovit nodded his head in agreement as Lel released him. 'And you Vidar what do you think you were doing attacking my men' he said to a very nervous Vidar standing at the tent opening taking in the confrontation. Entering further he took his position standing shoulder to shoulder with Kovit who just grunted at him and moved away. 'I have to follow my father's orders; he is still head of the Elders and Leader of The Crowden. What would you have me do? he said a little too shaky for his own liking. 'I would have you do your damn job' Lel screamed at him not caring if he woke the woman or not, if she said a thing he would make her wish she hadn't. 'Did the Elders sign the treaty? he asked through his teeth. Vidar swallowed hard 'No! but . . . ' he stopped not sure if he wanted to continue. Lel walked towards him menacingly 'but what?

Vidar took a step backwards until he was back out of the tent with Lel still descending on him.

'Some of the Elders are unhappy with the decision. They feel that bitch Nox spoke of things that can no longer be ignored and are beginning to break into groups. Elder Dreakwood is amongst them, he arrive two days past.' At hearing this news Lel stopped and looked at Vidar. 'This Kiril of Zantar' he asked with a sneer as he faced Vidar. 'What kind of a man is he? Vidar looked at him in amazement 'have you not seen my face Lel? He is jealous and over bearing who doesn't let her out of his sight for more than an hour if she's lucky. Not that she minds of course. When he's not looking for her she's already right behind him. Their never apart.'

'Interesting' Lel said as he looked out into the distance. Seeing this as an opportunity to reinstate his authority Vidar braced himself and turned on Lel who was just about to walk away. 'As far as doing my job Lel I think you need to reassess your situation in this.' Lel turned on him with a murderous stare that made Vidar wish he had kept his mouth shut, but taking a deep breath he squared his shoulder and continued. 'During your little gathering last night Nox's first in command Hakan and the twins Gaius and Toran were right under your very nose. They even managed to take a girl that you had given as a little prize to one of your men only the idiot didn't finish the fucking job, leaving her to squeal like a pig. You'll be glad to know they took her with them' he said looking at Lel with smugness. When he didn't reply to this information Vidar continued 'you'll also be happy to know that the woman your men also left alive when they attacked a homestead in the gap between the Floyden and the Shia has now been claimed by Toran. So surprise, surprise they fucked up there too. Your men are getting sloppy Lel and you wonder why the Elders are edging closer to Nox and her damned treaty. At this Lel's face paled with temper making Vidar decide the best thing now was to leave. Turning he strode away feeling his heart beat so fast he thought he wouldn't make it down the mountain.

Chapter Seventeen

Nox woke to the feeling of rain falling onto her face leaving wet tracks free to run down the sides of her face and soak into her hair. Feeling groggy and slightly nauseous she tried her best to force her eyes to stay open and focus on something. That something turning out to be Kiril who was kneeling over her with a very worried look upon his face. He was she realized talking to her, but as she put both her hands to her face she groaned making him stop abruptly. Placing his big reassuring hands behind her head and back he raised her enough to be sitting against him.

'What happened? she spoke in a weak voice. 'You fainted' he answered as he leaned down to look at her properly. She was pale and clammy and clearly needed some space and time to gather her thoughts. Without warning he slid his arm under her knees and lifted her to himself and carried her away from the campsite and prying eyes. Not arguing she nestled her head closer in under his chin and fed on his strength. It didn't matter where they were going and she relaxed her whole body against him letting the tiredness and soreness of her muscles drain away with each step he took. When he had eventually reached is destination he sat onto what seemed like a tree stump. Still holding her he sat down, drew her across his lap and wrapped his arms tightly around her waist. He rested his head on the top of hers and placed his hand lovingly and gently upon her stomach and breathed in a deep breath. Lifting her head she looked straight at him as tears welled up in her eyes. Laying her hand on his her lip began to quiver again at everything she wanted to say. Hating the feeling of being so weak she was beginning to battle with her inner voice for answers to her questions and as always receiving none to her total dismay.

Closing her eyes the tears she was holding back overflowed leaving her yet again cursing herself for being incompetent to control her emotions. Just as she was about to break away, something that felt as gentle as a feather floated over her skin. Kiril planted kisses upon her still closed eyes and continued downward along her tear stained face until he arrived at her lips. He didn't kiss her. As he held back she could feel his breath on her face. 'Nox' he whispered as she opened her eyes. Placing her fingertip to his lips she looked at him pleadingly. Taking hold of her hand he held it against his chest. She could feel his heart beating solid and fast and knew he was struggling with everything in him to keep calm as much as necessary. He couldn't force or demand to know what was going on. Taking a deep breath she shuffled to get a little more comfortable and began her story.

I was sixteen and as usual never listened to my father. I had to sneak into the stables as he had banned me from ridding Snowflake because I refused not to mount him properly. He felt it to dangerous. Well I had managed to get him saddled, out of the stables and out of the castle grounds without alerting anyone. I liked to ride along the Floyden Mountains, it was always so peaceful and the wide open spaces were fantastic to run Snowflake to his ability. He was so fast and powerful. I felt so free when he galloped without being held back. Never going further than half way I had just reached my turning back point when I noticed a horse with a single rider in the distance. I ignored him at first thinking he was just a hunter from Arella. Turning I began to make my way back, only to hear the horse grow closer. When I turned I realized I didn't know this man and he seemed more intent on a different type of fun other than hunting. I kicked Snowflake into a gallop and trusted him to get me away, which he did until like a fool I turned to look behind and bang, I was on my back.

A low hanging branch hit me, I didn't even see it. Before I knew it he was on top of me . . .

'Stop! Kiril said his face contorted with fury as he looked at her.' . . . skip the details I beg you' he pleaded unable to hear the rest. But she had to continue, she had to say it out loud at long last.

He was on top of me, I couldn't move him. He was so strong and intent on finishing what he had begun. He tore are my clothes and raked my flesh, drawing blood. I kicked, and screamed as loud as I could but no one was anywhere near to help me. He laughed as he pulled up my skirts and dug his fingers into my thighs . . .

'Nox please' Kiril whispered as he lowered his head incapable of looking at her. She noticed he was shaking and as much as she didn't want to cause him distress, he had to know who this man was. What it means that in spite of everything still has her in his thoughts.

He was close enough to reach so I bit him as hard as I could until I tasted blood, only to be left tasting my own. I thought I was going to pass out from the force of his strike but I fought against it. I had to stay awake, I had to try and get away. I knew he was trying to rape me and for the first time in my life I never felt so much fear. He leaned back up off me to lower his trouser and when he did I grabbed my blade from my thigh and waited. When he lowered himself again I struck him as hard as I could. I didn't realize it had gone into his face until he moved back screaming. I wrapped my legs tight around him and with every bit of strength left in me I took hold of my blade and pulled it down along his cheek. His blood spurted out from between his finger and down along his arms. He fell off me and rolled around screaming in pain. I didn't think of seeing if he was following me when Snowflake ran to me. I never looked back.

'Oh my love' Kiril said in a torn voice, as he stroked her face soothingly. Has he been haunting your dreams? I swear if I could I would slit the bastards' throat for ever laying hands to you.' he declared in a tone overflowing with vengeance. 'I haven't thought of him in years,' she whispered. 'Then why now? he asked warily. Raising her head to gaze directly into his eyes now filled with anger and regret, she answered in what she hoped was a voice that contained anything but fear. 'Because he is the leader of the Mickisi,' she stopped to take in his response to see the tendons in his neck and jaws tighten and clamp together. 'Nasha has told me he speaks of me,' she continued only this time Kiril couldn't retain his temper any longer 'That son of a bitch. I vow to you he will die by my sword, I give you my word. He's mine do you hear,' he screamed. Look at me Nox! He said as he turned her around fully. He will not lay hands on you for a second time. Do you hear? Eyes burning with hatred and something more dangerous she gave in. 'I hear' she said in a whisper. As loathing and revulsion was replaced by longing in his eyes, she ran her fingers through his damp hair and kissed him with such passion it left both of them gasping for air. 'Please' she pleaded 'I need you.' Without any hesitation he pulled up her skirts in anticipation of feeling her soft flesh beneath his fingertips. Feeling her warmth he assisted her as she rose and lowered herself onto him. Right at that moment he knew he would die to keep her and what was his safe. 'Let the bastard come' he thought as she wound her arms tighter around his shoulders and drew him in deeper leaving him with complete and utter thoughts of her in every way possible.

Chapter Eighteen

The chill that had struck through her clothes had passed as they walked hand in hand back into the campsite which was strangely quiet as they approached. Bringing her to the conclusion that the men were obviously too busy stuffing their faces. From the scent that wafted through the air she knew eggs were definitely involved and once again her stomach growled. Glancing reflexively up at Kiril who glimpsed down at her and smirked. 'I'll get you some food' and at that he walked ahead. Disregarding the intent behind his food comment she moved towards the fire and sat beside Gaius who was still clearly upset at her fainting scene earlier. 'I'm fine' she said and drew her knees up under her chin, got comfortable and began to enjoy the heat that travelled over her. Above the flames she could just about make out the fields that lined the horizon and if she squinted that little bit more she could see were the sky darkened and became barely visible. 'So peaceful' she thought as a flush of heat rolled over her body, as vivid images of Kiril came to mind. 'What is wrong with me? I'm not thirty minutes satisfied beyond measure. This is getting ridiculous! Shaking her head she shuffled and moved position thinking maybe she was too close to the fire. 'Nox, if your uncomfortable we can move' said Kiril from behind her. She hadn't heard him approaching which clearly pleased him. 'Heavy feet was it?

He said smugly handing her a plate of what looked like nothing in particular but smelled divine. As he took a seat beside her he leaned in and whispered in her ear making her blush and slap him playfully away. 'You seem better' Anso said as he walked past the fires edge. He hadn't stopped but to her surprise but then he suddenly whirled on his heels and looking at her with a small frown that creased his brow that she decided could have been anxiety. 'How does my grandchild fare? Kiril tensed and frowned momentarily up at his father leaving her to nudge his foot ceasing him from any outburst that was brewing within. Smiling up at Anso she told him how she seemed constantly hungry when she wasn't feeling sick and to her dismay she had to pee every twenty minutes. Which to her surprise made his face turn a lovely shade of pink and made him splutter on about having to talk to one of the men. She could feel a vibration traveling through her arm which obviously could be deemed as amusement coming from the father of the child in question. Until finally it turned into a chuckle making her lean against him and laugh.

Her spirits were higher and for now she was finally relaxed, but evidently Gaius wasn't in the same frame of mind as he mumbled incoherent things under his breath. Elbowing him in the ribs, he grunted but looked at her in question. When she just cocked and eyebrow and said nothing he turned and glared at Toran who was happily cuddled up with Tianna. 'The man's deserted me for a damn woman! He huffed and to her amusement pouted. 'And would you begrudge him his happiness? Kiril jumped in before she had a chance to speak making her want to hit him for the intrusion. 'No!'Gaius snapped as he threw what was left of his food into the fire. As though reading his mind or just having heard his brother's outburst Toran whispered something to Tianna, rose and walked with purpose in the direction of his clearly unhappy and disheveled brother. On arriving he stood directly in front of him casting a shadow over his huge form.

'I'm going hunting Gaius. I can't eat this shit anymore. You'll come?

One corner of his mouth twitched, as he was noticeably reassured as Gaius jumped to his feet and began to fumble through his things. Clearly not being able to find what he was searching for he let out a line of blasphemies until he was pushed hard and unceremoniously out of the way by Toran. After a quick look he emerged with a good looking blade, which was grabbed by Gaius and shoved into his belt. A moment later they were walking side by side from the camp. When Toran slapped Gaius on the back and they both grinned at each other she was left not knowing whether to laugh or cry as she watched them, she was in total awe of their relationship and friendship. 'Let's just hope they don't kill each other' Hakan said as he took Gaius's seat beside her. 'It seems your chat with young Nasha transpired into something worrisome' he said looking at his feet. Growing quiet it took a lot of prompting and coaxing from him but finally he got the whole sordid story. When she was finished retelling her encounter with Lel she noticed how both his hands were clenched into fists and he looked deeply angered by what had happened. She wondered if it was because he never knew or the fact she had never told him, but whatever it was the tension at that very moment surrounding them made her almost afraid to move an inch or speak another word. Stealing a brief glance in both directions to either side where two powerful men sat still, jaws clenched, lips tight, and frowning deeply and clearly fighting with their own emotions. Shrugging uncomfortably she rose slowly and without a word to either of them walked away. The whole affair had left her with a horrible taste in her mouth and she was finished discussing it. Taking one last glance at the man in her life, and her loyal friend, cousin and captain she sighed to herself. 'Well, it's up to them now' placing a hand protectively over her stomach that she could swear was beginning to swell and reminded herself that things were about to change.

~

Sunlight shimmered through the tree over her head casting shadows across the ground around her. She lay there just looking up at the morning sky and wondered about what would happen if she told Kiril what she had decided. Having argued with him passionately about Arella and Zantar and never coming to any type of agreement or compromise meant that they still had plenty to discuss in the next five days before they reached his home. Looking over her shoulder at his slumbering shape she longed to reach out and touch him but she sometimes just liked to watch him sleep. 'I wonder what he dreams of' she asked herself as he snored lightly. Feeling content to just stay where she was and take in her surroundings and the quiet peacefulness that accompanied it, that was until she caught the smell of fish waft through the slight breeze which resulted in her stomach responding in its usual fashion. With a grunt she rose herself up into a sitting position and stretched luxuriously drawing her arms high over her head as her back cracked and popped in quiet a disturbing way. Standing slowly she looked back at Kiril who hadn't seemed to move and deciding not to wake him, walked of towards Gaius who was bent over a steaming pan. When he looked up to acknowledge her, her eyes grew wide with worry when she seen his face. What the fuck happened to your face? she asked in panic, but turning around to see Toran making his way towards them and sighed shaking her head. Putting her hands on her hips she smiled down at Gaius who was in great spirits 'so what was it this time?

Resulting in Toran laughing, 'I don't know but I won' he said as he stared daring at his brother to argue the statement, but who to her surprise didn't even raise an eyebrow. 'Well at least things are back to normal' she said absentmindedly as she looked over his shoulder at the fish cooking.

Not noticing Tianna and Nasha approaching she jumped at the girl's voice that sounded close to her ear. 'They caught rabbit too' she proclaimed with excitement that made Tianna smile down at her and then at Nox, who was clearly happy to see that the child was beginning to come round and spend time with others. 'While you cook my breakfast, I might go and have a quick wash in the stream' she said giving Gaius a cheeky wink as she walked away. As much as the thought of food made her want to run and be speedy in her washing, as she began to make her way through the shrubbery and close knitted trees she found herself drifting in and out of daydreams about nothing in particular. Until she heard rapidly approaching footsteps. Realizing without doubt that whoever it was did not come from the direction of the campsite, she ducked in behind a gathered mound of a huge thorn bush, held her breath and waited. As the moments passed she stayed bent over watching and listening until she became increasingly aware of how close they were. Raising her hands back over her shoulders to retrieve her swords she cursed her stupidity realizing she had left them behind. 'Shit' she whispered, 'of all the idiotic things to do –' but stopped when she noticed two men coming in her direction. Wondering to herself if she shouted loud enough and ran fast enough would anyone come to her aid. 'You bloody coward' she hissed at herself. 'Since when do you go crying for help? With that she reached under her skirts and pulled her blade free of its snug place against her thigh. Holding the blade in her closed fist she knew she had only one chance and she would have to be fast. Whatever happened now she wouldn't go down without a fight. She stood slowly and moved with great care over the dried up leaves that to her total annoyance crackled loudly under her feet. But obviously not loud enough to draw any unwanted attention so she continued until she reached the tree she had in her slights and placing herself flat against it she waited patiently. Her hands were sweating and didn't know if it was nerves or the excitement of the oncoming confrontation as she remembered her abilities and talent in bringing down her enemy. 'Now would be no different' she thought to herself with great confidence. She could feel their closeness as the bigger one stood on the opposite side of the tree. Holding her breath she squeezed the handle of her blade gently and worked it through her palm. Spinning out of her hiding place she grabbed her opponent from behind and pulled as hard as she could on his heavy dark blue cloak. Resulting in him yelping in surprise and begin to struggle only to stop abruptly when he felt the cold blade against his throat. Glaring at his companion she shouted for him to drop his sword. 'I'd drop it faster than that if I were you' came a voice from behind her and she smiled inwardly as the very big and very angry Kiril stepped out from behind her and stalked towards an extremely worried looking young man.

'Nox! crocked out the man she was holding captive, making her spine grow stiff as he recognized the voice. 'Elder Dreakwood? She asked in total disbelief. When he nodded which was only a slight movement of his head still fully aware of Nox's blade that was still pressed tightly to his throat. Dropping her hand gingerly she looked at him with wide and questioning eyes. 'What are you doing here? She snapped. 'I could have killed you, you do realize that don't you! Rubbing his hand shakily along his neck as he looked at her while throwing her a weak smile which seemed to melt her temper just enough that she was not frowning anymore.

'I've come with news from the Glens of Crowden. I'm so glad I found you so soon, we have much to discuss but if it's not too much of an inconvenience would I be able to trouble you for a drink of some sort, we've been traveling all night' he said as he looked at the young man with him. 'Where is your horse? Kiril asked in a distrusting tone that made Nox cringe, and look at him with a warning glint in her eye. Before anyone could answer she turned sharply 'bloody men! She murmured leaving the three men looking at her back as she walked back towards the campsite.

When they arrived she was surprised to see Hakan and Arnav had gathered their swords and were making their way out into the field. Excitement ran through her and she had an urge to run and grab her swords and join them until Kiril walked up beside her 'don't even think about it

Nox' he said in a warning tone. She looked at him in total shock that he would have the gaul to think he could order her in such a way. 'That's it' she thought and with that she strode with purpose straight past Kiril and with a swish of metal leaving their sheaths her swords came free into her hands. Throwing a challenging look in his direction she lowered her eyes just enough to look at him under her long eyelashes and with a twist of her lip gave him a daring smirk 'first blood' she said tartly as she walked towards him. 'Absolutely not' he relied with such force he drew the attention of those sitting around the fire. 'No? she said mockingly as she turned and made her way towards the men already engaged in a battle of their own. Turning and pointing her sword at a glaring Kiril she winked teasingly. When he began to make his way towards her she didn't like the look on his face and she noticed he didn't have his sword with him. Growing anxious she began to back up taking sure steps to keep the distance between them. She couldn't stop herself from getting excited at the prospect of fighting him again as she remembered what had happened when their swords met before, but more so what had happened after. When he grew closer she braced herself and readied her stance only to have him rush her and without giving her any change to break away flung her over his shoulder. Totally taken by surprise she froze until it finally dawned on her what he was doing. Fury rose through every inch of her as she began to kick and squirm to get away. 'Kiril' she screamed through clenched teeth 'let me down this fucking instant.' Ignoring her striking fists and verbal threats he held tight and walked back to the campsite, until finally he put her gently on her feet to the cheers and laughs of the men, and the look of total confusion from Elder Dreakwood which changed to a look of approval when informed by Anso of her delicate condition. 'Damn him' she thought as she looked around. 'How dare you . . . you . . . bloody – only to be cut of mid sentence when she was pulled into a forceful kiss leaving her seething. Pushing him away she yelled at him to 'sleep with one eye open' only to have him laugh and point out that she'd know if he did considering he'd be sleeping bedside her. 'That's it' she fumed to herself again. 'You cannot stop me. In case you have forgotten you big bloody oaf I am the leader of Arella and I do not take orders from you or anyone else for that matter. If I wish to fight I will bloody fight, and be damned with you or anyone else that has issues with it' her bosom was heaving heavily as she spoke. At that he glowered down at her 'I always knew you were a selfish bitch. You have no concern for the child growing in you at all do you? He asked to calmly for someone who looked so angry. When she didn't answer he shook his head and walked away clearly not able to look upon her anymore.

'I'll give you selfish bitch' she said to herself as she looked around for something hard to throw at him. Spotting what looked like a lump of bark that had clearly broken free from its resting place; she picked it up and in calling Kiril threw it as hard as she possibly could. As he turned around to say something it hit him square between the eyes again, leaving her cringing as the bloody ran from his nose, down over his lips and dripped off his chin. 'Why doesn't he wipe it off' she wondered as he just stood there staring at her. 'Oh shit' she thought as he suddenly began to come towards her, only to have Gaius and Toran step in front of him blocking his way aiding in her escape. With fast steps not looking once in Kiril's direction, she made her way to Anso and sat down between him and Elder Dreakwood. When she finally looked up to where her very angry husband was once standing she sighed with relief to see him make his way out into the field sword in hand. Pity filled her for the two men who would be taking the blunt of his anger. Not taking her eyes from him she took in every inch and found herself wanting to run after him, drag him off to a private place and show him how sorry she was, but she didn't think he would do anything right now only give her a good hiding. 'Your marriage is definitely not going to be a dull one' Elder Dreakwood said in a warm voice, clearly enjoying the display.

Unable to stop herself from laughing when she looked at Anso who was smiling at her 'No, It definitely will not,' she said as she looked upon her warrior again.

'So are you going to inform us on the reason you're here? Nox said in a serious tone that demanded answers. Shuffling and making himself more comfortable Elder Dreakwood looked directly at Nox. 'Firstly Nox I must ask you. Do you think you have made the right decision in your marriage to Kiril, and before you attack me Anso you have to ask yourself if you actually think what went on today is normal for a newly wedded couple. They nearly killed each other' he said in a high pitched voice that drew a smile from Nox. Clearly he was upset about the whole thing which made her feelings soften towards him immensely. 'Elder Dreakwood please do not think you made a mistake in joining us together. I can say with all honesty that I am extremely happy and I love that man with everything in me' she stopped then and laid a hand on his arm 'he's a good man' she said with a genuine smile that seemed to make all the difference.

Taking her by the hand he squeezed it gently and began to explain. 'I have been having a feeling that there has been something out of the ordinary going on in the Crowden. People are on edge, committee members are having late night meeting that they seem to think are going unnoticed, whispered comments and looks between those who have plenty to say and are saying nothing.

But what I witnessed during your visit is what finally opened my eyes. If I'm going to be completely honest it disturbed me enough to look more into things. In talking to certain members I found out that I seem not to be the only one that is worried about the reason or lack off that Ulric gave for not accepting the treaty between our lands. The worst part of it all is the fact that he hasn't called for the army to form ranks and advance upon the Shia Mountains and the Mackisi. Especially after hearing the disturbing stories you brought to his attention' he stopped to catch his breath and think about the best way to continue only Nox got there before him. 'What are you saying? You think some ones hiding something? She said in complete surprise. Turning slowly and looking directly at her he quirked his eyebrow at her 'I know they are my dear.' At his comment Nox shot her head in the direction of Anso who was deep in concentration but clearly looking disturbed by the news. Nox needed more and damn it she was going to get it 'explain' she said in a stern voice. 'After you left a number of the committee members voiced their concerns over everything they witnessed. They were very upset at the pure lack of respect you were given.' 'I didn't see or hear any of these members stand up and speak their views when she needed it' Anso said with bitterness, 'she was thrown to the dogs and from what I remember you were there were you not? Elder Dreakwood lowered his head in shame unable to look at her knowing there was nothing he could do or say that could change the fact that Anso was in fact right in what he was saying. 'I think you'll find I am here to remedy that fact' he said looking at Anso now. Nox grew uncomfortable as she sat in between the two men. Placing her hand on Anso's arm she thanked him for defending her and placing her other hand on Dreakwood arms she reassured him that all was well between them and for him to continue with the rest of the information he had come to share. 'The committee is scared of the Mackisi and their recent expeditions from the Shia Mountains and into the surrounding lands and across the Glens. They are worried and they fear that if they are not stopped more deaths will be imminent' he paused when he heard Anso murmur something to himself that made both Nox and Dreakwood look in his direction. 'What is it Anso' Nox asked. 'Well I was just thinking that while these committee members were voicing their opinions and concerns where were Ulric and that son of his? Smiling at Anso Elder Dreakwood rustled the leaves under his feet continued with much more excitement at the fact that Anso had clearly noticed something of great importance. 'Ah, now that's what I was about to say next. Ulric remained in the gathering hall talking and trying to reassure and calm things down, but Vidar left not ten minutes after you left.

But not before he had a blazing row with his father about his inability to control his halls and the people that enter them.' Without any notice he ceased talking and just stared into the distance.

Following his line of vision Nox spotted Kiril walking towards them not taking his eyes from her. Cringing when she looked closer at him, his nose was swollen and his eye was puffy. Guilt gripped her tight in the chest and she cursed herself for striking him. Standing she moved position moving herself out from between the two men and sat on the opposite side of Anso.

'Will this be a problem? Elder Dreakwood whispered in Nox's ear. Shuffling up slightly she made just enough room for him to sit beside her on the log. 'No, its fine please continue' she said with a genuine smile that seemed to ease him somewhat. As Kiril took his place beside her he ran his arm around her waist and began to rub the lower part of her back gently making her lean back against him. 'You were saying Vidar left' she coaxed. 'Yes, that its. Well like was saying he left but he left me with a very uneasy feeling so I sent Lorso after him only he never ventured outside the castle walls. He seemed to have something of more interest to keep him occupied' he said with a wave of his hand in dismissal. 'The night after Erso followed him into the Shia Mountains and straight into the camp of the Mackisi. The boy relayed to me that he entered the tent of the leader and after a short and very intense argument they came barreling out still continuing the conversation not caring who was listening. He heard Vidar speak of the young girl your men brought with them and the woman who seems to have settled well with one of the twins' he stopped at Kiril's outburst 'why that little traitorous bastard' 'That's putting it nicely' Anso added. Nox on the other hand was far from satisfied and she set her full attention on the man sitting beside Anso beginning to look like he was regretting his decision to come to them. 'Elder Dreakwood is there anything else you can enlighten us on? She said in a hushed voice. Nodding his head he told her of Vidar informing Lel of Hakan and the twins sneaking around the camp and in addition to her marriage to Kiril which seemed to be of immense interest the Mackisi leader. Nox sighed at this news and as she pinched the bridge of her nose with her thumb and forefinger her heat began hammering in her chest so hard she thought they could surely hear it. Turning back to Elder Dreakwood she asked if he thought if Ulric was involved.

Shrugging his shoulders and rubbing his hands roughly together he gave her a look of pure distress 'I don't know, but I'm hoping the man had better sense' he muttered to himself. 'I think it frightens me to admit that he could in fact be the one who is involved more so.' Anso she noticed hadn't said anything in a while and in looking at him she seen that he was sitting with his chin in his hands as his elbows relaxed on his knees. Looking out over the land before him he finally broke the silence 'do you think the Mackisi are planning an attack with the aid of the Crowden? And as he voiced his concerns a chill rain down her back and throughout her body making her shiver. Elder Dreakwood's face already grim grew grimmer as he worked the question over in his head. Kiril brush a strand of hair out of his face allowing her a better look at his face making her want to lean over and kiss it but she noticed the blank look that had taken over his features, and suddenly his eyes cleared and he found his voice. 'It's evidently obvious Vidar is working with the Mackisi. Why? Damned if I know. But what I do know is the army of Zantar will be ready to fight for what belongs to them, and the army of Arella' he added hastily after he received a cool look from Nox who clearly felt left out. 'Giving such circumstances do you think the Crowden will fight with or against us? She asked Dreakwood bluntly. He turned his head slowly towards her, wiped his hands in his cloak and answered with a trace of triumph in his voice 'they will fight with you, and those who do not will be the enemies of the Crowden and the committee of Elders. Anso smiled looking amused by this bit of news 'well then there's only one thing for it. I am assuming that Vidar knows nothing of your journey? At his nod Anso continued. 'From judging from what you have said here tonight the majority of the committee has agreed with Nox's treaty even though it hasn't been put to paper. Either way we have the upper hand. So you'll find out of the worse situations we can always find the positive side and use it to our advantage. The only thing we need to do now is to decide the best way forward.

'So for now what do we do? Nox asked totally engrossed in what Anso was saying. 'Well we can't do much right now, we have to talk to Hakan and I will need to speak with Arnav so if you would excuse us I need to talk with my wife' Kiril said addressing the two men who just looked up at them both as he took her hand and led her away.

They had walked for what seemed forever to her but she said nothing and when she began to tire he just held her hand a little more tightly making her wonder if he thought she was going to run away if he let her go. The breeze was refreshing and she was glad of it. For the past hour her stomach twisted and turned leaving her fighting to keep the food she consumed already today. She fixed her eyes upon his face until he looked down at her and for some unknown reason she blushed rosily with embarrassment leaving him blinking as his thoughts were in turmoil. Finally he stopped walking and turned to her. 'Will you tell me what I'm doing wrong? All I want is for you to be safe, for our child to be safe, but you won't let me and I don't understand. Its persecution Nox! I'm like a bloody fool for you, only I seem to be getting nowhere.' She noticed that he wasn't angry and for that alone she exceedingly glad, especially when she knew she deserved to be shouted at and more. Still she couldn't bring herself to look upon him now that he was so close, she knew deep down she had wronged him. 'Forgive me' she whispered staring at the ground under her feet. 'You are right' she said taking a shy look up at him. 'I am selfish, but would by no means put our child in danger' she said in a rushed voice only to be stopped by his hand and his response. 'And what do you think you were doing earlier? Sure the men would have been as careful as they possibly could but things happen Nox you know this better than anyone' anger starting to build, he turned on her 'do you realize what I would have done to them if they had of hurt you? Virtually shouting as he turned from her.

Knowing she had to make him understand she followed him. 'You don't know how hard it is for me now. I feel my men are looking at me as nothing but a meager married woman who has her husband the heir of Zantar to fight her battles. That I no longer require to fight' she was getting emotional to her utter annoyance. 'To make matters worse they no longer come to me, they go to Hakan' raising her voice slightly she looked away from where he was standing. 'That's why I wanted to fight him, I need them to see I'm still as good if not better' do you understand? she asked pleadingly as she faced him once more. Sensing him move closer she took a step backward and continued before she convinced herself not to. 'Then you expect me to lie in a bed that has housed other women before me and the thought of that is worse than any other you can imagine. It makes my skin crawl. Envisioning you . . . I'm always going to be wondering who these women are, who you –' he cut her off when he walked to her and took hold of both her hand which he noticed were shaking and drew her closer. 'Nox, your men have never ceased to look to you for guidance, but Hakan is their captain. They have and continuously will look to him. You know this! As far as my bed goes' he stopped and tilted her chin up to so he could see her eyes and she could see his and know that he speaks with truthfulness. 'I have never brought any woman in Zantar to my bed or any other bed. Yes I have had women but never there. I swear it you! Not taking his eyes off hers he leaned forward and kissed her gently. As he drew back and she opened her eyes and looked at him he met her eyes bravely and decided he wasn't yet finished. 'Now! he said in a loud but lighthearted tone that made her frown slightly but she kept her mouth shut. 'I cannot and will not allow you to fight when you are with child. You can kick and scream all you like until your voice goes hoarse. But I tell you now Knox I will tie you to the first thing I see and I don't give a fuck who's looking. As your husband I forbid it and if that means I end up with a bleeding nose or worse on regular occasions, so be it. But be rest assured I will not be moved on this.' As he was talking she tried with all her might to fight the urge to argue as she shifted from one foot to the other, flicking her eyes to him and back towards the camp where she knew her swords lay unused. Just as she was about to tell him to jump from the highest cliff he stopped and just looked at her. 'What? she thought, but clearly he was waiting for her response so she threw him a smile and a nod of her head in acknowledgment that she would abide by his rules on the matter.

Smiling to herself as a look of male smugness drifted across his handsome features, she made a mental note that if a situation arose and she had no other choice but to fight she would.

He didn't have to know she reasoned with herself. She'd let him win this one, there would be other times and right now she knew to pick the right ones. Just as his hands dropped lower onto her waist pulling her closer she leaned over to the side in urgency and vomited.

Chapter Nineteen

Gaius and Toran stood before her in shock. 'You think I've made the wrong decision? She said in a tone of irritation. Looking at each other before saying anything Gaius took the first step and in taking a deep breath, ran his hand through his hair and obligingly answered. 'Have you spoken to Hakan? Giving a slight nod in response resulted in Toran whistling softly as he looked at his brother. 'What of Kiril? He asked. Seeing the direction of her gaze he knew the answer.

'Oh! Well I think you're going to have to at least tell him don't you think? 'I didn't say I wasn't going to' she protested. 'Why does everything have to be so damn complicated? She said squinting thoughtfully as she stood up and laughed hysterically startling the men enough to get up and walk to her. 'Nox' Gaius said as he reached for her 'never a dull moment eh' he said as she smiled up at them her emerald eyes glistened half shut by her smile. 'You do realize that if Elder Dreakwood is correct you will be forced to decide faster than you wish to. If the Mackisi attack either Arella or Zantar we will needed to be ready and we will most definitely need our armies to know who rules them and who does not. Nox you need to tell them' Gaius said with great seriousness. 'So what exactly do you expect me to do? She answered testily. 'We expect you to lead your people' Toran said with a cool eye. 'Well then I'd better go and do something useful' she snapped. 'I didn't mean – ' Toran said but she wasn't having any of it and walked back the way she came leaving them alone and cursing themselves for not handling it better.

Walking alone back towards the campsite she stopped dead in her place and found herself finding it hard to go any further. 'What would you do? She said with a defeated sigh as she thought of her father. 'What would who do? Came a voice to her right, which made her jump placing her hand upon her chest cursing. Arnav smiled at her response and walked to her. 'Do you have to sneak around? Where were you anyway? She said heatedly clearly not happy about the intrusion. If she had wanted company she would have stayed in camp. 'Firstly I wasn't sneaking and secondly I was taking a piss. And since you're by yourself I'm assuming you snuck off leaving Kiril looking for you' he said with a sidelong glance, as his mouth twitched slightly but managed to keep a straight face. 'I did not sneak off, I was discussing an issue of great importance with the twins if you have got to know.' 'That's funny, I could have sworn I heard you talking to yourself' he said throwing her a cheeky smile that made her want to wipe it clean off his face. 'What do you want Arnav? She said heatedly making him laugh. 'Your insufferable, you do know that don't you? To her annoyance she smiled at his facial expression of shock at her statement. 'Why do I find the man extremely amusing? She asked herself looking at him. 'What is Zantar like? She asked playing with the folds of her skirts. Seeing that her question clearly surprised him she rushed to explain her curiosity. 'I've never been.' As he looked upon her face he relaxed sufficiently to allow him to find his voice. He described absolutely everything even down to the colour of the walls in the cells. This made her scrunch up her nose and imagine what kind of cell would have yellow walls. 'Anso is truly a peculiar one' he thought as Arnav continued with his description of Zantar. These he told her were under the right side of the castle but never really got that much use as Anso didn't like to use them even when the occasion arose. 'What of Arella? He asked her suddenly and noticing he looked clearly interested she smiled and started to tell him everything. Not leaving any detail out, she even talked of Tressin who she described as an absolute nightmare but he could see how fond of the boy she was.

'You know I visited Arella before with Kiril but I've never looked at it as you do' he said with a smile. 'Mmm! That's because you probably spent the whole time looking at the women' she said tartly. Laughing at her bold statement he couldn't deny she was wrong and just shrugged his shoulders and sighed theatrically. 'Well I had to find something to keep me occupied while Kiril skulked around looking for you.' This made her laugh. 'My father always found a way of informing me of that little piece of information, as if I didn't already know' she said as she threw him a mischievous grin. 'You're wicked' he said in shock as he looked upon her. 'Do you realize how difficult it was to be around him every time we returned from Arella?

Even Anso avoided him. Honestly he was convinced even though your father told him he was wrong that you had a man in your life. The pain he afflicted on the men during training sessions had gotten so bad they refused to train with him.' This made her laugh even harder at the thought of Kiril attacking with all his power. Just to aid in drowning out images of her locked in an embrace with an unknown lover. 'And now? She asked looking at him through watering eyes. He took a deep breath through his nose and let it out wondering if he should say anything.

Would Kiril thank him or kill him he contemplated as he looked at her waiting. 'Now? Well now I guess he's scared.' Clearly not the answer she was expecting she found it quiet unsettling that her big strong man would have a weak point. Knowing Kiril as she did she knew he wasn't used to feeling powerless, useless and most of all scared. It aggravated him immensely.

Thinking of Arnav's comment she began to think of things that could be causing Kiril upset.

Well of course he was worried constantly for her and their child, and thinking of the Mackisi surely must not be helping matters. But it wasn't until Arnav spoke again that she was left open mouthed and looking at him like a fool. 'He fears you will leave him and return to Arella' he said as his eyes travelled over her until eventually resting on her stomach. Following his eyes it hit her like a jolt of lightning. 'Does he speak of it often? She asked in a small voice. 'He worries of nothing else Nox, but surely you can see why. He has always wanted nothing only you, and now you're carrying his child and it terrifies him to mull over the idea of you leaving, and with you goes everything else he has dreamed of.' Sighing she at long last knew what she had to do. 'I have to go' she said to Arnav and as she walked away to her shame she was afraid.

~

Stumbling back through the over growth, her elbows were red and scrapped from the thorns. 'I definitely do not remember all these blasted

147

thorn bushes' he said as she turned her body away to the side as much as possible to edge through. She began to think about what would happen if she did try and return to Arella. 'I'd definitely have a fight on my hands' she thought as she stormed through the last of the bushes that lined the campsite. On spotting Hakan she changed her route and headed straight for him. Unfortunately he was in deep conversation with Kiril who on seeing her gave her a brilliant smile only when all he got in return was a look of what he felt was distaste leaving him frowning. On getting close enough she spoke to Hakan in a tone that made him somewhat glare at her. 'I need to speak to you now! At that turned and called for Gaius who to her surprise had already made it back to the campsite. 'Gather the men. Were leaving! And at that she moved away from the two men only to have Kiril grab her hard by the arm spinning her around. 'What do you mean you're leaving? He snapped. 'Remove your hand' she hissed as she looked from his hand to her arm and back at him. 'Now! But she only received a look of challenge from the big man. Tugging hard against his iron grip she peddled backward and pulled with everything she had until she heard a rip as she freed herself and stalked towards her swords that she was finally fed up looking at on the ground. As she attached the harness to herself she felt strangely guilty for having weapons on her person, but just as fast as the feeling filled her it passed and with one final pull they were held tight against her back once again.

While she was adjusting her deadly arsenals' Kiril glared at her. 'Take them off' he said in a voice she had only heard him use on others, and she shook a little. Pulling back her shoulders she looked up into his eyes and readied herself yet again for an argument. 'I will not! she said through clenched teeth. 'And if you think for a second you can make me I suggest you give it a go' showing complete and absolute control of her emotions on the outside while her stomach performed a familiar lung that made her feel like the selfish bitch Kiril once called her. She had to convince him that she was leaving, there was no other way. Craning her neck to look around Kiril she let a scream at Hakan. 'What the fuck are you waiting for? Taking a look at Kiril she could see his anxiety was sharp and not having to point out the obvious that he was on the verge of losing his temper, she had to get away from him. She had to focus on the task at hand before she changed her mind. Turning in the direction of Toran who she seen laughing at something either Tianna or Nasha had said, her patience grew thin and in her sweetest voice called him.

'Would you be so kind as to go and help your brother gather the men? Something flashed in her eyes that told him today was not a day to argue and he all but jumped to his feet. 'That is if it's not too much fucking trouble, make sure they gather outside the camp on the other side of the hill' she yelled at the man who towered over her. As he ran to locate Gaius he cursed himself for speaking so freely with her early, clearly it did not help. 'Nox' Kiril said in a hard voice.

'What! she returned just as hard but bitterness lined her word. Realizing that right at that very moment he was the last person she wished to talk to and deep down she wished he would just leave her alone, as she balled up her fists in the attempt to stop herself from slapping him. He hesitated and she knew he was torn between what he wanted and what he knew he might not be able to stop from happening. She knew her bluntness totally ruffled him when he said nothing else. Without another word she turned and walked away. 'Tianna, Nasha help the men with the horses and make sure nobody touches Snowflake. That's my job, and if you think of it would you try your very best to root out some food. I don't care what it is as long as it's eatable.'

Tianna smiled in her direction at her request and in leading what seemed like a very panicky looking Nasha away, as they went about their chores. A diminutive amount more relaxed and if she was completely honest she was reluctant to do what she had set her mind to do. Her reasoning was as mumbled as her thoughts as they ran over and over in her head. 'No! she said to herself sternly 'It has to be done' and with that walked with determination towards the gathered men, who were busy saddling and packing whatever supplies they could get their hands on.

Hakan who had pulled back from her had now began to grow closer in his step until finally he was right back on her heels. 'That was a bit harsh' he said quietly hoping she wouldn't hear him but at the same time hoping she did. Turning with a glare 'I didn't realize you wore your feelings on your sleeve Hakan. I'll be sure to mind your fragility next time' she hissed sarcastically as she stormed away from him. 'I wasn't speaking of me; I was speaking of the man you married in case you have forgotten' he returned just as sarcastically, which resulted in her drawing her sword so fast he didn't have a chance to defend himself. Caught in a dilemma where she found herself incapable of a response. Exploding unable to withhold her inner turmoil any longer, her inner voice screamed loud and clear. 'How bloody dare he speak of such things.

What does he know? Nothing! He knows nothing of what I am having to do for that man I have in his eyes forgotten. Bloody man! 'Do not concern yourself with such matters Hakan, you'll find it will bring you nothing but trouble' she said as she glared at him through green eyes that warned to watch his words. On any other day he would have made an attempt for his blade but he had in no way seen Nox so frustrated. He stepped overconfident to intercept her only for her to laugh at him. 'You're not worried? She asked with a smirk. 'No' he answered plainly. 'Well maybe you should be' she replied but leaving her emotions run riot across her features. 'Nox' he said in a soft tone as he reached for her only to have her turn quickly and continue on her way.

Shaking his head and letting a defeated sigh leave his lips as captain of Arella, he followed his leader with determination. Whatever her reasons for departing he would do his job. Finally she stopped and called for the attention of the men who looked upon her in confusion.

'When my father died I was terrified of taking his place. Not until today have I been able to acknowledge that fact and say it out loud for you all to hear. It's a strange thing to not want your weaknesses to show to the people you have always looked up to and respected. I was afraid you would not accept me as leader of Arella. But you did' she said with a smile as she looked at all the faces she had learned by heart. 'I brought you to the Glens of the Crowden to attempt to finish what my father had started and in doing so three friends died, and a traitor was named.'

Taking a breath she took a look over her shoulder where the campsite lay and forced herself to continue. 'Today I have had a decision to make that has taking me some time, and has not been easily made.' Turning to Hakan she took hold of his hand and squeezed tightly. 'Hakan, captain of the army of Arella, my friend and most importantly my cousin and blood.' Finally it dawned on him what she was doing and he had a sudden feeling of panic run through him. 'Nox, please think about what you are doing' he said pleadingly. Looking out at the men before her she finally knew she was making the right decision, and instead of addressing Hakan she spoke to them with earnest. 'I have thought of nothing else since being in the Glens. I had been afraid that who I was would change. Being known only as the wife of Kiril the heir of Zantar. But I know that will never happen. Arella will always be my home, but from this day and more importantly this moment I am no longer it's leader.' Turning to Hakan she smiled up at him sincerely. 'Hakan, you will take my place, and I know in my heart you will be a great and compassionate leader. I am to travel to Zantar so there is no reason for you all to be away any longer.' She said as a wave of the emotions she had reined in so hard to keep control of made her eyes water and lip quiver. Suddenly remembering the women who now travelled with them and were to start their lives in Arella she turned to Tianna and Nasha and looked upon them fondly, strolled to them and took both their hands. 'You will both enjoy the life Arella has to offer. I think our home is lucky in receiving two very strong and beautiful women.' At that she looked at Gaius and through him a wink, and then with a final soft gaze over the women before her turned and walked back to Hakan. 'Nox' he said sadly. 'It makes sense and we both know it. It's my decision to make and I know I've made the right one' she said leaning in and kissing him on the cheek. 'You should go before the light fades' she said looking up at the sky frowning. 'Remember the Mackisi Hakan. They can't be trusted and with Vidar on their side we may find ourselves fighting alongside each other sooner than we –' she stopped mid sentence when she notice from the corner of her eye that the men were all on bended knee before her. Her breath caught in her throat and her heart felt so much compassion for them at that very moment she couldn't bear the thought of any of them having to go to war. These were the men who had fought with her, protected her and been part of her life since she was able to lift a sword. From behind she could feel large hands on her shoulders as she fought to control her tears yet again.

Turning to who she thought was Hakan, only to find Toran and Gaius both wearing equal looks of despair. She had not thought of how they would feel. 'You fool Nox, how would you feel?

Annoyed with herself yet again for not thinking. 'I'll be fine' she said in a persuasive tone, which earned her with raised eyebrows and squinting eyes. 'There so much alike' she thought as she looked up at the two big men. 'How did I never notice that before? Because you took for granted they would always be with you' you idiot' she cursed herself. Reality all of a sudden sank in when the call from Hakan came loudly and unmistakable for the men to mount. 'All you have to do is tell us you want us to come with you' Gaius said as he gazed down at her. She had to convince them that she would be fine and subconsciously she knew she would always be.

'Don't even think about it' she said laughing slightly making them smile. 'I'll never be able to have a good argument with Kiril if you too butt in all the time' she said as she playfully punched Gaius in the arm. Suddenly she was pulled securely into an embrace that left her fighting for air making her cough and gag causing Toran laugh loudly and squeeze her tighter. When he finally let her go she had go through the same ritual with Gaius but when he went to let go she was reluctant and held on. Sensing her hesitation he hugged her gently and kissed the top of her head. 'We'll miss you sister, and remember Gaius is a strong name for a boy' he whispered and at that she wept.

She had watched them ride of until she could no longer see even a slight imagine of what might be a horse and rider. Taking a deep-seated tearful breath she walked to Snowflake who as usual chomped peacefully. 'Hello you' she said approaching him. Running her hand through his lengthy main she laid her head against his shoulder and for the first time since waking she found peace. Hearing footsteps come behind her she smiled secretly into the softness of Snowflake.

'Nox' Kiril said in a quiet voice that held no anger or mockery. Not answering she turned to him with eyelashes heavy with tears until she was finally unable to hold back her feelings and erupted into loud sobs. At once he gathered her to him and whispered soothing things into her ear, while he stroked her hair and back and kissed her head gently. 'It must have been a difficult decision to make and –'Sliding her fingers into his she looked up at him through a haze of tears 'It was one of the hardest things I have ever had to do. They are my family.' She said through her tears but taking his hand she placed it on her stomach ' You both are my family now and I will never leave you' she said as her tears fell along her flushed cheeks. Rubbing his thumb across her tear streaked face he cupped her cheeks in his big hands and drew her mouth to his. Her kiss was sweet and tasted of salt from the tears she had wept for the men she loved. Breaking away her voice came softly to his ears.

'Kiril.'

'Mmm'

I'm hungry.'

Throwing his head back he laughed more in shock at her statement but more from the happiness he was feeling. She hadn't left. 'Well I better feed you then' he said with a smile that made her want to forget about food and just let him take her anywhere he pleased. As if he could read her mind he sighed, rolled his eyes as he took her by the hand and led her back to the camp. 'What? she asked in a voice that would have got her anything she wanted, and if it wasn't for the fact she rarely asked for food he would have given it to her. 'Later' he said with a wink that made her smirk and flutter her eye lashes at him in a manner that left him howling with laughter.

'Chivalry truly is not in your nature' he said choking back a laugh. 'I'll show you how chivalrous I can be' she said as she pulled him to a stop on the hill. Holding his hand she stood directly in front of him. Moving slowly towards him she leaned in looking up at him from under those long flirtatious eye lashes and pressed herself against him. His broad shoulders rose inhaling a deep breath as her breasts rubbed against his chest. She could feel his heart beat thumping through his shirt and through her bodice which was beginning to get slightly unpleasant around the mid section. She was left her with a feeling of ecstasy at what she could do to his body. Drawing herself upwards she flicked her tongue along his bottom lip and held back just enough to torment. When he moved in to take her mouth with his she eased herself away and leaned towards his ear 'later' she whispered, and with that pulled away leaving him with an erection that clearly wouldn't wait too long.

Chapter Twenty

THE GLENS OF THE CROWDEN

'You dare to accuse my son of such a thing? Ulric roared standing abruptly from behind his desk.

His face became pale with fury but Elder Dreakwood would see to it that Vidar be brought before the committee and punished for his actions against his own people. 'Ulric see sense. The proof is there before you and is too great to ignore' he said pleading for the man to open his eyes and look past his emotions and loyalty towards his son. 'To great to ignore? He repeated bursting into what could only be described as hysterical laughter. 'What! You expect me to believe that my son has formed some sort of alliance with Lel of the Mackisi. Do I have that right? His face showing the shock. Raising his head Elder Dreakwood squared his shoulders and looked straight into his eyes 'yes I do! He declared clear voiced and with some force. Ulric stood straight and sever unable to believe what he was hearing. 'You've know Vidar from childhood and you truly believe that he would do what you say? He asked in total bewilderment.

'Ulric look past your role as a father in this. Can you honestly say that Vidar has been content of late. He undermines and questions you're every decision, insults guests to our great halls and has disappeared at numerous intervals during the recent weeks. He refuses to acknowledge his part in the downfall of the treaty with the south and west, and you do not find it in you to question any of this. Ulric the Committee of Elders are on edge and they are looking for answers and results.' Ulric sat back into the chair and stared out into the star filled night in a daze. 'If he is found guilty' he turned and looked at Elder Dreakwood with dark eyes, 'will he be brought before the committee? He asked in a stern voice. 'Yes, he will! Dreakwood responded 'And if found guilty? Ulric pressed. 'Ulric you know the answer to that, and I am truly sorry but traitors to the Glens of the Crowden do not get second chances' Elder Dreakwood replied with an edge to his voice and made Ulric open his eyes wide and glare at him. 'You would kill my only son?

'If he is found guilty, he has sealed his own faith' Ransan answered moving towards the door.

As he reached it a loud knock came before he had a chance to place a hand to it. Hearing Ulric stand behind him and call for whoever it was to enter, leaving him with a horrible feeling of dread in the pit of his stomach. When the door opened he cringed at the sight of four guards of the Glens standing before him. Ulric turned from pale to gray as stone as he braced himself for what he couldn't accept. 'Elder Ulric, we have come to inform you of your son's arrest. He has been brought to the cells were he will await trial by the Committee of Elders.' At this Ulric sank into the chair placing his head in his hands and told them all to remove themselves from his sight. Sudden memories of recent weeks filled the silence that engulfed him. He forced himself to acknowledge that Elder Dreakwood's words were correct. Vidar had become aggressive in his dealing with the committee, disagreeing with everything that was voted on. When it came to the stories that Nox had shared with the council before leaving his skin crawled, only Vidar had laughed and called it 'Interesting' Ulric suddenly felt ill. 'Why would he do this? He said suddenly breaking his silence as he looked at Elder Dreakwood giving him the look of a broken man. 'Only he can answer that' he said moving towards the man slouched in the chair. Laying a hand on his shoulder he squeezed gently hoping it gave him some reassurance. 'If you do not wish to see him, a message can be passed on' he said as he looked upon his long time friend.

'When will the Committee gather? Ulric asked with no emotion in his voice as he shook of his friend's hand. 'Tomorrow' Dreakwood responded as Ulric stood and walked to the window.

'Good. Have word brought to me when his trial is set to begin.' 'Ulric' Ransan said in a saddened voice that it had to ever come to this. 'Thank you Rasan for bringing this to my attention, now if you would excuse me I'd like to be alone.' Not turning to face him again Elder Dreakwood left Ulric to contemplate what the morning would bring.

Unable to sleep Ulric knew he had to see his son. Making his way through the corridors that led to the cells he paused briefly to speak to the guards on duty. Their eyes held both pity for the man who was so clueless to the fact his son was the near ruination of them all. Followed by suspicion that left him with a feeling of both anger and understanding towards them. Biding them a good night he continued on his way. He had never thought he would see the day that his son and heir would be locked in the cells and facing imminent death for treason. Eventually he reached Vidar's cell and froze looking upon his son as he sat on the edge of the thin mattress of the bed. The cell he noticed was clean enough, but the smell was overbearing coming from what seemed to be an overused wet space. Walls holding freedom within their blocks and mortar loomed from all sides of the cell almost teasing the occupant. Even though no windows visibly took their place within the cell the air that seeped through the corridor was cool enough to give him a chill. He had a sudden feeling of pity for the man before him as he noticed the size in which he was confined. Measuring what looked to be a mere six feet long and wide, and holding no light or candle except for the shimmering light coming from the already burnt down candles lining the corridor he had just ventured down. Vidar stood abruptly when spotting his father.

They stood facing each other from a distance, and for the first time since being arrested Vidar was afraid.

'Father' he said in words that were dry and emotionless.

'Why? Ulric asked pleading with his son to explain.

'It doesn't matter now' Vidar replied as he walked towards the bars separating them.

'Of course it matters' Ulric bellowed making Vidar cringe. 'You have put your own people in danger, betrayed them and most importantly betrayed me. You had everything Vidar. But it was never enough was it? He said with such anger he was beginning to shake. Vidar's eyes grew angry and lashing out he smashed his fists against the bars making Ulric take a step backwards when he heard cracking bones. Unblinking Vidar smirked as he spoke with smugness that gave Ulric a sudden urge to call for the guards to open the cell so he could get his hands around his neck.

'Everything! Is that what you think? And how was that so? Maybe you would care to inform me on how easy I have had it.' He was so angry his face flushed a dangerous red as beads of sweat formed on his brow. Walking away from the bars of the cell he pivoted again on his father who just stared at him in shock. 'What I wanted you could never give me. Can't you see the possibilities of an alliance with Lel? It could have been a revelation for the Glens. You and that bitch Nox and your little treaty were going to ruin everything. Don't you see? An alliance with the Mackisi would have made us stronger than Arella and Zantar together. But you had to make friends.' He shouted as his voice held venom and hatred that Ulric finally seen what was there all along. 'Lel and his men are nothing but bloody murders. You heard Nox tell us of what her men witnessed. They are burning and hanging, while they take young girls and women to whore them. And you look for alliances with these people? Ulric shouted back. Only to be met with a laugh that sent a chill down his spine. 'Blind old man, you think I was unaware of that little fact. I had my share' he said as he licked his lips and grinned. 'Where did I go wrong?

Ulric asked himself as he lowered his head in shame. He was answered with a wicked laugh that came from the man he no longer seen as his son. Straightening his back he took one last look and left.

~

'Vidar son of Ulric of the Glens of the Crowden you have been found guilty by members of your peers of treason. The punishment for such a crime against the Crowden is death by archers. Do you understand? Receiving nothing but a slight nod of his head Vidar stood looking out over the men before him. 'By our laws at this time you are entitled to plead your case one final time. Do you have anything more to say? Moving just a few inches away from the guards that flanked him on both sides he took his time. Finally he spotted the one man he didn't think would have attended and right there he knew he no longer had the love of his father. Setting his attention on him he spoke. 'Father, you're a fool to think that my demise will halt what has already begun.'

Without another word he focused his eyes on Elder Dreakwood and sneered at him. 'Ransan, my father's oldest friend it seems you have failed your Lovely Lady Nox. It's almost a pity I wouldn't be there when she returns to Arella to find it in ashes' he said as he laughed bitterly.

Seeing Ransan's face grow pale with worry looking around frantically for Anso's man, Vidar continued to laugh. 'Awe, what's wrong Ransan surely you're not worried? Don't be, when they kill that psycho husband of hers Lel will make her feel right at home.' Laughing madly he informed them of the Mackisi forming ranks and marching for Arella three nights ahead. 'You rotten son-of-a-bitch, what have you done? Ransan screamed lunging forward only to be grabbed by Ulric and detained. 'No! I need to know'. He shouted pulling away. Vidar's mouth twitched on one side as he stared at the elder trying fiercely to break through the barrier of guards. His heart was racing so fast he thought it might actually stop from the pressure in his chest. 'Tell me damn you! Only to be drown out by Ulric's domineering voice. 'Let's get this over with' he shouted in a rough tone with demanding authority. 'Archers! He bellowed. Stepping forward twenty archers readied their bows and waited for the order to fire. Looking dangerous as they stood strong and focused on their target Ransan's stomach tightened. Each man held one arrow.

Their feathers black from raven's wings for the occasion while their tips were hard steel, made for one reason alone and that was to kill. Their bows were nothing but spectacular to look upon.

Each archer held a magnificent display of craftsmanship. Reaching a meter in length as the gold designs engraved into the wood held a secret story behind each bow and each archer glistened in the morning sun. A slight bend on either end that were carved into a half moon shape held tight to the bow string which was made of vines and rawhide as the center grip was molded to fit each archers grasp. When the order was given he broke free of the gathered crowd of elders and began to run towards the stables. As the sound of arrows whistled through the air his skin tightened as goose bumps ran over his body leaving him cursing himself for wasting time, but he turned and watched as they hit home into their target. Vidar let a loud painful groan seep from his mouth as the arrows hit one by one. Striking him through the abdomen, legs, arms and two struck with precision into his neck resulting in fresh red blood squirting from both neck and mouth. Falling heavily onto the ground he watched as his blood soaked through his clothes and into the green grasses of the glen.

'Ransan' Ulric beckoned as he began to run to him. 'Ulric, really I have no time to waste' he said in a rushed voice, as he turned toward the stables once again. 'I'm coming with you' Ulric stated as he ran to keep up with the older elder. Leaving him pleasantly surprised at his friend's fitness at his stage of life. Turning to Ulric as they entered the stables he took a deep breath 'I don't mean to seem ungrateful of the offer of your company but I don't think right now is the time to be leaving. Besides I have a horrible feeling both Arella and Zantar will need more than just the both of us to make a difference.' He said defeated. 'I will right my son's wrongs Ransan. We have an army ready to go, and the Mackisi need to be dealt with before it's too late for us all,' and with that walked to his horse, mounted and rode from the stables with purpose.

Looking briefly to were his son now lay dead he called for the men to mount and ride with haste.

Some distance along the trek that led off the glen Ransan rode up beside Ulric and informed him of Nox's decision to travel to Zantar before returning to Arella with her men.

'Shit' Ulric said as he looked back over his shoulder and called of two men Ransan didn't recognize. When the men approached Ulric set them on their way to travel at speed to Zantar to relay a message of the impending war. Only to be told that the man that had travelled with Elder Dreakwood from the west had already left to bring word to the Lady Nox and Anso of Zantar.

'He can't have gone far' Ulric said looking out into the distance. 'Continue on your mission and we will see you within the next two days. Give word to Nox and Anso that we are travelling to intercept the Mackisi. At this the men bowed their heads in acknowledgement of the task assigned to them. 'You will have to ride through the night if you are to make good time' Ransan said to the men and looked at Ulric for his opinion and was glad to see him nod his head with agreement. Turning their horses in the direction of the West they led two thousand men into what they could only assume would be a battle to remember.

Chapter Twenty-One

Anso allowed himself a few seconds to shake off the look of surprise that ran across his features at the sight of his son coming through the campsite hand in hand with his wife Remembering the difficulty he had not an hour past in his attempts to make Kiril rein in his temper when she stormed from here with her men in tow. He couldn't draw his eyes from the scene before him of the now laughing and cuddling couple. On hearing approaching footsteps he turned to see Arnav coming in his direction. 'Told you she wouldn't leave' his voice holding just enough smugness.

Anso gave an exasperated sigh through his pursed lips as he looked at the young man beside him.

'He was so sure she was gone' Anso said with sadness at the heart ache and panic that showed on his sons face before he left the camp in search of her. 'Well it seems she did listen to me after all' Arnav said in surprise looking at Nox. 'Her responsibilities to her growing family out weight that of ruling Arella. She made her decision when she wed Kiril. The day was bound to come' Arnav stated as he watched his lifelong friend smile from ear to ear. 'Your right' Anso said as he looked at Arnav. 'When did you get so in touch with matters of the heart' he asked him teasingly. 'Ah, I never said I wasn't. But that doesn't mean every woman has to know about it' he said with a cheeky grin. Strolling down along the grassy edge of the campsite Kiril turned and made a grab for Nox only to end up face down with her kneeling on his back giggling. 'You have to be faster than that my love' she said mockingly, resulting in Anso laughing loud enough for his son to hear him and Arnav to walk to them just so he could jest Kiril of becoming weak. Rotating beneath Nox so that he lay on his back, he pulled her down into a passionate kiss and when they broke apart gently lifted her off him and rose with a smile on his face. 'I'll show you how weak I am if that's what you want. But as far as being put to the ground and mounted by a beautiful woman goes, I think I'll allow myself to feel weak any day' he said with a sly grin in the direction of his friend., who just grinned back shaking his head. 'So do you want me to join you in the field? Kiril asked Arnav who just laughed 'I'm not that stupid!

'I don't know about that' Kiril returned in a good-humored voice that held a hint of challenge.

'Hello! Nox said dramatically as she pointed to her stomach. 'Food remember.' 'How could I forget' and laughing he took her by the hand and led her towards the fireside. The smell of the remaining rabbit the twins had caught drifted through the air making her stomach growl and her mouth water at the thoughts of eating something with taste. She suddenly felt guilty for not giving the men a chance to gather their remaining supplies for their return journey to Arella. Her heart sank as she thought of her home but when looking up at the man at the fireside gathering her a plate of food and laughing at something one of the men said she smiled to herself. As she took a seat beside Malachi she pulled and tugged at her bodice. 'What's wrong Lady Nox?

Malachi asked in a genuine voice as he watched her struggle to arrange her skirts to a more suitable position for sitting in. This drew the attention of her protective Zanni warrior who blinked in surprise to see her blush at Malachi's attentions causing Kiril to glare in his direction.

'I was only asking' Malachi said defensively, 'she looks uncomfortable.' And before she could come between what looked to be an agreement in the making something gripped her hard along her side making her gasp in pain. Kiril practically lunged himself across the fire to get to her as Malachi bustled around like a mother hen with his hands on his head. When she found her feet she stood slowly from her sitting position allowing Kiril to help her. 'What is it? he asked in panic. All of a sudden Malachi was running through the camp screaming for fresh water, which to her surprise drew a small smile from Kiril as he looked at the young man trying to help.

'Nox? he asked again growing impatient with her for not giving an answer. Bunching up her shoulders and lowering her eyes to the problem at hand. 'It's gotten to tight, I can't sit comfortably, it squeezed when I walk and the pain of it digging into my sides is excruciating when riding long distances.' She was rushing through her sentences and as frustration grew in her Kiril knew there was only one thing to do. Placing the plate of food in one hand and taking hold of her hand in the other he walked from the fireside and made his way through the camp until they were out the other side. 'Where are we going? She asked in a soft voice. 'To get you more comfortable, that is presuming that is what you want' he replied with a wink in her direction. Focusing on the man if front of her she squeezed his hand harder and picked up her pace. Surveying the forest around them Kiril tried to find the right place to help his wife relax sufficiently. 'I was just thinking, is there not some sort of river around here? Nox said as she looked up at him in question. 'I really need to freshen up' she continued. 'That's a great idea, I think I'd like that myself. Come on we'll try this way' he said as he led the way through the vast landscape. Catching a branch just before it flung back and hit her in the face he cursed and snapped it clean off the tree. 'Was that . . . ? She had started but the sound of running water stopped her. 'Do you think there are any waterfalls in this part of the West? She asked in a hopeful voice. 'I doubt it; I've been all over these parts and never seen one.' At that she froze remembering his words "I've had women but never in Zantar." Sensing her sudden mood change he knew that clearly something was going on behind those emerald eyes. He stopped to face her. 'What? He asked in a gentle voice. 'Why would you have spent so much time around here? She asked shyly feeling like a fool for letting it bother her but damn it, it bloody well did.

'Would it surprise you if I said hunting? 'Really Nox do you honestly think me such a man to be spending my time chasing women through the bushes? I think you may be confusing me with Arnav.' Clearly put out by her line of questioning, but he knew why she had to know. He hated the idea of another man sharing what she shares with him, and unconsciously he clenched his fists. 'No, it's just . . . ' He shifted closer closing the gap that had formed between them.. 'Nox you know that I have been with other women but you seem to think it more than it is. I'm ashamed to say she was . . . well anyway she was what she was and I cannot do anything now to fix it.' 'Wait! She was a whore? She said in complete and utter shock that he would have gone with such a woman. 'The fact is I have loved no other but you. When you say you love me, that you chose to stay with me, that you want me as I want you is all I can wish for. Nothing and nobody else will ever come before that.' 'She? Nox said quietly as she looked at the man before her pouring his heart out. 'So you've only . . . 'she started. 'Yes once' he said 'now come on so we can get you freshened up,' he said kissing her gently before continuing on their way. 'Seems I've been proven wrong' he said as they came through the trees that lined the water's edge. She jumped up and down clapping her hands and once again he stood back watching her childish excitement over the littlest things. 'Is it not the most beautiful, breathtaking thing you have ever seen? She gushed. The water was a bluish green and the spry that came from it lay cool and welcoming upon her face. Stagnant pool lined the opposite side of the water pool leaving her to wonder what lived in them. 'Surely nothing dangerous' she thought as she moved closer.

Before he knew it she was stepping out of her clothes and making her way through the water towards the base of the waterfall. Smiling to himself he bent down and took his boots off followed by his pants and shirt. It wasn't the warmest day but he had experienced worse, and as he placed his feet into the water the memories of the last river he had ventured into came to mind. Placing his hands over his testicles he walked cautiously deeper and gasped as it ran between his legs and over his abdomen.

'Honestly Kiril, it's not that cold. I think Arnav might be right after all, you are going soft' she shouted at him jeeringly as she laughed. 'I'll show you soft' he replied and began to swim out to her. When he reached her she was lying on her back in the water. Her breasts displaying firm nipples which he realize had began to change colour slightly. His fingers tingled with the urge to lean over and touch them but he held back as he looked at the beautiful woman who was finally his. There was a slight swelling of her stomach and he wondered if she should be showing yet? It was an unnerving thought. She had become on edge lately complaining of her gown being too tight, her breasts growing achingly tender and now her nipples. A sudden thought came into his head. Should we be making love? The thought distressed him. 'Nox, how do you feel? He asked as he drew nearer softly caressing her from underneath as she lay her weight in his hands. Without opening her eyes she smiled 'I'm fine, your touch feels good' she whispered. This sent a delicious chill up his spine making him incline his head and take her nipple in his mouth. Licking, biting gently and kissing he lifted her to the heights of unbridled passion as she turned herself into him and wrapped her arms tightly around his neck. 'Will you finish what you start this time? 'I need you' was all he said as he lifted her onto his stiff shaft.

'You feel so good, it feels wonderful to hold you in my arms,' he said as he kissed her so passionately it left her frazzled and gasping for air. Entwined around each other they panted with the effort of their lovemaking. Arching her back she leaned herself into the water as he met her trust for trust. 'You're so beautiful . . . I love . . . so beautiful' he said through gasps as he held her tight against him. Moaning deep in her throat she rose herself up to face him. Taking a grip of his hair in both fists she took his mouth and kissed him thoroughly, enjoying the feel of his lips molded against hers. Every touch of his tongue restless as it explored her mouth made her nibble on his lower lip. Suddenly he remembered his concern and stopped 'please don't stop now! she said in a deep breath as she kissed his neck. 'Nox, stop' he said making her face him.

'What is it? she said looking worried. 'I'm sorry I can't' he said as he blew out a breath not looking at her, afraid of what he would see. 'What! she replied in amazement that he would do this twice. 'It's just . . . well it's . . . ' 'Oh just spit it out Kiril, I cannot believe you are doing this again.' She said agitated pulling away and glided back through the water facing him. 'Don't do that Nox, come on' putting his hand out to her, only for her to splash the water in his face. 'Me! your joking right? Don't do what exactly? Stop making love to me because, oh wait that's it, because you fucking can't' she screamed at him. What can't you do? Finish what you damn started maybe' she hissed with sarcasm as she glared at him. 'Nox please, I'm sorry, let me explain' he said pleading as he moved towards her. 'Obviously you're mistaken me for someone who gives a fuck, your such an asshole' she shouted back over her shoulder as she moved further from him and closer to the waterfall. 'It's the baby' he shouted out a little louder than intended as he looked at her. She turned in a whirl of water that moved in circles around her body, until she stopped leaving them to branch out like waves towards him. Her face had softened as she looked at him. Making her way back to him slowly he braced himself for the onslaught as bit his bottom lip hard enough to draw blood. 'If you draw blood on yourself she might be less inclined to do it' he said to himself as he waded through the water to meet her. She drew herself up along his length and kissed him gently on his cool lips, leaving him feeling confused and a little uncomfortable. 'You're going to hit me aren't you? he said pulling his face back just enough to protect himself. 'You're worried you will harm the baby by making love? She asked softly.

Shocked by her response he blushed slightly at the fact that, that was clearly not the case.

Placing her arms tighter around his neck she went on to tell him how women sometimes even make love to bring on labor, and that unless there are unforeseen complications love making is perfectly fine and more important safe. 'How do you know all this? He asked in shock. 'Kiril, this might be my first child but there are other women in Arella that took it upon themselves to share the wonder of child birth with me' she said laughing. 'Now can we finish what we started or am I going to have to find something to hit you with? He laughed loudly and moved in to take her mouth. 'Thank the stars' he said through kisses which made both of them laugh. 'Hold on' he said as he walked through the water and under the curtain that was created by the cascading water that fell from a height over their heads. When coming through to the other side the sheet of water left a constant background sound while they were surrounded by an almost eerie feeling. Although he felt it he didn't was time in placing her boldly against the wall of the cave within and proceeded to ride her solidly. 'I'll always regret not waiting for you' he said through stolen breaths. Her insides felt like they were turning to liquid. Holding on tightly she dug her nails into his shoulders as he bit her neck hard enough to mark her. He shut off all other things going on in his head and focused on putting all his strength into satisfying the woman in his arms and his shaking muscles. Feeling his testicles tighten he plunged deeper into her wetness and when she finally buckled and gasped for air with the force of her own climax, he let himself go and came with a force he could barely sustain. Relaxing against his firm body gasping for air she chuckled thinking about the fight they just had, making his very sensitive cock grow more sensitive that he begged her to stop moving. 'Okay, okay I'm sorry' she said leaning her forehead against his. Kissing her on the nose he lowered her to her feet gently and took her in a loving embrace. 'I don't want to go back to the campsite tonight' he whispered. As she raised her head to look at him she smiled and kissed him on the chin 'Anything you want.'

~

During the night he woke with a terrible urge on him. He wasn't sure if he wanted to disturb her sleep and fought the throbbing between his legs that is until she turned to him naked and nuzzled up under his neck. He began to feather her with soft kisses along her neck and down along her chest bone until he reached her breasts. Instantaneously she woke and moaned his name making his heart race and hands sweat. Raising his head he gave her a look from his yearning filled eyes and in moving and placing himself behind her, drawing her to the shape of his body. He was devastatingly accurate in his intentions and when he entered her she shivered pushing herself back against him to take him deeper. His arms held her tightly anchoring himself in her and when she shuddered with her climax he never let go, even when he lost himself in his own. Not releasing her they both feel back into a deep, restful and very satisfied sleep leaving him with thoughts of never being happier.

An hour later Nox exploded from her sleep in a terrible panic. 'I have to go' she said loudly enough to wake Kiril. 'What? Kiril replied drowsily as he tried to focus on Nox and reach for her at the same time. 'I said I have to go, I forgot Snowflake. How could I forget him? she said clearly upset with herself. Kiril let out a sigh and in reaching her pulled her to him.

'Snowflake is at the water's edge Nox and has been there for as long as we've been here. I swear that horse has better senses than any dog' he said kissing her gently and proceed to settle them both into a comfortable position. 'You're sure? She asked. 'I'm positive, now go back to sleep and in the morning I'll make you anything you want to eat' at that he closed his eyes as she sniggered and nudged him playfully. 'I don't eat that much' he hugged her tight and laughed at her attempt to get away as he tickled her. 'Okay stop, I thought you were going to sleep' she said through giggling. 'Oh I never thought to ask you how you managed to get two rings for our wedding at such short notice? 'Arnav went to the stone mason who lives just an hour from the castle in the Glens.' She said looking at him with a smile. 'Why? You don't like it? asking as she twisted it around his finger. 'Of course! I love it' he said with meaning afraid that he had hurt her feelings. 'But maybe you can tell me why it's black? He said in a worried voice as he looked upon the ring himself. 'It's stone carved from the Pillars of Uros. They say it is stronger than any metal. It will never change shape and never break,' she stated with a smirk in his direction. 'I asked Arnav for his help when we arrived in the Glens of Crowden. You had no idea? I would have thought Arnav would have found it increasingly hard to hide it from you.'

Laughing he kissed her as he rain his hands over her stomach and around to her backside.

Moving back slightly 'It's not that I don't trust you, but I really want to just have a quick look to see if he's okay' she said quietly as she began to rise from their makeshift bed on the floor of the cave. 'You're not serious? he asked in shock that she would actually be unable to rest feeling the horse was not cared for. 'I'm beginning to understand what your father meant,' said smiling in her direction. 'Shut up and go to sleep' she threw back at him with a hint of annoyance in her voice. 'I was only jesting you' he said as he nestled into the space she had just left vacant.

Turning back to him she sighed and went to sit beside him. 'I know, it's just I feel he's the only part of my father I have left' she said sadly looking at Kiril for understanding. Taking her hand he kissed each of her knuckles with feeling. 'The day he gave me Snowflake I knew he was heartbroken about it. But he did it anyway. That day he handed over a piece of himself to me and I have cared for it since that day. But Snowflake grows old and I feel him beginning to slow in his movements and abilities,' she said but then laughed. 'Not that he doesn't still try little tricks I thought him as a foal. I thought he might have broken his leg on a few occasions over the recent months. You think it's silly? she said looking at her hands as they twisted in his. 'No, I think you're very fortunate' he said 'now go and check him, I'll be waiting for you as I always have.' Leaning down she kissed him with feeling and rising she walked towards the entrance and looked out into the starry night as the moon shone its brilliant radiant glow down on the water before her. 'So spectacular' she thought to herself. When the light reflected off the water she spotted him. Her white stallion was standing peacefully by the water's edge. She watched him for a long time taking in the muscular shape of his back and legs and kicked herself for never leaving him out to stud. Imagining what it would be like without him her heart skipped a beat. Having made very little friends growing up in Arella which at the time didn't bother her and if she was honest still didn't. She had kept to what she did best and formed great relationships with her fighting partners which of course happened to be her father's men. Of course her father always blamed the fact she never truly tried, and of course that she spent way too much time in the stables and unlike her not every little girl liked smelling like horse shit.

Smiling at the memory she took another look at Snowflake. She had always deemed him the only one she needed. But as age crept its boney fingers upon him she realized she would never find another to take his place. Taking a look back over her shoulder at the slumbering form on the ground, it was amazing to her how easily Kiril fell asleep. Looking out at Snowflake once again she smiled 'goodnight old friend' and at that she returns to the arms of the most important man in her life. 'I never thought someone would take your place father, but I think you would approve' she whispered looking at Kiril as he slept. Leaning over she planted a kiss on his cheek closing her eyes allowing herself to drift into sleep.

Chapter Twenty-Two

As they made their way across the land that was relatively low and gently rolling. Forests and woodlands expanded towards mounds and hills in the distance that seemed to peak in some areas of the landscape while it dropped from sight in others. Trying to make up time and distance to bring about an attempt to intercept Lel and the Mackisi army, Ulric cursed his son again.

'How could he do this? He thought as an overwhelming feeling of irritation and disapproval went through him. He had been finding it problematical blocking out Vidar's excruciating whine as the arrows pierced his flesh. He was cruel, harsh and callous but damn it he was his son. He could still remember his joy the day he came into the world, and the promise to always defend and care for him. 'I've failed both of us' he said to himself sadly. Reaching what seemed to be the border between the West and South he was flabbergasted by the intimidating sight that lay before them. Ransan drew in a jagged gasp of horror as he looked upon the scene facing him.

'Those brutal bastards' he hissed. The landscape was littered with enormous fires that burned far above the ground. 'We should keep moving' Ulric said as he forced his horse forward toward the devastation. Moving slowly they took in all around them but found some things unbearable to look upon. As a number of Ulric's men dismounted and threw up he wondered if it was due to the smell of scorched fleshy tissue or the sight of bodies left to decompose. These people had perished and they were too late he deliberated as he hung his head. Passing through the village they had found no survivors to their distress. 'How far do you think they have travelled? Ransan asked Ulric as he squinted through the smoke. 'We need to pick up the pace' Ulric said forcing his horse into a gallop. He had seen enough and the repulsive and gruesome scenes they had just witnessed were going to be revenged. Breaking through the last of the fires they finally spotted who they were looking to stop in their tracks. Holding his hand up high Ulric called for his men to prepared their bows. Ransan looked on in awe as the two thousand braced themselves for attack. Grasping their bows in skilled and practiced hands they drew their arrows and held them in place. Drawing back on the bowstring they waited unwearyingly for the order to allow them to kill those who had killed so nauseating and sickeningly. With a swift movement of his arm arrows in their thousands glistened through the air and shed darkness upon the Mackisi.

~

The clatter of hooves echoed breaking the silence that surrounded them as Anso rose from his slumber only to find three men approaching rapidity in the direction of the campsite. Jumping onto his feet he shouted for the men to ready themselves for a confrontation. Commotion took over the camp one end to the other as the men rustled and dug through their possessions looking for their arsenal. Grabbing for his sword he paused when he recognized his own man amongst the three riders. Walking in a brisk stride he placed himself between the impending riders and the campsite. Halting when they reached their destination, they dismounted, and with somber and unsmiling expressions approached him. Noticing the men had undoubtedly been riding for what looked like days he proceeded to welcome them and shouted for refreshments. Turning to his own man and scout 'what news from the Crowden? Before he answered all three men looked to one another making Anso restless and unnerved at what would be so ghastly as to have two of Ulric's men accompany his man back. 'Speak now, or I'll see to it that all three of you are run through' he bellowed drawing the attention of Kiril and Nox who had just arrived to the rear of the camp. Without hesitation Kiril made his way to his father who was red faced with fist clenched. 'When did they leave? He asked just as Kiril was in earshot for the conversation.

'Three days not including the day and night it took us to reach you' Ulric's scout replied in a hoarse voice. 'What's going on? Nox asked as she wrapped her arms around Kiril from the back. Unexpectedly Ulric's men stood and faced her looking unsettled and gloomy which made Kiril take a step towards them menacingly causing them to flinch. 'She asked you a question' he said towering over the two men before them. 'Kiril! Anso shouted at his son giving a look that bothered him so considerably he froze. 'Vidar has been executed for his traitorous behavior against the Glens of the Crowden. He faced his faith yesterday morning by archers,' one of the men said looking from Nox to Kiril. 'Who called for his execution? Kiril asked in a harsh tone.

'Elder Ulric' Anso answered. Nox said nothing as she stood looking from Anso to the men before her. 'His own son' Anso said sadly as he shook his head. At his statement Kiril glared at his father. 'What do you mean his own son? His son was in allegiance with the Mackisi in case you have forgotten. The very men who tried to kill my wife and her men . . . ' Stopped mid sentence by Nox as she laid a hand upon his chest to soothe his temper. 'Your father meant nothing from his comment Kiril, you know this.' Turning then she focused on Anso who was staring at his son. 'Apparently you meant how considerably hard it must have been for Ulric to make such a judgment, did you not? she asked sympathetically when she seen the wounded expression that lined his face. 'Of course. He's a better man than I' he said in a whisper as he turned his eyes from Kiril. 'That is not all' Ulric's man spoke as he turned to face Nox. 'Vidar declared the Mackisi formed ranks and . . . ' he yielded as Kiril moved to stand beside Nox. 'And?

Nox asked tensing. 'They marched for Arella three days ago' the man said nervously as he waited for her response. Taking a step backwards dumbfounded by the news shaking her head slowly mouthing the word no over and over again. 'You must be wrong' she said willing the man to change his story but as she looked at the man face she could see the truth etching into the lines of his brow. Without warning she turned and ran out into the clearing and gave a high pitched whistle that made Kiril's ears ring. 'Nox! he screeched as he realized exactly what she was about to do. He took off running after her at such a speed his legs ached and complained.

Mounting she faced Snowflake in the direction of Arella and forced him into a gallop, leaving Kiril seething with anger and racing to find his horse. 'Blasted woman' he yelled as he barreled through the camp of men who were looking to Anso for his instruction and command. 'We ride to Arella' he bellowed. 'Damp the fires but leave everything else, prepare yourselves for battle' with that he took off in the direction of his extremely irate son. 'Kiril calm yourself' Anso said as he mounted his horse. 'I will not! I warned her. How many times do I have to tell her I forbid her to fight! He said shaking his head as his eyes grew more and more angry. 'You forbid it? Anso asked in shock. 'Please tell me your joking. Of all the things to say to such a woman as your wife,' he said laughing. 'I forbid it' he mocked. 'Oh, I would have loved to be there to see her response to that' still laughing he risked a glimpse at him son to find him glaring at him.

'You think this is funny? Kiril asked in disbelief. 'I do as it happens' Anso replied as he kicked his horse into a canter.

~

Nox rode with a singular purpose and that was defending Arella with her life. With a sturdy tug on the reins Snowflake came to a skidding halt buckling slightly under her. Reining him in she leaned down and whispered soothing and comforting things. As she rubbed behind his ears she thought about what she was about to do. Could she take the risk? What if the unbearable happened, would Kiril ever forgive her? So many questions were running through her head leaving her feeling inadequate once again. Having not felt this way since her father died she clenched her jaws tight and cursed at the top of her voice. 'Damn it! What would he have me do? Fingering her hair roughly she turned and risked a glimpse behind her almost expecting to see Kiril approaching like lightning over the hill. As usual he didn't disappoint. Seeing him she wasn't sure if she wanted to laugh or cry but she knew she was in for a interesting ride to Arella.

Following him was Anso with his two thousand men geared up and prepared to fight. Drawing up beside her she threw him a sly smile which didn't go down as well as she hoped. 'What are you smiling at Nox? Maybe you can tell me what you intend to do once we get to Arella, because I definitely know what you're not doing. You think I won't follow through on my threat just keep trying me' only to receive a snort of amusement from her. 'Well let me see. Firstly I intend to do whatever the fuck I like. Secondly I have every intention of fighting to defend my home and thirdly I'm actually looking forward to seeing you try to follow through on your little threat. Now if your finished I think we should keep moving.' Leaning over he took a firm grasp of Snowflakes reins and pulled him tight alongside his own horse. 'Listen and listen to me good Nox, you can do as you please. But I will see to it you do not raise one of those swords. Do you understand? At that he kissed her on the nose and smirking he released the reins. 'You wouldn't! she said as he turned and began the decent onto the level soft southern grasses. 'Oh, my love' he replied sarcastically 'just try me.' 'Kiril . . . ' she said in the progress of retaliating to be stopped by a commanding and dominant call from the distance. This drew their attention towards an accumulation of trees not an hour's ride away. Awareness of their surroundings rapidly doubled as the men became even more watchful and conscious of every diminutive sound. Not understanding why she felt anxious about what lay in waiting she shook of the feeling and reminded herself that this land was hers and damn it whoever it was definitely didn't know it like she did. Rising in her saddle she looked out beyond the tree line and knew that either their enemy or Ransan and Ulric stood on the other side. 'Only one way to find out' she said to herself and without hesitating she kicked Snowflake and proceed to lead the way. She had contemplated passing Kiril at a great pace just to piss him off but it was categorically not the time for games. When they were close enough to speak without shouting, she took one final look into the distance and turned giving him her full attention. 'Just beyond the trees there is a rundown homestead. No one has occupied it in a long time so it has been left to ruins. If it is a band of straggling Mackisi we have the advantage.' Looking at her to continue she went on to inform him of the unlevel ground that lay to the left of the dwelling. The ground rises and falls but it gives the ability to lay in waiting without being discovered. When asked how she knew this she just laughed and told him that, that was definitely a story for another day.

'What do you think? Arnav asked Kiril as he lowered himself face down on the ground beside him. 'Well it seems there are no occupants other than the Mackisi that have taken up residency. If we move downward cautiously we will maintain the advantage. Take a number of the men and work your way towards the rare of house.' As Arnav began to rise Kiril leaned up he pulled him back down to his level. 'Arnav, keep low, quiet and hidden as best you can.

Don't attack until we are all positioned.' Nodding his acknowledgment he rose still crouching and moved away to call upon the men he would take with him. Silently beckoning them with a head motion they set off to corner in the men below. 'Were are you going to be? Nox asked in a muted tone. Glancing at her from the corner of his eye he gave her a half smile while his eyes twinkled. 'Wherever you are.' Seeing her face drop he chuckled softly as her eyes bore into him.

'Well in that case I think it impartial that you be aware that this child is the only one I'll be giving you. I'm surprised I can piss alone, or have you been hiding in the bushes? At this he laughed loud enough to have Anso hush him and cast him a 'what do you think you're doing' gaze. Moving up Anso placed himself between Nox and Kiril and began to talk tactics.

Listening carefully Nox made the decision to make her way towards the sheds, which from the look of them were once fine stables. 'Pity' she said to herself as she looked upon the buildings.

As high and wide as her own in Arella. Guessing that at least ten to twelve horses had been housed there at some stage she began to allow her mind to wonder. 'Nox! Kiril said elbowing her gently. 'Huh? She said snapping back into reality. 'Do you think we have missed anything?'

Taking a final look out over the area in consideration. 'Arnav is behind the house, men are to the right of the trees and surrounding the stables inside and out to the left just below us. I don't think they will have any opportunity to escape once we advance on them.' Talking with confidence. Without waiting for any of the men to respond she gathered her things and with determination headed towards the desolated stables. A firm grip caught her around the waist and lifted her clean off the ground. Pivoting she found herself heading back the direction she had just come. Not even bothering to struggle against his strength, she tolerated him carrying her back, placing her down and telling her to stay in that precise spot. 'This is one of those battles' she thought to herself as she kept her features neutral, which resulted in him being the one to start the argument that she had been waiting for. 'You know the rules Nox! he said trying to sound stern but failing. She smiled to herself 'this is going to be so easy.' Walking towards him she placed her hands on his chest and smiled apologetically up at him. 'That's easier said than done. Not being involved is so hard' she said shrugging her shoulders. Seeing he wasn't moving she pushed it that little bit further 'I'll stay, I promise' she said giving him her brightest smile. Leaning down he kissed her leaving a satisfactory feeling run through her. As she watched him relax and more importantly believed he had won yet again she smiled. Looking down he sneered at the Mackisi, 'this won't take long' he said through clenched teeth. An impulsive need to drag him off into the bushes went through her which clearly must have showed all over her face. Rolling his eyes and shaking his head, 'you're unbelievable! What am I going to do with you' he said laughing as he nuzzled her neck making her squirm. 'Got you' she thought as she moved even closer to him. 'What do you want to do? she asked tartly. 'He hasn't got the time' Anso said with a chuckle. 'Honestly Nox' he said winking at her. 'I'm not going anywhere' Kiril told his father as he continued to look at her. 'Did I not just promise? She asked trying her very best to sound affronted. 'Kiril' Anso said as he pushed past him. Brushing his lips across the top of her head he took one last look at her before leaving. 'Finally' she thought as he went out of view. Giggling she took off towards the stables for a second time.

Taking the corner of the stables at an immense speed she was unable to stop herself before running directly into Kiril. Glaring at her in total disbelief, evidently not impressed at being lied to, took hold of her hand roughly and led her towards a colossal sized tree which lay to the edge of the ruins. Tugging against his grip, she dug her heels in and leaned back with all her might to no avail. 'He's so damn strong' she said to herself as he walked with ease while she struggled with earnest. When they reached the tree he grabbed a long vine that had wrapped itself around a mound of fallen rubble. Whirling to face her she cringed slightly, squaring her shoulders with every intention of standing her ground she glared back. 'Do you remember what I told you? he asked in a sinister way making her take a step back. Only to have him follow casting a shadow that surrounded every inch of her. 'You can't make me sit up there watching while you are all down here fighting for my home and my people. I won't do it' she yelled as her anger escalated. 'Do you hear me Kiril? 'And if you think for a split second that you are tying me to anything, you are sadly mistaken' she said leaning forward placing her hands upon her hips. 'I suggest you try and see what happens when you do,' she shouted. 'Fine' he shouted back and grabbed her again. With a sly smirk upon his lips he wrapped the vine around both of her hands and tied tightly, as she cursed, kicked and to his disbelief actually tried to bit him.

'You really are wicked' he said backing away from her. 'Did you just try to bit me? he asked shocked. 'Come closer and we will find out' she mumbled in a dangerously low voice. 'Maybe I'll just bloody leave you here,' he said smartly. 'Really? She said suddenly smug. 'Maybe you should learn to tie knots' she responded throwing the vine at him. 'Idiot! She laughed and before he could react chaos broke loose in the direction of the homestead. Sensing how torn he was between staying with her and aiding Arnav she made the decision for him. Tearing herself out of his clutch she ran into the clearing. Drawing her swords she braced herself and attacked with every once of strength her muscles possessed.

Fighting back two Mackisi who obviously assumed they had chosen the easier target, making her anger grow with such intensity she gritted her teeth and glared from under her eyelashes. Overflowing with their own patronizing self-importance they left themselves wide open for attack. Not waiting for a second opportunity Nox displayed why there was no need for her to be hiding in bushes. With lightning quick movements she blocked strike after strike. As time went by she noticed how they were beginning to grow fatigued, she drew back just enough to permit them to catch their breath. 'When you're ready to recommence just let me know' she shouted at them jeeringly, as she held her swords before her face as if examining them. From a distance Kiril hadn't taken his eyes from her. 'What is she waiting for? He asked himself heatedly as he struck another with such power he lifted him from the ground. Falling at his feet he wasted to time in finishing the job as he moved onto another, which he realized were diminishing at an alarming rate. Deciding that perhaps Nox was right and he was being a little too over protective he watched her from a distance who to his amusement was toying with two men, who were growing exceedingly pissed off. Her laughter filled the air making him smile to himself as he made his way towards her. Reaching her he wasn't a bit surprised to see his father and a group of men already there enjoying the show. 'When the rest are taken care of we will interrogate these two. Well when Nox is finished having fun' he said laughing. 'Mmm! Was all he received as an answer but in looking at his son he knew why. Kiril stood staring at his wife as a small smile teased the side of his mouth. 'Skilled is she not? he said proudly looking on. Nox was evading, blocking and striking as she went. The two men had an abundant of injuries to their bodies, face and to his astonishment even their hands bled. 'When you're finished teasing your pets, do you think we might have a word with them? Kiril shouted at her. Risking a fleeting look in his direction her face split into a grin that that lit up her eyes. At that moment he realized what she had been missing.

~

Burst lips and swollen eyes later the two men lay resting against a wall of the house at Kiril's feet. 'Well did they tell us anything we didn't already know? Arnav asked positioning himself to his right. 'No nothing.

It's amazing how deep their loyalty runs for a sadistic bastard such as their leader' shaking his head in disbelief. Noticing one of the men making themselves more comfortable he glared at him and in doing so followed his gaze in the direction of Nox with a sneering expression. Fury took him as he lashed out kicking him full force in the stomach, resulting in the man buckling over himself moaning with pain. Nothing short of shock ran through Kiril as the man began to laugh nastily up at him while he wiped frothy blood from his chin. 'It's a pity you won't live long enough to hear your wife scream' he said through blood stained teeth. Arnav seized Kiril as he lunged forward with a deafening screech. Struggling to restrain the big man he couldn't help sighing with relief as Anso arrived to offer assistance. Kiril fought against both men with such intensity that he pulled them alongside him as he edged closer. Arnav's eyes widen when he realized how strong he actually was. Having never been on the side of withholding him from killing someone he made a mental note never to attempt it again. Looking at Anso he could see he was red faced and sweating from his efforts. 'Kiril!

Nox screamed. Unfortunately for the men holding him, his hatred seemed escalate towards the two men at the sound of her voice. 'Kiril! she screamed once more coming to stand right in his line of vision. Grabbing his face between her hands she pulled his face down to her level forcing his eyes to meet hers. 'Kiril calm down, now! she said though clenched teeth. His eyes were wide with fury and she knew he was ready to kill at that very moment. 'Let him go' she said to Arnav and Anso never taking her eyes from his. He was breathing heavy strangled breaths that made the men look at each other. 'That is the most ridiculous thing I have ever heard you say' Arnav said as he held fast to Kiril's arms. When they didn't release him she broke away from Kiril glaring from one to the other. 'I said take your hands from him.' Not particularly liking the way her eyes bore into him Arnav dropped his hands and stepped away. When Kiril didn't move Anso did the same as he looked at his son nervously. Kiril stood staring at the man before him as Nox took his hand. 'I don't know what the problem is. Their of no use and we are finished with them are we not?' speaking never taking his eyes from the men before him. Nox rubbed his arm soothingly as she lead him away. Unable to switch off he could still heat what he had said to him, 'pity you won't hear your wife scream.' His hand tightened upon hers as he looked down at her. He'll kill them all. Leading him to his horse who was oblivious to what was going on and grazing alongside Snowflake she stopped and spoke as she stroked his face gently. 'We cannot waste any more time here, we have to move on.' Looking back over his shoulder at the men who lay on the ground his blood boiled. 'Kiril' she said as she began to bustle him onto his horse. 'They will die but not by your hand.' At that she turned, pulled her swords free and went to finish the job she started earlier. Having watched her saunter back in the direction of the men he so wanted to suffer at his hands, he knew she would always be in Arella.

This place would always be a part of her. It runs through her veins. 'While you defend my home and my people.' 'She's never going to settle in Zantar' he said forlornly to himself but loud enough for Arnav to hear. 'Why do you think that? She made the decision to make Hakan leader of Arella' he said looking at her as she rode up front deep in conversation with Anso.

Sighing Kiril never answered. 'You're a fool Kiril. What else would you have her do to prove her love for you? Arnav said testily as he left his friend to his own self pity.

Chapter Twenty-Three

'Is it just me who thinks we are going in the wrong direction. Should we not have continued on the way we were traveling? Arnav asked as he rode up alongside Anso as he looked around baffled. 'Nox knows of a better way and we do have to bear in mind that this is her home, and the reason her father was near driven to tears on numerous occasions. The woman knows too much about the land she was born to. If we continue on the trek we were on we will come within reach of Ulric and the army of the Crowden. We will be of no use stuck behind them. This way we end up directly at the rare of the castle were we can join the Arellian army and head the Mackisi off from the front. The element of surprise is a unmatched thing in war Arnav remember that' he said facing him, until he turned his gaze to Nox his eyes holding nothing but pure approval. 'Nothing to do with the fact that Hakan will be there with her armor in hand' Arnav replied wearily as he chanced a glance back in Kiril's direction. 'If she is going to insist on fighting Arnav she needs to be protected properly does she not? she said frowning at the young man. 'Of course . . . it's just . . . ' sighing he shook his head 'Kiril believes she will never settle in Zantar' he said apprehensively. Anso laughed rotating to look at his son. 'She'll settle.

She's looking forward to turning the place upside down. You know there hasn't been a strong woman in my home since Kiril's mother.' Anso said looking directly at Arnav. 'Kiril thinks he has his hands full? He said in a pitch higher than his usual voice with the excitement. 'Believe me Nox is a kitten in comparison. He doesn't comprehend what I had to deal with' he said looking back again at his son laughing directly at him. 'I'll tell you now Arnav I'm deeply looking forward to having the castle in total uproar again. It will finally feel like the home I remember.' Before Arnav could answer Nox came up fast on the left drawing their attention to a gap in the landscape. Turning they followed her at speed to keep up with her as she raced through the fields and towards a break in the forest that lay to the east of the castle. By now Kiril had joined them flanking Anso to his left while Arnav continued to ride on his right. They couldn't forget their own job in all of this and that was to protect and shield their own leader.

This was war and their priority was the man between them. Feeling a great sense of appreciation towards the two men, Anso knew only too well what his son was going through. He faced the same when his own father still lived and Mara had insisted on fighting as does Nox. The woman feared nothing and nobody while he feared everything when he looked upon her. Stopping abruptly he pulled on the reins of Kiril's horse and drew them both to a standstill. Arnav halted also only to be told to continue on. Even though not ecstatic about it he did what he was commanded leaving Anso and his son to talk. 'What are you doing? We will fall behind' Kiril shouted as he watched the army but more so Nox gallop off into the distance. 'I'm doing what my father did for me' Anso said looking at his son who was being torn in two before his eyes.

'What? He answered truly confused. 'I know you have your job to do, you are after all captain of the army you see in front of you. But you are also a husband now and soon to be a father and I hope that when the day comes you will do the same for your son.' 'Father, what are you talking about? Kiril asked frowning. 'Nox! His father answered as he looked out into the distance. 'Today you will not be needed to protect me' he said in a relaxed tone as he smiled at his son. 'She will fight whether that pleases you or not. Your job is to keep what is yours safe' he said as he laid his hand upon his shoulder. 'But I can't just leave you open to attack' Kiril answered hotly. 'I have Arnav and two thousand others to make sure that doesn't happen. Your job is to protect my grandchild, and the daughter you've brought to my home.' Giving one final squeeze he turned kicking his horse into a gallop he followed as fast as it would carry him.

Arriving just at the rear of the army he noticed how Arnav had held back enough to ride back to him and place himself into his position. When Kiril grew closer and went to do the same Anso threw him a wink and bid him good luck. Without waiting Kiril forced his way through the Zantarian army until he at length caught up and flanked Nox who jumped in surprise at his abrupt and unexpected arrival. Not asking any questions she grabbed his reins and drew him near enough to permit her to lean over and kiss him briefly. Taking his look to signify he wasn't going anywhere she smiled back at him. Deep down she was relieved. Today they would be each other's protector.

Coming face to face with a wall that went as far as the eye could see the men all looked to Nox who only laughed as she dismounted. Beckoning Kiril to assist her she walked with purpose to a huge slab of stone that was overgrown with grasses and thorn bushes. 'Don't worry we don't have to push it' she said when she seen Kiril eyeing the slab with apprehension.

Leaning in she tugged at the vines that had grown thick over what gave the appearance of an entrance of some sort. There spiky protuberances caused her such discomfort she thought of giving in, only pure stubbornness made her grit her teeth and continue. The thorns prickled her are so badly that the pain and irritation was so bad she cursed. Withdrawing her hand she hissed as the blood weld up and trickled down the length of her arm. 'Damn things are razor-sharp' she said moving aside to allow Kiril to make his way in past her to take over. After an abundance of choice words from him and stifled giggles from her the opening was clear. 'That's huge! Arnav said in amazement. 'And nobody knows of this entrance? Kiril asked her in total disbelief.

'Just the twins and Hakan' she said as she moved towards the entrance to guide the way. 'Your father didn't know? Arnav asked. Her laugh echoed through the underground passage.

Completely enclosed except for the opening and the exit the passage was hidden from sight. It was the greatest escape route from the castle. 'Does that answer your question? Kiril said smiling at Arnav. 'Make sure the last one in blocks it back up again' Nox shouted from the front. 'We don't want any of those bastards discovering it' Making their way through the passage the atmosphere changed as it grew black as night as the entrance was blocked once again. Knowing herself the distance between the entrance and exit she was relaxed but when she thought of the men walking four a breast and on top of one another she felt a pang of guilt. 'I should have warned them' she said to Kiril who had his hand resting upon her waist. Lowering his face to her check he kissed her so gently her legs went weak and all she wanted to do was take him in her arms and forget about what was coming. 'I love you' she whispered to quiet for him to hear as she squeezed his hand tightly not wanting to let go. Reassuring the men that it would not be long before they reached the exit they all followed in unison. Listening to the noises and what they hoped was progress coming from around the castle. Being unsure if it was coming from within or beyond its walls made Nox's anxiety intensify beyond measure. After walking one hundred feet from the entrance they finally came to the opening on the other end.

'You're going to love this' she said looking in the direction she assumed Kiril was standing.

Shoving forcefully upon what looked like any other part of their stone surroundings, it moved without difficulty displaying a huge and elaborate gathering hall. Shocked by the large space that housed a roof measuring at least twenty feet high, he looked around in wonder. It had been decorated from wall to wall with ornamental works ranging from metal, wood and to his surprise glass. Drinking vessels, glasses of all sizes, vases and unbelievably a single flower. Its glass petals trapped the light and threw shapes across the floor and over his feet. Rotating his head to take in the painting that hung far above the ground upon the walls, but almost reaching floor level. One in particular caught his eye. Set on canvas this representation was made up of gold leaf and other material. Establishing a strange but brilliant merge of colours. He tilted his head to look upon it in a variety of positions. The room clearly had been designed by a keen eye for detail. Light and shadow were of equal quantities, and he decided there and then that if he had lived here this would have been the place we would have spent most of his time. 'You can't be serious? Kiril said when he completely came through out of the darkness. Nox laughed at his expression. 'Were did you think I hid for three days' she said winking. 'Clever girl' Anso replied wiggling his finger at her. 'Unbelievable' was all Kiril said as he looked at her.

Bursting through the heavy wooden double doors came Gaius with Toran close behind along with about fifty men swords at the ready. Gaius laughed with delight as he walked to Nox, picked her up and proceeded to swing her around like a child. 'Might have known it was you' he said as he placed her down and went to shake Kiril's hand. 'Couldn't stay away? Toran said as he hugged her tight. 'Hakan will be glad you've made it' he said as he led her out of the gathering hall and towards the main entrance. 'The army of the Crowden are just beyond the southern borders with Ulric and Elder Dreakwood' Nox told him as they rushed along. 'Wait!

What? Toran asked totally shocked by this revelation. 'Vidar was executed for treason against the Crowden' Kiril said as he and Gaius were exchanging stories. 'When did this happen? Gaius said before Toran had a chance. 'Not three days after we left. Elder Dreakwood rode out to enlighten us of his fears that Vidar was hiding something. All of a sudden he was arrested and sentenced to death by archers' Arnav joined in. 'Archers!' Toran whistled through his teeth.

'What a way to go.' He said shaking his head. 'I'm assuming Ulric wasn't too pleased' Gaius said looking at Nox. 'It was him who gave the order. Now stop gossiping and tell me what has been going on.' She said with a bite to her voice. 'Nox! came a voice to the right of them as she walked past a hallway leading towards seamstress's rooms. Stepping backward she spotted Nasha bounding full force down the length of the hallway with an ear splitting grin. Without stopping she hurled herself into her arms and squeezed tightly as she laughed hysterically. 'I knew you'd come back. Nox your bleeding' she said loudly as a worried face grew worried.

'It's just a few scratches' Nox told her. Obviously the words she needed to hear Nasha jumped to the next subject. 'Just wait until Tianna learns of your arrival, she'll be so excited' breaking her embrace she stepped back and looked at her strangely. 'Nox' she said as she tugged her away from the men. 'Do you desire me to get the seamstress to make you a more comfortable gown? 'It looks that bad? Nox asked extremely paranoid of her appearance. 'Well no of course not' Nasha rushed her words afraid she had caused offence. 'It's just . . . well do you not find it . . . ' leaning in she whispered 'too tight.' As Nox pulled and tugged on her bodice Nasha decided that she would go and organize it straight away and also to fetch Tianna to dress her arm much to Nox's delight. 'Thank you Nasha' she sighed.

As they came into the main entrance hall of the castle she was beckoned again by another enthusiastic voice. 'Lady Nox, lady Nox' scanning the entrance hall she spotted Tressin. She couldn't help but smile at the young boy. 'In trouble again? Nox asked teasingly, but when he shrugged his shoulders shyly and sniggered she sighed. 'Well it can't be the stables anymore so what now? Talking as she placed her hands on her hips. 'The work shop' he replied quietly.

'Tressin! She bellowed. Sensing that everyone in the entrance hall was glaring at the child she lowered herself to his level. 'Tressin, you know you cannot be in there. Hot metal is nothing compared to the horses in the stables.' Noticing his head was now bowed she rose his chin and smiled at him. 'How is your father? At that he laughed, 'he said when he sees you he is going to have words.' Nox laughed along with him upon hearing that piece of news leaving the onlookers wondering why they would find that so entertaining. Finally she caught a glimpse of Hakan.

Rubbing the top of the child's head she whispered the same thing as she did before and left him to run off and do what he did best. Torment his father. As Gaius called to Hakan she turned to Kiril who was still looking after the boy running riot through the hall. 'You wish for a son' she said smiling up at him. 'I wish for whatever you give me' he said tearing his eyes away. 'You're a horrible liar' she said tenderly. 'What have you done to yourself?' Tianna fumed as she forced her was through the crowded entrance hall. Toran's eyes lit up at the sight of her. Nox noticed that even though she received hardened eyes, he received a love filled look. She almost felt she was intruding upon something private between them both and looked away. Spinning on Nox she remembered her reason for being in the entrance hall and with force she grabbed Nox's arm as she inspected the damage. 'Mmm! Not too bad I suppose. Nothing I can't fix' she said as she took a bottle of what looked to be iodine plus an unsoiled wet cloth from Nasha. Devoid of any notice Tianna added the mixture to Nox's arm forcing a gasp and an intense glare in her direction. 'Ouch' Nox exclaimed. 'Do you have to be so damned rough? She asked while trying to wriggle free of Tianna's startlingly strong grasp. 'Well if you were more cautious not to mention sensible this would not be happening now, would it? Now shush.' Tianna retorted, which drew a startled look from Nox and a snigger from Toran. Slightly abashed by the scowling, Nox held as steady as she possibly could while keeping her mouth shut. As Tianna worked at mending her arm, Nox noticed Hakan who was approaching enthusiastically.

'Welcome home' he said embracing her. Only to gain a mouth full from Tianna about his stupidity 'honestly Hakan, can you not see that we are in the middle of something? 'I do' he said just as heatedly in return. Tianna took a step backward, place her hands on her hips and just as she was about to let him have it Toran put his hand tight across her mouth. 'I would not like to be him right now' Kiril said inclining down to her while still looking in the direction of the now fuming Tianna and a very bashful Toran. 'I see the tunnel is still in use' Hakan said smirking.

Tearing herself away from the confrontation about to take place she threw him a sly smile.

'When has it never been in use? 'True' he answered laughing but soon the playfulness left his voice and he became serious. 'We have a great deal to get through. I have seen that your armor was taken out and let in your room along with your shield.' Stopping he risked a glimpse in Kiril's direction. Knowing his feeling on the matter of Nox taking part in any type of fighting while pregnant, he really didn't want to be seen as enticing or encouraging her. Catching Kiril's eye he shrugged leaving Hakan with a feeling of pity for the man who obviously didn't stand a chance against Nox and her willpower. 'We expect to be leaving within the next two hours as the Mackisi are drawing close to the forest of Huri. ' Meet me by the gates' Nox said walking without lingering any longer in the direction of her rooms, leaving Kiril standing shoulder to shoulder with Hakan. As he watched her stroll away Hakan sighed deeply. 'I hope you don't mind me saying this but . . . 'he stopped to make sure he had Kiril's attention. 'If she was my wife' looking in the direction to where Nox was he turned back to Kiril, placed his hand upon his shoulder and smiled. 'I'd tie her to the bed and leave her here' he said shrugging his shoulders.

'But that's just me' smiling a brilliant smile he sauntered off leaving Kiril thinking the very same thing. Setting of after her he watched how she held herself. Forever the proud and fearless warrior she had grown up to be. Could he leave her here by force? Thoughts ran through his head and every time he liked an idea he always came back to the same outcome. 'She would kill me.'

'You know I've never seen your rooms before' Kiril said coming beside her. 'No man other than my father have ever seen my rooms' she replied in a low almost embarrassed voice.

'Not even Hakan and the twins? He answered stunned. 'No. There is a meeting area where we always would gather but never my bedroom.' This gave Kiril an immense feeling of exhilaration that he would be the very first man to enter her domain. Coming to a halt outside a huge heavily built wooden door, Nox opened it and stepped in without looking behind to examine Kiril's expression. The living space was a vast area that was lit to some extent by a huge window facing the Floyden Mountains. Left him to wander around inspecting everything she walked through to her bedroom. Following her the first thing he noticed was the enormous four poster bed that lay against the middle of the wall facing the door. Four columns supported the upper panel which held white flowing curtains. Enclosing whoever lay within away from the rest of the world seemed like a great idea Kiril thought as he lifted back the corner of the feather light curtain and took in the inner sanctuary of her abode. Covered from head to toe in white blankets, with the exception of a fur that lay across the bottom and fell to the floor. Taking a closer look he realized it was the same as his own. Frowning he found it extremely odd considering his father gave it to him as a present after a hunting trip. 'Nox, were did you get your fur? He asked not looking at her. 'From your father. Why? She asked walking over to him and pulling back the curtain looked up at him. 'Why would he give it to you? he frowning at her clearly not understanding why a man of his father's age would give a young woman a fur to line her bed. He felt a sick feeling in the pit of his stomach. What was behind his father's gift? Is that why he insisted on accompanying him to the Northern territory? 'It was a birthday present. I had seen yours and said I would love my own' she said cheerfully. 'And Anso said you thought it warm in the winter.' 'You were in my rooms? He asked in shock. 'Yes' she replied shrugging her shoulder as she smiled up at him, clearly not seeing why that would be a problem. Walking off she left him to his thoughts. 'So bloody intrusive' he said a little too loudly, and as he heard her laugh in his direction he cringed thinking that she thought him so petty. After all they would be her rooms now. Returning his attentions to her bed he caught a glimpse of the four good sized pillows at the top of the bed that he could have sworn were calling his name. 'I'm definitely in need of sleep' he said. Noticing the width of the mattress he found it considerably larger than most but it was the headboard that grabbed his courtesy. Beautifully handcrafted it had an immense amount of detail going from one end to the other. Obviously having taken a considerable amount of time he wondered if she would like to have it moved to Zantar. coming out from under the curtains he was bewildered that the first thing he had noticed was her bed. He was sure that hers was unlike any other woman in the castle hers was decorated with every type of sword there was. 'Is there any sword you don't have? He asked in amazement. Proceeding to give him the story behind each sword he had learned that most of them had been given to her throughout her life by her father but one in particular had its own special place. His sword hung alone over the window which gave a view of the whole landscape surrounding the castle.

Walking back through the doors into the living area she was left in a deafening silence. A slight frown creased her brow as smoke bellowed into the atmosphere from the distance. The most ghastly, horrifying things ran through her head as she imagined the cause of the fire. Her mind went to the images it still held when coming upon Tianna's homestead. 'Is this your armor? Kiril asked running his fingers lightly down along the smooth metal. 'Why do you want to wear it? she asked tartly. Throwing her a good-natured look he turned back to the armor. 'What does the design mean? Of course I know that the horse is obviously Snowflake but the rest . . . it's strange' he said frowning. Walking over to him she looked warmly down at the armor on table. 'It's not Snowflake, its Chacha' seeing his expression she laughed faintly and continued. 'This was my mother's armor. Chacha was her horse. A beautiful black stallion with a wicked temper' she said as a far off look filled her eyes. 'Well so my father told me. As for the rest, some are names of ancestors and some are just flowers that she loved. My father gave it to me when I turned fifteen. I was beginning to train with the older men. I think he was beginning to panic as he watched.' 'Do you remember her? he asked tenderly as he lay his hand on her shoulder drawing her near. 'I remember some things' she said smiling to herself as she touched the armor with a fingertip, as if afraid she might damage it. 'She died when I four. Sometimes I'm not even sure that the things I do remember actually happened.' Shrugging her shoulders she strolled back through to the living area. 'I know that no matter what I say you're going to fight but please tell me you are going to wear it aren't you? he called carefully not wanting to upset her. A knock sounded at the door before she could respond much to his annoyance. Opening the door Nasha stood with her red gown in her hands. 'Maggie send's her apologies for being unable to produce a new gown. Time is in short supply at the present moment. I was not sure which gown to bring her so I brought your red one. I hope that was alright? 'I'm sure it's perfect' Nox said throwing her a smile of reassurance that she did a wonderful job. Stepping close Nasha hugged Nox yet again. 'Be careful' she whispered as she left. Watching her as she walked away Nox wondered what would have happened to the young girl had Hakan and the twins not saved her from the Shia Mountains. 'You do realize how challenging it is going to be for me to concentrate if you're going to insist on wearing that dress' Kiril said as he worried his bottom lip between his teeth.

The recollection of her wearing that dress made his hands sweat with the need to touch her.

Laughing out loud Nox strode to the bed, laid it down and began to strip off her green gown and was extremely pleased to be free of it once and for all. 'So' Kiril said as he ran his hands around her waist and onto her slightly swollen stomach. Resting his chin on her shoulder he began to kiss her gently. Relaxing herself back against him she let out a sigh of contentment. They hadn't made love in a bed since the night he rode with Anso into the Northern Territory. 'We don't have time' she said teasingly prizing herself away from his heat, leaving him to pout looking from her to the bed that lay unused before him. 'You know if you put that red dress on it won't take that long, so really we will have all the time in the world to waste. It will only take a minute' he said throwing her a sly wink. She had begun to wash enjoying the heat of the water that ran over her breasts, stomach and down along her aching legs. Giggling she turned her head slightly 'only a minute? she said as a smirk formed upon her lips. Walking slowly to him she ran her fingers lightly down and around her breasts never taking her eyes from his. Reaching him she stood naked as the chill in the air drew the steam from her body. Placing her hand within his trousers she took a firm grip and gently massaged, while he groaned as satisfaction took over.

Releasing him she took a step backward as those hazel eyes bore into hers. Removing his clothes feeling the intensity of her watching him drove him crazy. He wanted her so badly.

Laying her hands upon his naked chest she forced him little by little back on to the bed were she proceeded to kiss, lick and nibble him gently up the length of his body. Wanting to show her dominance she slapped away his hands when he could no longer take the teasing of her tongue.

Rising she lowered herself onto him slowly until he filled her completely. Forgetting all sensibility or appreciation of those in the near vicinity she threw her head back and made love to him until he screamed her name so loud she was sure everyone could hear.

Laying naked entwined in each other's legs and limbs he played with a length of her hair.

Twisting it over and over through his fingers he needed her to know how he felt once and for all.

'I need you to know something that I have never told you before' he said quietly. Getting her attention she rose her head and rested it upon her arms which now lay across his broad chest.

Quirking her eyebrows at him to continue, he leaned forward and kissed her on the nose. 'Do you remember when myself and Arnav came to Arella? 'Which time? she asked smiling. 'The last time, when my father didn't accompany us.' Nodding her head he pressed on. 'Well it's just . . . well you were never around when I looked for you . . . and . . . well . . . ' shooting up into a sitting position she stared at him with wide eyes. 'Please don't be tell me you had affections with one of the women that insisted on following you everywhere? She asked in total shock.

'No! I did not' he replied heatedly as he let out a sigh and rubbed his forehead roughly. 'Well what then? She asked a little wearily. 'I followed you' he said quickly. 'You followed me?

Where? She asked curiously. 'I was convinced you had man in your life and when you were constantly absent I needed to know for sure. And

I know your father told me there wasn't but I just couldn't relax. So I followed you the day before we left for Zantar.' he was running through his words and she was totally confused. 'What is he talking about? she thought looking down at him in a total fluster. Laying a hand upon his chest she could feel his heart beat so hard it must have been deafening to his ears. 'So you followed me. And what did you find? Sitting up to face her he leaned forward again and kissed her thoroughly leaving her laughing at his strange behavior. 'Kiril will you just say what you have to say.' 'I seen you naked' he blurted out loudly. 'In the forest by the gathering streams. I didn't mean too . . . I came upon you while I was . . . ' stopping he took a glimpse in her direction to see her glaring at him in total disbelief.

'I'm sorry' he whispered. 'So you followed me thinking I was with a man? And what exactly we're you going to do if I had of been in an embrace or worse making love to this man?

Clenching his jaws tight and forming a fist he jumped from the bed and smacked his fist on the table making everything on it fall onto the ground with a loud smash. Whirling on her face flushed with anger he grabbed for his trousers and shirt. 'What are you upset about? I'm the one who was being spied on as I washed for fuck sake. Honestly! You wouldn't speak to me but you thought it alright to find me naked in the forest and stay there to get an eye full.' 'I would have killed him' he screamed at her. 'I wouldn't have cared who it was or if you loved him or not, I would have killed him there and then.' Closing his eyes and taking a breath he lowered his voice and went to sit beside her on the bed. The silence filled the air and Nox knew she had to be truthful also. 'I knew you were there, did I not tell you, about your heavy feet' she said looking up at him with a cheeky grin. 'For the record I also warned at least five women to keep their distance from you when you visited.' At this he shook his head. 'You knew all along? 'Would you really have killed the man if there had of been one? 'Yes' he said as he faced her directly.

'Well then it's a good job I kept my virtue intact' she said laughing as she drew him to her for a second time.

Waking some time later they rose and began to dress readying themselves for what was to come. Slipping into her red dress she was overjoyed to find that it was precise and accurate around the mid-section. She was totally taken back when what Maggie had done with the sleeves caught her eye. Having added gold and black feature that covered all sides of the cuffs while, leaving an adequate amount of space around the hip line for her armor to fit snuggly. A tingling sensation ran through her with thoughts of standing before her adversary looking like a true Arellian. 'Maggie, you truly are a marvel' she said with a smile while running her hands down the length of the velvet. Hearing Kiril draw near she twisted to face him. Standing before her holding the armor she had only worn to keep her father happy and content in his hands.

With a slight motion of his shoulders and a curl of his lip he moved to her and carefully set it in place. Unhurriedly he tied it tight enough not to move but lose enough not to squash the fragile contents she held within. When he had finished he moved to her rear and began to buckle her swords into position. Leaning down he kissed her neck while drawing his arms lightly around her. 'Please be careful. I don't know what I would do if you got hurt or worse' he said in a choked voice that once again left her feeling like the selfish bitch. Running her hands along his arms she squeezed him tighter to her and sighed deeply. 'I promise.' Turning she hooked her arms around his neck and looked up into his troubled eyes. 'I swear to you I will not let anything happen to your son' Unable to hold back a deep sigh he forced himself to ask her again. 'Please stay here' he said pleadingly. 'If you need me on my knees I will do it' he said as he lowered himself to the ground in front of her. Feeling her eyes glaze over she knelt down and faced him.

Placing her hand upon his cheek she bowed her head as her tears flowed. 'You would have me choose? she asked as she held firm to her emotions. 'I'm sorry, I must' he said raising her jaw to look affectionately upon her tear stained face. 'Then I'm sorry but I cannot.' She said looking directly at him. 'You would rather keep face with the men than do as I ask? He said looking at her in utter disbelief as he went to gather his feet beneath him . Grabbed tightly to his hands to kept him there before her she leaned in closer to him so that her nose touched his chest. 'No. Not for the men . . . for you' she replied running her fingers lightly over his lips. 'I will not stay here and watch you leave. You are within my circle and I will protect you. ' At this Kiril broke away and stormed to the other side of the room leaving her to pursue him. But just as she had it would seem he had learned to pick his battles. 'Please understand' she begged as he laid her hands upon his chest and willed him to look at her. Leaving her room in a dangerous temper he wanted nothing more than to do what Hakan had suggested. The sound of her heaving things brutally against the door while calling him every name she could possibly think of made him want to do it even more. Walking all the way through the hallway that led to the other rooms he tried to gather his wits and his self-control before he bloody throttled her. 'You're doing this deliberately' he shouted back in the direction of her bedroom. Willing himself to agree with her he found he just grew more angry at the concept. He could not, just as she couldn't do as he asked. 'Why does she have be so damn stubborn? He shouted punching a wall as he passed. Pain shot up throughout his arm, but ignoring it he turned on his heel returning the way he came.

'Blasted woman' he said clenching his teeth together. Not noticing Arnav coming towards him he stopped to greet him, while still eyeing her bedroom door with disgust. Sensing he wasn't in the humor for joking he approached him with caution. 'Come for a drink Kiril' he said following his gaze. Without speaking Kiril nodded his head in agreement and allowed Arnav to lead him away from another possible argument.

Sitting opposite each other Kiril explained what had been going on between himself and Nox making him grow angry once again. Passing him his drink Arnav enticed him to continue.

'What do I do Arnav? Because at this present time I really don't know what I'm doing but I seem to be constantly in the wrong, I'm definitely not doing anything right' he said displeased. 'What kind of husband cannot keep his wife from wanting to bloody kill him.' Taking in his friends expression he laughed and rubbed his hands hard across his face. 'Ignore me Arnav, truly I do understand where she is coming from but why does she have to push me so fucking much? He said looking to his friend for guidance. 'You're really talking to the wrong person Kiril. I've never been in a relationship that lasted longer than one night.' He said shrugging his shoulders as he took another gulp of his drink. 'But I will say one thing to you that I really think you should remember. You have wanted this for as long as I can remember. Can you sit here before me and tell me that as much as she's driving you crazy you are not the happiest you've been in years?

Taking a deep meaningful breath Kiril shook his head slowly. 'No I cannot.' He said as he sighed leaning is head upon his folded arms. 'I love her more than anything in this world' he said into this arms. 'Well then I suggest you go back and sort out this mess, and for all that is good try not to kill each other.' At this both men laughed. 'I have something of great importance to ask of you Arnav, Kiril said unsmiling and somber. 'Of course anything, what is it that troubles you so much? Arnav asked deeply bothered that something would upset the great man before him. 'You know Kiril I have never seen you look so terrified, what is it man? he asked placing his hand on his shoulder. 'If she insists on fighting I need you to protect her if I am unable to reach her if she needs me. There is a score I need to settle.' Arnav's shock ran all over his face and he leaned in abruptly grabbing him hard by the arm. 'Remember you are to be a father Kiril. Whatever you are planning rethink it, I beg you' Arnav pleaded. Irritated Kiril turned on him with heated words that he wished he could take back as soon as they left his mouth, leaving him furious at himself. Running his hands through his hair he cursed and stood up to move away from Arnav who's mouth hung open as he frowned up at his friend. 'You're a damn fool but I'll do it.' he called after Kiril who was skulking his way back through the crowded room. 'If this goes amiss you have only yourself to blame and I will not defend you when she does actually try to cause you grievous harm.' Smiling back in the direction of his friend and first in command he nodded his appreciation. 'Thank you Arnav' at that he turned and walked back to where Nox would be waiting. Standing at her door he could still hear her.

Between laughing and shouting about his outright arrogance, and stupidity to think she was not fight, he stood back and listened intently to every heated word that came from her mouth. 'Of all the unintelligent, foolish and ludicrous things you could think of doing' he roared as he stormed back into the room. She stood before him no longer concerned for his feelings, but reeling and prepared to go against everything he said and more. 'Why you conceited, egotistical, condescending bloody man' she yelled back just as loudly. His face grew red as he glared at her, only to have her straighten her back and give him a dangerous and challenging look. 'You will be the bloody death of me, damn it' he screamed marching towards her and pulling her into a tight embrace he kissed her senseless. Not fighting she responded to his ferocity with her own.

As their passion grew she raked at the flesh of his back trying with all her might to bring him closer. Desire and yearning left them both breathless and disgruntled at not being able to continue. He pulled back displeased and looked upon her hungry eyes that glowed like the morning grasses after the drew. Leaning to her ear he whispered 'He's mine.' Without another word he took her hand and led her from the room. Holding tight she risked a quick glance at him.

Only to find his face still held the look she wished never to see again. Her heart shattered for the man who swore to shield and protect her with his life. Wishing with all her might that she could find it in her to give him what he asked of her, she squeezed her eyes together and sighed. She could not.

Chapter Twenty-Four

The multitude of the mass of men who stood before her as she ventured out through the castle gates was so overwhelming it took her breath away. Weaponry varied considerably and like her father, Hakan did not force his ways upon the men. They were a sight to be feared by any enemy. Anso sat tall in his saddle fronting his own army flanked by Arnav. Her breath caught as Kiril mounted his horse, bowed his head in his father's direction and came to rest at her right. He would ride into battle flanking her as husband and protector. Deep within she was yet again conscious of how she was wronging him. His men stole glimpses at their captain who would not be leading them into battle. 'Bloody man! Closing her eyes as she allowed a gentle gust to run over her features. Turning Snowflake she rode to Hakan who was positioned between Gaius and Toran as she once was. 'I will find you all on the field' she said smiling. Quickly turning before she had a chance to change her mind she led the horse to were Anso sat looking out into the horizon. Leaving the three men watch as one of their own joined the Zantarian line. 'She has finally found her place in all of this' Gaius said looking upon the woman who was clearly not a girl anymore. 'I guess your right' Hakan replied while leaned upon his saddle on folded arms.

'She will always be an Arellian' Toran snapped clearly not impressed that both men seemed to be in agreement that she would never return.

The physical altercation that would possibly lead to many being injured or killed left Kiril's mouth dry. Thinking of Lel and his men he wondered what kind of manipulation he used to control them. 'Reinforcement created by a climate of fear, leading to hostile, angry and very dangerous men. 'Why didn't I just tie her to the damn bed' he grumbled. But his face softened when he thought of her choosing to ride alongside his father, giving him back the opportunity to watch over them both. When he arrived behind her she couldn't resist a snipe at how long it was taking him to organize himself. 'Really Kiril it doesn't take that long to choose a riding companion. I was beginning to think you were going to leave us and travel with Hakan and the twins.' Laughing at his facial expression she reached across grabbed his thigh and squeezed.

'Are you ready? She asked more seriously as they began to set off. Placing his hand over hers he gave her a one sided smile. 'I'm always ready. Just don't cause to much trouble' he said giving her a stern but pleading look. 'Me? she answered jokingly laying her hand upon her chest totally scandalized he would say such a thing. 'Give me strength' he said rolling his eyes as he kicked his horse into a gallop. Coming over the hilltop the roar of men in battle echoed through the countryside left her fingers tingling with the need to touch her swords. A unified strategy would be needed if they are to make a dent in the Mackisi army. Looking closer at the terrain in front of them she knew only too well how the weather could affect the ground they would have to travel on. 'I think we should try capturing the high ground' she told Anso without taking her eyes from the vast spance before her. 'If we stay high they will have to climb to attack' turning her attention to Kiril who seemed in agreement, but voiced his own thoughts. 'What about an area of dense vegetation like the forest? The way I see it if they have not reached the Huri Forest it's ours for the taken' he said looking from his father to Nox. 'But if we take the higher ground they would be drained from the grueling climb by the time they reach us' she replied. 'We will stay high enough to look out over the battle as it is now. I can't recall many hills on our journey here but I do realizing we took another route . . . ' stopping in mid sentence he turned to face Nox.

'Nox I am trusting the lives of my men into your capable hands until you see us to a suitable position.' With that he through his hand out for her to lead the way. Taking the lead of the two thousand strong Zantarian army she felt strangely at home. 'Well played sir' Arnav whispered to Anso as he came beside him. Anso smiled as he looked at Nox before him. Head held high with purpose, he knew she needed this, and Kiril needed to see her as others did. Having rode at a steady pace they finally came to a standstill. Beneath them stood the Mackisi army who were deep in battle with Ulric and his dynamic and skilled force of archers. Attacking from a distance was always an advantage but she always loved the feeling of her sword clashing against another.

The screams of injured men rose and fell with the wind that had by now grown into a blustering current of air that encircled them. Her tight braid that hung heavily down along her back had begun to loosen leaving wisps of hair to ran over her face and shoulders. Coming close behind Hakan who was followed by Gaius and Toran stated how he had decided to bring his men around to the entrance of the forest if Anso had settled upon attacking from their present position. Bidding farewell and good luck they left with much hast towards their attacking point.

She had noticed that Kiril was preoccupied taking in the progress of both sides below. A hardened frown formed across his brow as something disturbing caught his eye. Following his gaze she cringed. Lel stood over a man who had fallen under his sword. 'The worse part of depending solely on a bow' she said to herself sadly looking at the scene before her eyes. ' It was no match for a blade' she thought in sympathy as they watched him plunge his sword into the defenseless and already beaten man. 'Make the call' he called to his father not taking his eyes from Lel who had entered his dreams too often. 'Arnav! he said in a clipped tone. 'Understood' he replied leaving Nox to looking from one to the other. 'Kiril, don't ! Nox shouted as he broke ranks and began his decent into the chaos. Not thinking about anything other than making it to him before he was killed Nox kicked Snowflake hard and galloped fast in pursuit of him.

Anso was in complete and utter shock as he watched his son and wife storm down the hill towards the mayhem below. 'Charge! He bellowed drawing his sword and following without hesitation. Two thousand Zantarians ready for battle rose their swords and screamed loud enough to shake the ground beneath them. Making his way onto the battle field Kiril had not taken his eyes from Lel.

Driving his horse forward through a mass of bodies he made a swipe for the man's head as soon as he was close enough. Cursing as he seen Lel move swiftly out of view, he rotated as fast as possible and not chancing another miss jumped from his horse landing heavily as he rolled in bloodied grass. Standing to his feet he braced himself and waited for Lel, who to his delight was running directly for him. 'Come on you bastard' Kiril said as he watched. Lel rose his sword and with solid force came down on Kiril's sword with pure hatred. As they fought Kiril's ferocity leaked from him in waves as he thought of Nox being hounded by the man at the other end of his blade, and his wrath grew. Nox couldn't believe her eyes. 'You'll be the death of me' was all she heard in her head leaving her hands shaking and heart racing. 'He'll be the death of me more like. Bloody fool' she said hotly as she dismounted and readied herself for battle. Not given the chance to catch her breath she was approached fast from the side by a screaming Mackisi soldier who was blood crazed and overly excited by the circumstances surrounding him. As he attacked wildly she jumped around him and with one swift movement she drew her swords simultaneously and plunged them deep into the depts of his stomach. As he turned to face her he barred rotten teeth and fell to the ground at her feet. Before long she was under attack again by a man who was by no means small. He was in no shape to be in a battle, definitely not the healthiest person she ever seen. His so called armor didn't fit him right due to his alarmingly full-bodied mid-section while his trousers were too small in the leg. 'Honestly what a mess' she thought as he moved in closer. Making a lung in her direction she braced herself for his worst, only before his sword lowered itself upon hers he fell to the ground with an unmerciful moan. Standing over him was Arnav with his usual charming smile and cheeky wink.

'Thought I'd save you the trouble' he said, but not waiting for anything else she looked around scanning the battle field for Kiril. Not being able to spot him panic rose in her chest and tears prickled her eyes. 'Kiril! she screamed into the inhospitable noise and confusion. A deep and callous voice made her freeze in her steps. 'It would seem he is preoccupied' said Kovit as a sly grin washed over his face. 'Nice to see Lel keeps his dog close' Nox hissed at him as she worked her swords though her skillful hands. Kovit's face turned a dark crimson as he fought the urge to attack her. His face hardened as he looked upon the woman standing so easy for the taking.

'Why doesn't he attack? She wondered to herself as she continued to watch him carefully. 'Don't tell me you were allowed to show your face but only to watch is that it? Nox said sniggering at the maddening Mackisi captain. Gripping his sword tightly he wanted nothing more but to kill her. Thinking of the warning they all received, Lel would gut him like a pig if he took what was his. Taking slow steps in her direction he held his sword high and smirked. 'Maybe when you're husband falls we will meet again' and with that he turned fast and rejoined the battle only to have her follow him. 'Bloody bastard' she shouted as she attacked. Stumbling forward he scrambled to retrieve his sword that had slipped from his hand as Nox shoved him. 'You will stand and fight like a man and you will die at my hand like the dog you are' she said as he gathered his feet below him. Attacking with a murderous scream he was met half way by Nox as she withheld nothing and as she lunged both of their weapons met, and she knew they were well matched. He was strong she noticed and held his sword with ease. His movements were flawless and somewhat graceful but she was angry and damn it she was hungry again. Ducking, blocking and attacking she met him blow for blow until he caught her hard with the hilt of his sword, and even though her armor was strong her stomach tightened leaving her breathless. Buckling over herself she rolled up into a ball on the ground. As she waited for him to come closer she reached for her hidden blade which as always lay against her thigh. The smooth handle was warm from her skin and as her fingers molded to it all she could think of was Kiril. 'This fool is wasting my time' she said angrily to herself as he stood over her laughing. Perseverance to continue and sheer determination led her to grit her teeth as he reached down taking a firm grip of her hair and heaved her onto her feet. The sensation of hair being ripped from the root was horrendous.

Placing her free hand to his she spun around as fast as she possibly could, resulting in her wincing and allowing a small whimper to escape her lips. With all her might she drove her blade high up under his chin until the handle lay against flesh and blood spurted over her hand. His fingers that were formerly dug deep through her hair loosened and as blood oozed from his mouth he slumped to the ground in a heap. She spat her distaste at the body at her feet. A piercing exclamation came from behind her and in turning she saw Kiril upon bended knee before three of Lel's men. Bleeding from lips and nose she ran immediately to his aid. Driving his fist fast and powerfully into Kiril's face as two of the men held him tightly, Lel erupted with laughter at the delight of having such a great enemy on his knees.

Nox wasn't sure what she was feeling. Rage? Hatred? Her jaws clenched as she gripped her swords until her knuckles turned a pale white as pure resentfulness ran through her veins. 'How dare you lay hands upon him! she screeched arriving with the intention of interrupting Lel and his men, and thus giving Kiril a chance to find his sword. At hearing her voice Kiril's swollen eye bulged and with a sudden burst of energy tried to fight against his captures, only to be attacked once again with brutal blows as Lel moved away to intercept her.

With her blades raised and ready she came at him with deep-seated revulsion of the man who was unable to better Kiril without the need of three of his men. 'You fucking coward' she yelled as her sword met his with a loud clash of metal. 'No! Kiril called through stolen breaths as the assault upon him continued. A cruel agonizing pain went throughout his side as blood weld up running hotly down soaking all the way through his cotton shirt as Nox watched the blade go through his flesh and deeply penetrating his side. Groaning he keeled over onto his side at the sound of laughter coming from his attackers, and before he passed out Nox's screams were all he heard . As Nox moved to avoid Lel's attack she caught a glimpse of Kiril lying lifeless and bleeding. With all her might she drew back and punched him with an accurate under-cut that left him falling backward and giving her the time she needed. No longer concerned for her own life she went as fast as she could before Lel advanced on her again and threw herself to the ground at his head. 'Please, Kiril open your eyes' she pleaded as her tears fell uncontrollably down her face and onto his. 'Please! I'm sorry! Please! She shrieked as she rubbed his face with shaking hands.

Leaning above him she screamed his name hysterically drawing the attention of Arnav and Gaius who were coming at high-speed in her direction. Again she found herself jerked roughly backwards and dragged over blood soaked ground as Lel struck her over and over again. Kicking and screaming she wrestled against his muscular grip. Realizing she wasn't going to be able to get free by these means she rooted once again for her blade and as hard as she possibly could drove it straight threw his hand. She knew almost immediately she had also caught herself and wriggling free her own blood trickled down the middle of her forehead.

Standing glaring directly at the heinous man who once she had feared and now all she wanted was to kill him and leave his decaying body to the earth. Hearing Arnav shout for Kiril to wake and his curse when he received no response brought her crashing back to reality. There would be another day, as much as she wanted him dead Kiril was the only person important now.

Without looking behind at the Mackisi leader for the second time she went to her husband, passing Gaius on his way to finish what she started. The feeling of being struck from behind didn't leave her until she knelt to the ground between Arnav and Kiril. His face wore a look of total distress, and her heart sank. 'No, damn it he's not dead, do you hear me Arnav! she shouted as he sat staring blankly at his friend. 'Hurry on we need to move him away from here.' Without waiting for a response she blew the hair from her face and began moving him by means of dragging and pulling him along the grassy ground beneath her feet. Through her tears and sobs she looked for help. Bodies fell all around her as men fought ferociously. Arrows still pierced the air as the archers moved so close she could hear the bow string snap back into place after their arrows were discharged. Heaved to her feet from behind she whirled ready again for battle only to find Hakan move her away from Kiril and with Arnav's help rose her wounded warrior into the safety of their arms.

~

Kiril slept for the two days as the battle continued unrelenting on the lands of Arella, but to the relief of everyone within the castle walls so far losses were not great. The Mackisi were three thousand in comparison to the six thousand of the Zantarian, Arellian and the army of the Crowden. But to her upmost annoyance the bastards wouldn't give up. Wishing Kiril would wake she ran her fingers gently along his cheek following the line of his jaw. Anso had returned on hearing the news of his son falling, and had been calling by on regular intervals with food for her. 'If I don't keep you fed he will have my life when he wakes' he said when she insisted on getting her own food. His beard had grown at an alarming rate but she found herself deeply amused by it and was constantly played with it. Leaning in over the bed she rose the blanket from around him and carefully removed his dressings. The blood had finally stopped flowing from his wounds but he was still such a pale and sickly colour which only put emphasis on the bruising to his face, chest and neck. As she looked at him she wondered how long it would take him to recover. 'Forgive me' she said kissing him gently upon his lips, wishing he would wake and respond as he always did that made her knees go weak and breath catch. Walking over to the wash basin she rinsed out the clean cloths and in returning to Kiril she gently began washing him from head to toe. Going as fast as she could it still didn't stop the goose bumps forming all over him. Drying him quickly she stopped and looked at the man who lay in front of her. 'Please be careful. I don't know what I would do if you got hurt or worse you said, only it's me that finds myself not knowing what to do.' Moving softly and carefully into the bed bringing her warmth with her, she cuddled up lying herself down beside his battered body. Drawing the blankets back up over them both she giggled when her stomach growled. Laying her hands gently upon it she whispered affectionately 'Your son is always hungry.' Closing her eyes she let herself drift into sleep with her warrior enfolded in her arms and hoped the morning would bring new beginnings.

~

Waking to the feeling of fingers running along her face she opened her eyes sleepily and near squealed with delight to see Kiril smiling down at her. 'Your stomach has been growling for the past hour' he said laughing as she jumped on him wrapping her arms around him tightly.

Forgetting his injuries she winced when he cursed and jerked away slightly. Blushing she apologized profusely leaning in more carefully to lay a kiss upon his now very awake lips. He responded as he had in her dream, and out of nowhere her tears flowed once again. Drawing her face to his he wiped them away gently kissing both of her eyes as she sniffled. 'I'm sorry' she exclaimed through her broken breaths. 'It was my fault, I should never have gone.' At this she exploded into a load and heart wrenching cry that shattered his heart. 'Nox' he said forcing her back to look at him. 'If you had of stayed I would be dead.' Shaking her head in disagreement he shook her gently by her shoulders and spoke with a little more force. 'I would have gone after him and died, Nox do you hear me? You saved my life and I will not have you blame yourself for my stupidity, do you understand' he said almost shouting with emotion.

Wiping her nose with the back of her hand she informed him of how Arnav and Hakan had helped in his rescue. 'Poor Arnav thought you were dead' she said with a weak smile. But when she drew her hand away and laid it upon his cheek he knew there and then so had she. Grapping her hand and kissing each knuckle hard he cursed himself for nearly leaving her widowed and his child fatherless. 'Forgive me! he said pleadingly as he looked up into her emerald eyes that still held so much passion for such a fool of a man. Giving him a striking smile that lit every inch of her once dispirited face she leaned down and kissed him thoroughly, tasting the passion and excitement that surged from him leaving her unable to comprehend her life without him in it.

'You are forgiven.' She whispered. Wincing as he pain shot through him he took her into his arms and with unadulterated bliss reacquainted himself with the feel of her silken skin.

Chapter Twenty-five

LEL

Watching as Nox left the battle field with Kiril and two other men aiding his escape Lel's temper was at the verge of erupting. 'Somebody stop them! He yelled into the chaos only to be met by a huge lump of a man who's sword was drawn and ready. 'Damn it' Lel hissed bracing himself for the attack. As Gaius dealt blow after heavy blow Lel could feel himself weaken. Looking around frantically for someone to aid him with the angry and very strong warrior in front of him as he collapsed to the ground. Rummaging around for his lost sword he sighed a sigh relief at the sight of Zev running to intercept the attack. With the sound of clanking swords Lel scurried out of harm's way. Taking the route Nox had presumably traveled he followed in hot pursuit. After running in the one direction for what seemed an excessive amount of time without spotting her he cursed and spun around looking wildly through the mass of fighting men. 'Well done Lady Roundgate' he said with a smile as he called for hi men to check every entrance and exit in and from the castle. 'You've just made this a very interesting chase Nox' he said licking his lips.

With every man that returned empty handed the more aggressive Lel became. 'They didn't vanish into fucking thin air. Find them! He roared at already exhausted men who looked ready to slump where they stood. As the sun set beyond the horizon each army seemed to verge off in their own directions to recuperate and calculate the damages done and numbers lost.

Stepping over at least ten identifiably his own men he knew even before counting they had suffered greatly. 'Zev! He called as he gazed at the army of the Crowden. Suddenly wondering how he had found himself in battle with the mighty Ulric of all people. 'Vidar you little bastard.'

He said with disgust. 'Eh sir, he was executed by orders of his father not four days past' one of his men spoke up while passing. Reaching for him Lel dragged him back with so much force he nearly tripped them both. 'What? When did this happen? Not sure what to feel about the news of Vidar's demise and the circumstances surrounding it he dropped his hands allowing the stunned man to make his escape. 'Seems you got your treaty Nox.' he said shaking his head in disbelief that she could out do him once yet again for a second time.

After another two days passed of fighting and scrapping, while still having no luck gaining entry to the castle Lel called for Zev. On his arrival Lel commanded him to gather the men and attempt to move out quickly as soon as darkness fell. Stunned Zev questioned his reasons. 'In case you haven't noti . . . 'Interrupted by Zev he clenched his fist. 'But what about . . . '

As Lel's hand came around his throat he froze. 'Zev if you interrupt me one more time I'll cut your tongue out. Do you understand? He said through clenched teeth..Sensing the young man was about to piss himself, he released him roughly. 'Now like I was saying every entrance and exit from here to the castle are being tended with either Arellians or Zantarians. Have a good look around you Zev we are all but down to a mere thousand men.' Pinching his nose with his thumb and forefinger he began to shake his head. 'Kovit would have at least understood that much.' Turning to the younger captain he waved his hand in dismissal and walked in the other direction. 'Zev' he called on turning. 'Sir' the young man replied as he tried his best to fit the profile of captain. 'How did Kovit fall do you know? 'Lady Nox' was all he said and all Lel needed to hear. 'Bloody bitch. Gather the men and be ready to leave, and Zev leave the dead' he said , his voice holding a warning that shouldn't be taken lightly.

Chapter Twenty-Six

'What of the Mackisi? Nox asked Anso as they left Kiril to his sleep. 'Well it would seem Lel created a chance to escape capture and took it, bastard could have killed my son,' he said slapping his hand with force against the wall. 'So Gaius was unable to kill him' she stated more than questioned. 'He was very close in defeating him' Anso said with a raised eyebrow. 'Oh?

What happened? Nox asked as her curiosity grew. 'Unlike us men' he said with feeling. 'Lel needs the aid of his men when fighting. Seems the man is unable to fend for himself.' He said getting worked up as he looked straight at her. 'Did you ever hear of such a thing as a leader of an army having to let his own men fight on behalf of him? I mean honestly Nox what a bloody joke.' Leaving him to his rant she remembered how he had three men arrack and near kill Kiril for him as he stood back and watched. 'In some ways you may be right Anso but I believe there is more to what meets the eye.' She said glancing at him. 'In what way? He asked interested in her opinion. 'It might be just an educated guess, but reflecting on what we have learned of the Mackisi I believe the power he holds within his men runs deeper than any of us could imagine.

Just ponder about it for a moment Anso. What does he award his men with when they squabble between themselves? The look of disgust that came over his face said he knew exactly what she was talking about. 'Yes,

Anso he hands over the spoils of their duties in destroying everything they touch. Now just think about what you would do for a man that offers you back what you believe you already deserve, without question.' Anso's face grew pale as he weigh up what Nox was saying. 'Pure manipulation' he said with disbelief. 'Exactly' Nox replied as they came into the gathering hall which was filled with men, women and children of all ages. Enquiries of Kiril's welfare came in swarms at the same time as she and Anso made their way towards the top of the hall were they found the twins, Hakan and Arnav deep in conversation. Seeing her Gaius rushed to her side 'Nox, I need to speak with you' he said in a worried tone. Leading her away from the crowd and into an alcove he turned to her sheepishly. She could see how troubled he was and walked to him. 'What is it Gaius? His grievance showed all over his facial features.

'Gaius clearly there is something you need to say, for the love of all that is good will you just bloody say it.' she said coaxingly. 'How does Kiril fare? He asked unsettled. 'Gaius' she said placing her hand upon his arm. 'Kiril and myself couldn't defeat him either.' Breaking into face splitting grin he pulled her hard against himself and squeezed tightly. 'Thank you' he whispered.

Breaking away from each other she punched him playfully in the mid-section and laughed. 'Your such a pansy' she said jeeringly looking up at him. 'Meet me in the field and we will see who's a pansy' he answered wounded by her jesting. Coming towards them Toran beckoned for his brother to accompany him on a task. 'Seems Hakan wants to help you save face' she said mockingly walking away with just the right amount of smugness. 'Toran do it yourself I'm busy.

Nox ready yourself' he shouted grabbing his sword as he walked in her direction. Turning she drew her swords with deliberately slow and measured movements sniggering. 'You sure you want to do this? she inquired on turning to face him directly. Freezing on the spot she returned her swords to their rightful place upon her back promptly and without delay as Kiril stood arms folded upon his chest with an astonished look across his face as his complexion paled before her eyes. 'Incredible' he said shaking his head.

Looking shamefaced and embarrassed she strolled to him. Her face blushed and to her amazement a grin forced its way onto her face. 'What? she asked as innocently as she possibly could when reaching him. All of a sudden she remembered he was standing there and not in bed where he was supposed to be. 'Nox . . . ' He began before being cut off by her. 'Don't Nox me' she said in her most stern voice. 'Did I not tell you to stay where you were? You need your rest.'

She continued. 'Don't try and change the subject Nox, you promised me no more fighting until the baby is born. Well did you or didn't you promise me? he said sternly while trying to stay as calm as possible considering how many people were watching. 'Well . . . ' she said thinking of something to say. 'Well' she said wiggling her finger in his direction. 'Did I not ask you to promise me you would get some sleep? And here you are. A bit of a double standard don't you think? She said dramatically throwing her arms in the air to exaggerate the fact he was indeed standing in front of her. Knowing this was definitely not one of those arguments, she reached back, took her swords from their resting place and handed them over. 'Fine' she said sulking as he took them with no care of their value which made her want to grab him by the scruff of the neck. Chewing the inside of her cheek she turned back in the direction of the men who were tolerantly waiting for them. Throwing Anso and slight shrug of her shoulders and a smirk she stood by Arnav who was deeply amused by the show of her having to hand her swords over to her husband in clear view of everyone . If she was completely honest with herself it made her blood boil. 'Arnav! Kiril said in warning as he brushed past him. 'Son you really should have stayed to rest yourself' Anso said as a tone of disapproval etched into his voice. Rolling his eyes he threw the swords onto the table and set his attentions on Hakan. 'Bloody man, how inconsiderate' she hissed under her breath laying her hand upon her hips staring angrily at the back of his head. Choosing to ignore Nox's gasp and line of insults he threw a cautious look over his shoulder in her direction only to have her snort in amusement. Smiling to himself he turned his attentions back on Hakan and to what his plans in dealing with the remaining Mackisi. 'I have called everyone here to the gathering hall to discuss just that' he said tiredly as he rose his hands and called for silence.

Stillness filled the hall as they waited to hear their leader tell them what they were to expect. Not having anywhere high to stand to be seen by everyone he climbed onto the table rewarding him with crude comments about showing his arse and giving them a show. Leaving the women blush and the men roar with laughter. Raising both hands while he laughed along the crowd he waited as all went quiet once again. 'You all know what has come about in recent days.

So you also know that this was something that was eventually going to come to our door. Our men fought with great courage, intensity and strength but like any war we have suffered losses.

Men that we have loved as husbands, brothers, sons and mostly friends. They will never be replaced but will be remembered fondly by us all.' Stopping he looked at Nox who stood motionless and subdued within her own thoughts. 'As you are all aware Nox handed the protection of Arella and its people into my care. When this happened we were in the middle of nowhere and with no other choice to make, but she is here now and as Arella law demands a vote must be reached in the proper fashion.' Putting his hand out for Nox to take he thought Kiril was going to drag him from the table and beat him senseless. As sweat formed upon his brow as he waited for a very shocked and what looked to be a very angry Nox, he swallowed deep and torn his gaze away from Kiril. Taking his hand Nox climbed onto the table and took her place by his side to the cheers of the crowd. 'What do you think you're playing at? She said through clenched jaws as she threw him an askew look. Alarm spread over his face as he realized what he had done. 'You fucking idiot, couldn't just leave well enough alone could you.' she hissed glaring at him. Breaking away from him she took a step into the centre of the extremely large round table that she had spent many occasions trying to persuade her father to bun the disgusting ugly thing.

Smiling at all the expectant faces her heart felt heavy as she tried to think of something that would be full of meaning and favorable to hear. 'Hakan is right in what he says. It was an arrangement that was made when I had no other choice.' At this she chanced a look in Kiril's direction to see him fret about her next words. 'Make no mistake in thinking this choice was easily made, for you would be wrong and it couldn't be future from the truth. It took days for my heart to allow me to acknowledge what I had to do.' Shaking her head she faced Hakan who's nervousness showed making her laugh. 'I have made my decision as you know, but for those of you who do not' pointing at Kiril she winked and turning to her people 'this man's name is Kiril Zanni of Zantar, my husband and father to my unborn child, and my reason for stepping down as your leader.' Witnessing shocked, understanding and smiling faces she shrugged her shoulders and smiled. 'I will always be an Arellian and you will always be my people and most of all my family, and I'm pretty certain and in no doubt some of you thought no man would ever be capable of handling me' she said to the laughter that filled the hall making her smirk. Sudden seriousness came upon her as she thought of all those who had died over the past days rushed back into her mind and crushed her with their presence. 'We have lost many over recent days some more than others' she said looking at Ulric 'but look around at the person beside you who you don't know and have never met. Inside these halls for the first time together are the armies of The Crowden, the army of Zantar and the force of Arella, and here we are as comrades and hopefully now lifelong friends. This is a good day for us all even though it may be shadowed by grief and sorrow.' Catching Hakan's hand she called for all present to give their leader the appropriate and accurate respect that he deserves. As the Arellian army fell to their knees before him, she let his hand go and knelt at his feet.

~

As they entered her bedroom and settled Kiril back into bed to rest she had to ask. 'What happened on the battle field Kiril? When I seen you last you were fitting well and looked to be bettering Lel, then when I looked again you were on your knees.' Lying back on her soft pillows he sighed worn-out and depleted. Patting the bed for her to sit beside him he placed his arm across his eyes blocking out whatever light was available. 'It all happened so fast, I was beating him on all accounts and the next thing I know I was being attacked from all angles.' Looking at her he searched her face for any sign of disappointment that he was in fact not the strong warrior she had thought he was. But instead he seen frustration and distress. 'I'm sorry I didn't make it to you faster' she replied with regret. 'Nox, please don't I have enough guilt of not being there to defend you let alone having to face the fact that it was you who had to save me.' he said as anguish made its way into every inch of him. 'I had three of his men hold me while he punched and kicked me and I could do nothing.' Anger rolled from him in waves as his face grew more and more disturbed by the memories. 'I could hear him laughing as he left them to their own devices and every time a blow hit all I could think of was you and where you were, and if you were safe.' he said facing her now with eyes wide with sorrow. 'Then I heard your voice and I thought I was going to die where I lay. Here I was your husband, the man who vowed to revenge you. Instead I lay upon the ground like a coward as you fought to save me. Fought against the man who tried to . . . ' 'Nox do you know he told me over and over again how he was going to ravish you once I was dead. That I claimed something that was already his, and no matter how hard I bloody fought those bastards never let up. I had to listen to every word while I waited for the chance to slit his fucking throat. What was his!' He screamed so loud enough Hakan who was passing the hall wall burst through the door with sword in hand.

'What is it? he bellowed ready for action. Removing herself from Kiril's side she went to Hakan smiling at his ridiculous stance. 'Hakan really do you actually look like that in battle? She said laughing. Not at all upset by her insult he lowered his sword and looked at Kiril. Lunging from the bed and nearly keeling over from dizziness, he swayed dangerously making her move towards him only to have him push her away again. Wounded by his rejection she took a step backwards and waited for him to continue. Breathing heavily as he stared at Hakan, who instantly got the message and retreated from the room leaving them once again in privacy. 'Nox you will never know what it is to have your pregnant wife save you and have to carry you out of battle before your own men.'

Preventing him from talking any more she moved with speed and with one swift movement pulled a sword from its holding place on the wall. 'Really so you would you have preferred me to leave you there you ungrateful swine' she said pointing the blade close to his chest. 'Do I have to prove to you that you that you are a great fighter? She yelled at him while circling his battered form. 'Well do I? she screamed. 'Even broken and wounded as you are you would still bloody beat me if you set your mind to it, and if you think for a second that I am happy to acknowledge that little fact you are sadly mistaken. Tell me Kiril do you remember the day I bettered you?

She said peeking out from below her eyelashes to look at him. Smiling he turned a shade of bright pink. 'Of course I remember' he said softly. 'Well then that was a battle you won was it not? I would have thought that would have been the hardest you would have ever had to face.' she said with a smirk as she moved closer. 'You are a great fighter but all great men are undone on occasion . Surely you're not so pig headed that you thought it would never happen to you.'

She said beseeching him to stop and listening to himself. 'I don't think I will ever be able to face them again, let alone lead them into any future battles.' Walking towards her now he placed his hands on her face and lowered his forehead and rested it against hers. 'Tell me you can at least understand that' he whispered. 'I understand' she replied. 'But you understand this Kiril Zanni you are no coward and I will never after this day hear you say it again. Your men will follow you anywhere, because you are their captain and they trust you.' Closing his eyes he leaned back against the bed post. 'Open your damn eyes and look at me' she shouted. 'Do you understand?

Kiril? Giving her a weak smile he nodded and drawing her into a tight embrace he ran his fingers gently along the length of her arm and took her sword from her grasp while he stroked her hair and caressed her curves with adoration with his other hand. Leaning in slowly he kissed her with passion as he explored along her neck and chest. 'Thank you' he whispered against the hollow of her breasts.

~

Strolling through the castle towards the kitchens she decided it was time to visit her father. Her grave was high upon the hill along beside her mother's. The day she took her last breathe he left the castle and walked for miles to find the picture perfect resting place that he could leave her in quiet tranquility. Throughout her childhood she had ventured there on many occasions, mostly when she was hiding or in trouble. He would always find her and when he did they would spend hours just sitting enjoying their surroundings. Smiling she recalled how he had went there first when she disappeared for days but when she wasn't there he had every man rip the castle apart looking for her. Hiding within the walls of her secret tunnel she could hear him shouting orders, and his dismay when man after man came to him with no news of her whereabouts. That was the first day she had ever heard Kiril speak. Laughing as his words came flooding back to her she turned for the narrow hallway that led to the kitchens. 'I don't know why everyone is looking for her? She's probably off playing with her dolls sticking knives in them.' At this she heard Anso's voice echo through the hall as he let a roar at his son. 'I've never owned a doll in my whole blood life' she said chuckling to herself. Entering the kitchen she found Maggie in a heated discussion with her husband about the bread he had prepared. 'It's disgusting! You cannot give that to any of our guests you silly man.' she said as she stormed out in the opposite direction.

About to retaliate he came to a stop when his eyes set upon her. Lowering his shoulders he sighed. 'How are you Lady Nox? Smiling she walked in and sat beside his work bench. 'I'm well Abner' she said glimpsing in the direction Maggie had taken. 'Do I need to ask how you are?

Asking with a slight laugh in her voice. 'Well, no Nox you can see what I have to deal with.

Besides that what can I do for you? Not answering she threw him a shy glance making him laugh. 'Hungry? He said smirking. 'I'm always hungry Abner' answering as she slouched on the stool. 'I'm eating so bloody much I'm beginning to think I ready will burst' she said as she ran her hand across her swelling stomach. As he fussed to prepare her something fast he continued to give out about his life's ordeals, especially 'that son of mine' he said tiredly. Seeing her lips twitch he stopped what he was doing and faced her. 'But did you have to encourage him? Truly?

Unable to stifle her giggling she laughed out loud. 'Yes' was all she said as he glowered at her. 'I suppose if I haven't already killed the boy I never will' he said laughing with her. 'How does your husband fare? Is he recovering quickly? Throwing him a sly stare as she chewed on the bread Maggie was screaming about. 'Why are you hoping I leave faster? Honestly Abner I haven't set eyes on Tressin since the day in the entrance hall.' 'Good' he replied as he handed her a bundle of bread, meats and fruit wrapped tightly. 'Thank you' offering him her sweetest smile she walking out of the kitchen and towards the door Maggie exited from.

Stepping out into the open she took a deep breath and set on her way. The land was a picturesque setting of striking and all inspiring views of a landscape that days before had been a mass of men fighting for their survival. 'Beautiful' she whispered. It amazed her how anything that looked so much like her worst nightmare could transform itself back into something so breath taking. Putting her head down she walked with purpose towards her destination. As the sun rose she knew Kiril would awaken soon and wonder where she had vanished to. Not leaving a note of her whereabouts he was sure to stumble from bed and through the castle in hot pursuit.

They had spent hours the night before speaking of Zantar leaving him laughing at all her questions and how she grew excited when he described the stables. As they cuddled she asked him if he would be fierce disappointed if the baby was not a boy but a girl. Sighing he drew her nearer reassuring her that it truthfully did not make a difference as long as she was safe and sound and out of harm's way well when it was all over. Smiling she recalled some of the names he had suggested. 'I swear he made up half of them' she said giggling to herself. They would be leaving for Zantar at some stage today and for once she wanted respite to enjoy what she grew to love and always known. The next few hours would be her time to bid farewell to her home and life before she sauntered blindly into her new one. Humming to herself she at last came to her parents resting place. Gently laying her food package upon the soft leaves she went to take her place between the graves were she rested herself. Laying a hands on each of the once swollen mounds of earth now covered beautifully by an area of wonderful stone. Tears fell freely down along her flushed checks. 'I have much to tell you' she said in a soft voice. Relaying everything that had happened over the past couple of months she felt mentally exhausted by the time she had finished. Reaching for her package she grinned as the smells and aroma of the fresh bread and meats rushed out to meet her. 'Mmm! She said with delight as she took a huge mouthful of bread. Moving away from the gravesite she stood and looked out once again at the terrain that stretched out before her. Having eaten to a satisfactory amount she was delightfully content.

Smiling she placed her hand once again upon her stomach and the amazing individual that rested within. 'You have already been through so much. But I think you will be my greatest battle' she said lovingly as she wrapped her arms tightly around her most valued and cherished possession.

~

Arriving back at the castle just after midday she knew Kiril would have been looking high and low for her. However she was in no hurry to put his mind at ease. He had constantly been saying how he felt the Mackisi had something still to prove and she had to be careful. Which of course meant going nowhere on her own or preferably everywhere with him. this once again resulted in them having an argument about his overprotect urges. Sighing she walked through the halls and corridors slowly taking in every diminutive and large characteristic and feature. The halls were wider than she thought and brighter during the hour that was in it. 'Strange' she thought as it dawned in her that she had never realized or noticed such little things before today. Strolling leisurely she finally found herself standing directly outside her father's rooms. Placing her hand gently upon the handle she froze as the feeling of entering crossed her mind, and all of a sudden she felt she would be intruding. 'Why am I nervous? She asked herself frowning. Still not turning the handle she lowered her head and took a deep breath. If she was true to the laws of Arella and it lands she should not even consider opening the doors. Knowing no one would have cleaned out his rooms without her permission, plus to be sure to their laws and beliefs they would not be cleared of the previous leaders belonging for a year to allow him to leave of his own accord. 'Well who's going to stop me? Saying to herself taking a final glimpse up and down the hall way before she entered into complete and absolute darkness. Walking carefully through the room by means of her hands to guide her way to the windows. Tripping and stumbled over a series of objects plus bits and pieces that her father clearly had no time to clear away. When reaching them with no more than a small insignificant scratch on her knee from a table she had failed to recall, she took hold standing beneath the huge heavy drapes and with one swift tug she drew them across. As a cloud of dust drifted high into the air making her sneeze profusely she cursed waving her hand before her face to clear her vision thus returning her ability to see clearly. As light shone through the room she seen nothing had altered. Her father's things still lay where he left them except for his sword that now held residency in her rooms. Bringing to mind the night Hakan handed it to her as his face held such grief and sorrow for the man he loved dearly. It was strange that she could still catch his smell wafting through the room like he had just left. Which made her feel reassured in an odd and peculiar way. Letting her fingers drift softly over his uniform that hung neatly and ready to be worn brought back the memories of the morning he died. Having spent all the night before laying beside him while he fought for air so ferociously that when he coughed so relentlessly he tore at his throat. Seeping through the crease of his lips blood dripped from the corners of his mouth. Her eyes welled up with tears as she attempted to push the image to the deepest and darkest region of her mind. Hearing Gaius talking loud as usual she made her way towards the heavy door once again only the next time she returned to these rooms Hakan would belong here. Surprised that Kiril's voice was the next she heard, smiling taking a grip on the handle she stopped herself on hearing what they were discussing. 'Your jealous is that it? Gaius asked in disbelief as he broke into a loud laugh at Kiril's expense. 'What is going on now? she thought to herself. 'I never said that did I? Kiril answered hotly. 'You didn't have to' Gaius responded. 'Honestly Kiril be rest assured I have no feelings for Nox. But I cannot say what she feels for me' he continued sounding smug at the fact that Kiril would be uneasy about his relationship with his wife. A thunderous roar came from Kiril as he lunged for Gaius. Pinning him against the wall with extreme force Kiril glowered at the man he was in fact jealous of. Intervening Arnav grabbed for Kiril while Toran did nothing as he stood with his back to the wall sniggering. 'Kiril will you release the man before you choke him to death' Arnav shouted breathlessly as he tugged hard on Kiril's arm. Gaius who was no longer laughing had begun to turn a deep red. 'Do you think you can find it in you to lend a hand maybe? I'm just wondering.' Arnav said to Toran smartly. 'You know if we had of just let them kill each other years ago none of this would be going on now. The only difference is you fucking idiots you're not sixteen any more' Toran yelled clearly fed up. On exiting the room to numerous stares in her direction Nox didn't do anything but stared at each of them with an equal amount of bewilderment. As she let her eyes run over the four men before her she frowned in total astonishment that grown men like them would be near killing one another over something so trivial. Kiril still had Gaius by the throat; Arnav by now had both of his arms wrapped tightly around Kiril's waist and Toran stood there with a grin that spread from ear to ear. 'When you are finished measuring the size of your cocks maybe I could converse with my husband? Nox said in walking away at a brisk pace. 'Shit' Kiril's voice rang clear though the hall way as Toran, Gaius and Arnav erupted with laughter making her smirk to herself. 'Never a dull moment.

Bloody stupid man! It didn't take him long to catch up to her and receive a measured look for his childishness. 'You cannot be seriously jealous of my relationship with Gaius? It was such a long time ago and something I have put to the back of my mind. If it's alright with you I would prefer not to dredge up forgotten memories.' Stopping to face him she took his hand and held it tightly.

'If Gaius could only look back over those times and remembered how I only spent that time with him when you were not in Arella. He would also see how I kept my distance when you were.

Now will you stop with this male ego business and get us organized to go home.' She said as she went up on her tiptoes and kissed him gently on his now smiling lips.

Chapter Twenty-Seven

ZANTAR

Drawing in long deep breaths Nox braced herself yet again for another contraction. As her stomach clenched with the pressure of her child moving with force inside her she moaned from the bottom of her throat. 'Were is Kiril? she asked breathlessly as the mid-wife hung close by.

'I have sent word that he is to be found at once' she promised moving nearer to have a better look. 'Do you feel inclined to move back to the bed Lady Nox? Asking gently removing Nox's hair from her forehead that was now wet from fatigue. Bursting through the door stood Malachi stood breathless as an extremely worried look captured his face leaving it seem ten years older.

Slightly embarrassed at his intrusion he informed Nox and an very irate mid-wife that Kiril had in fact gone hunting with his father. 'What? Find him' Nox shouted towards the door as she gripped hard to the window sill readying herself yet again. Tiredness was getting the better of her at this moment in time and she was growing angrier by the second. 'Gone bloody hunting! I'll show him hunting' she said venomously. 'Try to stay calm Nox, he will be back well before this baby enters the world' the mid-wife said hoping she sounded reassuring. A thunderous commotion sounded outside the doors as Nox gritted her teeth holding her breath one more time.

'Why was I not informed? Kiril yelled.

'We thought you were hunting Kiril' Arnav answered nervously.

'Fuck' Kiril screamed from outside as he came barging in looking both vexed and exasperated, but it was replaced by a petrified look when he took in Nox's form. Bending over she moaned painfully resulting in him running to her, taking her into his arms and apologizing profusely. 'Oh my love I'm sorry I left. I swear I was not far.' 'I thought you were gone hunting? she replied snuggling up to the one person who could make her feel more contented than she had been in hours. 'My father asked me as much early this morning but I refused. You were so uncomfortable last night, I was afraid to leave the grounds in case anything happened. I was just in the stables checking the horses when I heard my name being called' he told her stroking her face lovingly. Moving away from him slightly she smiled for the first time all morning 'I'm so glad you're here. I never thought I'd feel unable to succeed at anything until now.' Still smiling she looked at him with such adoration he wished he had of been more careful the first time they had made love. The need that took them both left no space for common sense, and if he was to be completely truthful he wanted nothing more than to leave her pregnant with his child. Now he wasn't so sure looking at the broken, tried and pain stricken woman before him. As fast as her smile appeared it disappeared right before his very eyes and was replaced by an excruciating soreness that nearly brought her to her knees.

The night had passed so slowly Kiril had sworn never to put his wife through such agonizing pain ever again. Leaning in he whispered what he hoped where words she wanted to hear but the likelihood was very slim. 'Kiril my love' she said with a sarcastic smirk. 'If you tell me to relax and breath one more fucking time I will choke the bloody life from you. In case you have forgotten I have been doing just that for the last forty eight bloody hours' Nox screamed as another contraction gripped her stomach with such intensity sweat rolled from her brow and her hands shook. 'I'm only trying to help' he replied as he proceeded to rub her lower back. 'Don't' she hissed leaning upon the window ledge for what seemed the hundredth time in as many hours.

'I'm sorry' he said raking his hand through his hair feeling useless. 'Shut up' she shrieked leaving him feeling offended that his efforts were going un-noticed and un-welcomed. 'Get out' she screamed at him moaning loudly as she rocked back and forth. 'But you said you wanted me here' he answered shocked by her outburst. 'I said get out' she screamed again but this time faced him directly. 'She had been so happy to see me' he thought to himself as he tried his very best to accommodate and make her comfortable. Taking a step back he turned and headed for the door as the mid-wife made her way towards Nox. 'No, please I'm sorry' she said now in tears. 'Please don't leave' she pleaded into the window frame. Backing away from the window and the chilled air that she had begun to enjoy she made her way back towards the bed. Resting all of her weight on Kiril who had wasted no time in returning to her side, the mid-wife was waited anxiously. 'I think maybe you should go now' she said turning to Kiril who in turn turned to Nox. Wincing as she enlighten the mid-wife where she could place her suggestions he tried to hold back the smile that was for some strange reason forming. 'Now there's the woman I married' he said proudly glancing down at the little spit fire in his arms. 'But men are never in attendance during childbirth' she said persisting making her way to remove Nox from Kiril's arms. 'I said he stays' Nox repeated glowering at the woman challenging her to lay hands upon her. 'Lady Nox I really thi . . . ' She began all over again only to have Nox straighten her back with whatever energy she could muster. 'I said he fucking stays' she screamed in broken words as another contraction set in. 'Fine, have it your way' she replied cynically moving to the bed just as Kiril bent downward and with one swooping motion lifted Nox clean of her feet.

Lowering his head to hers he proceeded to kiss her gently while laying her upon the bed.

Positioning herself between Nox's legs the once narrow-minded mid-wife gave her a supportive smile. 'Are you ready to push? Nodding Nox gripped her knees and as fear washed over her she took a deep breath, closed her eyes tightly and pushed with all her might.

Lightning Source UK Ltd.
Milton Keynes UK
24 November 2010

163373UK00002B/14/P